"The lives of the homeless and high society are woven together in this cleverly plotted mystery. This is a book that will challenge your head and your heart."

Fiona Veitch Smith, author of *The Jazz Files*

"Richardson-Moore's latest is a tightly plotted mystery rich with southern grit and replete with twists, turns, and a surprising reveal. Reporter Branigan Powers is an unforgettable protagonist brimming with determination, compassion, and a strong sense of justice. Readers will be glad they've met her. Highly recommended."

Susan Furlong, co-author of the *New York Times* bestselling *Novel Idea Mysteries*

Deb Richardson-Moore is a former journalist, and the pastor of the Triune Mercy Center in Greenville, South Carolina. Her first book, *The Weight of Mercy*, is a memoir about her work as a pastor among the homeless. She and her husband Vince are the parents of three grown children. To find out more about Deb, you can go to her website: www.debrichardsonmoore.com.

Also by Deb Richardson-Moore

The Weight of Mercy: A Novice Pastor on the City Streets
The Cantaloupe Thief

THE
COVER STORY

A BRANIGAN POWERS MYSTERY

DEB RICHARDSON-MOORE

LION FICTION

Published by Lion Fiction
an imprint of
Lion Hudson IP Ltd
Wilkinson House, Jordan Hill Road
Oxford OX2 8DR, England

www.lionhudson.com/fiction

ISBN 978 1 78264 240 4
e-ISBN 978 1 78264 241 1

First edition 2017

Acknowledgments
Author photo: © Robert Bradley

A catalogue record for this book is available from the British Library

Printed and bound in the UK, April 2017, LH26

To Susan, Wanda, Jeanne and Allison,
generous givers of time and advice,
and
to Lynne and Lynn
brave women, title peddlers

Acknowledgments

Thanks to my writers' group for their unending patience and encouragement: Susan Clary Simmons, Wanda Owings, Jeanne Brooks and Allison Greene.

Thanks to my early readers: Lynne Lucas, Lynn Cusick, Madison Moore, Mary Jane Gorman, Elaine Nocks.

I am grateful to Becky Ramsey, Matt Matthews, John Jeter, Carl Muller, and Susan and Bill Smith for their assorted kindnesses.

The folks at Lion Hudson in England – whom I hope to meet face to face some day – have been delightful. That's Jessica Tinker, Jessica Scott, Remy Njambi Kinyanjui and Daniel Haskett.

At Kregel Publications stateside, I thank Katherine Chappell, Noelle Pederson, Ginny Kelling and Lori Alberda.

Thanks to my mom, Doris Richardson, for pushing my books at Senior Action. Oh, and for everything else.

And as always, thanks to my husband Vince and children Dustin, Taylor and Madison, who are always there to assure me I ain't anything special.

PART ONE

CHAPTER ONE

*C*harlie Delaney slammed her exam booklet against the desk top, shaking her wrist and forearm to ease the ache of answering three essay questions. She was happy with her discussions of Kurt Vonnegut and Alice Munro, less so with her take on John Updike.

But it was over, she told herself with a sigh. Over and done until January 7.

She glanced around the University of Georgia classroom, where another twenty-two students still worked, heads down, finishing one last thought even though the professor had called time. She was the only freshman in the upper-level class in Contemporary American Fiction, due to an error in registration. By the time it'd been discovered, she was a month into her first semester and holding her own. So her academic adviser tapped his pen against his lip and told her to enjoy the only small class she had.

Charlie stood and shrugged into her backpack, flipping her reddish gold ponytail out of the way. Over her athletic frame she wore the ubiquitous UGA black and red sweatshirt, plenty warm enough for a day in the high 50s. This was her last exam and she was headed home. She could barely suppress a grin as she nodded goodbye to youngish Dr Dorchester with the auburn braid, and walked into the mid-December sunshine.

She tapped Janie Rose's number into her phone, singing "I'm finished!" when she connected.

"Me too," Janie Rose answered. "I'm at your car."

The girls had agreed to forgo lunch so they could be on the road by noon. Charlie had packed last night during a study break, anxious to put academics behind her for awhile, eager to return home and see her parents, grandparents and brother. She'd been surprised when Janie Rose asked for a ride; she figured the off-campus sophomore would want her own car over the three-week Christmas break. But Janie Rose said there was an extra at her house, and Charlie didn't doubt it. Probably more than one. Janie Rose's father was CEO of Shaner Steel, headquartered in Grambling. Her mother was a professor at Rutherford Lee College, a private liberal arts school on the city's edge. Janie Rose was their only child, and she lacked for nothing.

The Carlton family had moved to Grambling when Janie Rose was in middle school. She and Charlie hadn't been close friends, and were a year apart in school. Still, they had several mutual friends and ran into each other occasionally. When they found themselves in a college math class that finished at lunchtime, they began eating together a couple of times a week.

Trotting toward her dorm, Charlie spied Janie Rose leaning against the faded red Jeep Cherokee Charlie had shared with her brother Chan all through high school. An enormous suitcase sat at the girl's feet.

"Looks like you're ready to go!" called Charlie.

Janie Rose jumped.

"Sorry," said Charlie, coming alongside her. "Did I scare you?"

"No. I'm just ready to get out of here. Aren't you?"

"You bet. My lit exam was a bear. Let me grab my bag and we'll hit the road." She unlocked the passenger door. "I could've picked you up at your apartment, you know."

"That's okay. I'll leave my car in your lot."

"Then go ahead and load up."

Janie Rose glanced around the parking lot, then lifted the Jeep's rear door. She looked around again before hoisting her suitcase.

"Just leave it open for me," Charlie called over her shoulder, but Janie Rose ignored her, closed the rear hatch and hopped into the passenger seat.

Charlie wondered momentarily at her friend's watchfulness, then forgot it.

Five minutes later, she was back in the parking lot, a navy pea coat in one hand, her old soccer duffle bag, stuffed with clean and dirty clothes, in the other. She tossed both into the rear of the Jeep, then climbed into the driver's seat.

"I am so ready for Mom's lasagna," she said. "And Grandma's biscuits. And cinnamon rolls. And hot chocolate."

Janie Rose smiled – nervously, Charlie thought. "Clearly you don't have gluten allergies," she said.

Charlie tried to make conversation as she turned out of the dorm parking lot. "Where do you guys spend Christmas?"

"At our house. My grandparents sometimes come for the day."

"We bounce around between my grandparents' houses and ours and my aunts'," Charlie said. "It's chaotic."

"Sounds nice."

"Yeah, it really is."

Janie Rose seemed to calm down a little once the girls had left the Athens campus and pulled onto US 441, a meandering two-lane road that would take them to Interstate 85.

"Is everything all right?" Charlie asked. "You seem a little… tense."

"Just tired, I guess. I had four monster exams."

Charlie turned on the radio, flipping through two versions of "Jingle Bell Rock" until she found the slightly more palatable "Little Drummer Boy".

"I can finally get into the Christmas spirit," she sighed. "Pah rum pa pa pum."

Janie Rose gave a slight smile, and rolled her shoulders and neck. "I am tense. Guess it was all that studying."

Charlie glanced into the rearview mirror. Every twenty seconds, she could hear her dad saying. Look in the rearview mirror every twenty seconds. She'd missed her dad this semester. His calmness. His steadiness. He was her greatest cheerleader, even when, as she was learning to drive, she'd spied vultures in the field alongside the road and slid slowly into the ditch. He'd let her, not hollering, not startling her. When she realized what she'd done, she looked over and her dad was grinning. Then he got out and pushed the car back onto the road. "Best way to make sure you don't do it when it counts," he'd said matter-of-factly.

Now, without him next to her, she startled when she looked in the mirror. There was a black car on her bumper. "Where'd you come from?" Charlie said aloud.

Janie Rose whipped around. "What?" she said.

"That black car. It's right on our butt."

Janie Rose peered at it for a long moment, her face draining of color. "It's a hearse," she whispered.

"How can you tell?"

"I can see the length from this angle. Curtains in the back. The old-fashioned kind."

Charlie pulled as far as she could to the right, inviting the hearse to pass. With a dotted line and no cars in sight, it would be easy.

To her relief, the car pulled into the left lane. As it pulled abreast, she saw that Janie Rose was right: it was an old hearse, its black paint faded to iron gray. Short black curtains hung the full length, stopping at the front seat. Or what Charlie supposed was the front seat: the passenger window was tinted, so she couldn't see anyone or anything inside.

But now, instead of speeding past the Jeep, the hearse began to edge to the right.

"Hey!" Charlie shouted. "Look out!" She took her foot off the accelerator, trying to fall behind. But the hearse did the same. It inched closer and closer to Charlie's door. Anxiety rising, breath quickening, she sped up, but so did the hearse. Side by side, the cars drove like hitched horses down the rural stretch. To her right, flat soybean fields flashed by one minute, a stand of trees the next.

But this was northeast Georgia, and now the road rose. Beyond the shoulders, the fields gave way to thick forests lower than the road bed. To swerve off now would be to slide down an embankment and into the trees.

Charlie looked frantically in her rearview mirror, hoping to spot another car. But the road was empty behind and ahead. She stomped her foot to the floor. The old Jeep hesitated for several counts, then shuddered and leaped ahead. The hearse momentarily fell behind.

What was going on? She chanced a look at Janie Rose, who was plastered against the seat, eyes wide, face white, one hand clasping the handle above her door, the other planted on the dashboard.

The hearse caught up with them, accelerated into the left lane and began nudging toward Charlie again. "Stop it!" she screamed, looking toward the car's darkened interior to no avail. "Stop it!"

Any driver behaving so aggressively would have been terrifying. Somehow it was scarier that Charlie couldn't see anyone inside the eerie old hearse.

Worse yet, she was going much too fast. She clenched the steering wheel, knuckles straining against skin, heart pounding. "Stop it!" she shrieked again.

The hearse, flying alongside the Jeep, finally stopped its sideways inching toward Charlie's door. She barely registered the change, then realized the reason for it. The hearse's nose now swerved toward her, leaving Charlie no choice but to yank violently to the right herself.

The top-heavy Jeep began to flip, side over side, down a shallow embankment, toward the tree line. Inside, Janie Rose's screams joined hers.

CHAPTER TWO

B ranigan Powers was thinking about eggs. Not cooking or eating them. She wasn't a fan of the poached, fried, boiled or scrambled egg, and kept them on hand only for rare cookie baking. In fact, she sometimes threw them out because she went so long between baking stints.

So, No. 1, she was wondering if there were actually any eggs at home in her fridge. She needed to bake cookies for tomorrow night's staff party.

No. 2, she was thinking about the economy of eggs in northeast Georgia. What had once been an area rich in chicken farmers was now rich in egg farmers. That might sound like the same thing to the uninitiated. But Branigan's grandfather had raised chickens in two long, low heated houses – bringing in loads of fluffy yellow baby chicks that squeaked and peeped and scurried to one end of the long house. Months later, he'd barely be able to get into the houses because the grown white chickens took up so much room. He entered carefully, cautioning Branigan and her twin brother against making any sudden moves, so the chickens wouldn't stampede and smother each other. Chickens, Pa said, weren't the brightest animals on the farm. When they got to that house-filling adult size, big trucks came in and loaded them up. Branigan didn't like to think about that part, about what came next.

But now Pa's chicken houses sat empty, and a lot of the neighboring farms had the word EGGS written in giant letters over wide, two-story buildings, complete with parking lots. MASON EGGS. SHIPLEY EGGS. EDGAR EGGS. Chickens were presumably somewhere around, but it was eggs that the trucks loaded and shipped to grocery stores all over the South.

That was the story Branigan was writing for *The Grambling Rambler*, part business story, part holiday feature. How an upturn in holiday baking affected egg sales. While there wasn't enough Hanukkah baking so you'd notice in Grambling, there was in nearby Atlanta and the other cities served by Grambling's egg farms. So she included challah bread and the double-baked Mandelbrot along with the sugar cookies and gingerbread men and coconut cake she was writing about.

She typed a final paragraph mindlessly. She'd had about all she could take of this Christmas baking cheer. She was not looking forward to making Crunchy Jumble cookies – the secret to the crunch being Rice Krispies. She was not looking forward to the newspaper's annual staff party. She was not looking forward, even, to Christmas.

The events of the previous summer still weighed on her. She'd covered the murders of several homeless people, and it had ended badly. Trying to get into the Christmas spirit was agonizing to contemplate. Branigan wished she could circle December 26 on the calendar and be magically transported. The only bright spot was her nephew Chan heading home from Furman University later in the week, and his sister Charlie coming in from the University of Georgia.

Branigan stood and stretched, her back and shoulder muscles stiff from hunching over a laptop. Across the largely empty newsroom, she could hear the familiar sound of the police scanner squawking irritably to life. Jody Manson, the paper's police/court/government reporter leaned in closer. He jumped up and grabbed his jacket, calling to the city editor, "Fatality out near 85. You want a photo?"

"How far away?"

"Thirty, thirty-five miles. Sounds like the Athens exit."

"I'll call the stringer in Athens," the editor said, reaching for his phone.

Somebody's Christmas just got ruined, Branigan thought. *Like mine.*

It was past noon, and Branigan was scheduled to meet her friend Liam Delaney at 12:30 for lunch at Marshall's, a downtown diner. She pulled on a hip-length camel coat, freeing her shoulder-length blonde hair from its collar with a tug. She added a navy and emerald plaid scarf, purchased when the saleswoman exclaimed over the green's exact match to Branigan's eyes. Her eyes, an unusually vivid shade of green, often drew comments from salespeople.

She strode down the sunny sidewalk with the easy gait of a longtime runner, a practice she'd kept since high school more than two decades before. Purple and yellow and white pansies hung in the iron planters on the streetlights, a touch of old Grambling charm. On the other side of the lamp poles were stiff banners of gold sprinkled with glittery white snowflakes. This part of the South seldom saw the real kind.

She arrived at Marshall's with five minutes to spare. She found a table near the plate-glass windows, warmed by noon-day sun, and ordered an iced tea. Then she sat back to read the morning's paper a little more thoroughly than she'd managed at 8 a.m.

Robbery of a Salvation Army kettle. Sheesh. Was nothing sacred?

The opening of the holiday ice rink on Main Street.

In the *Style* section, a preview of a Moravian love feast on the Rutherford Lee campus. And a production of *The Best Christmas Pageant Ever* at the Grambling Little Theater. Branigan smiled at that. Maybe she could talk Aunt Jeanie into going.

The waitress came back, and Branigan looked at her watch: 12:45. Maybe Liam had forgotten. She called his cell phone, and left a message. "Did you forget me? I'm at Marshall's."

She wanted to talk to him about a story that Tanenbaum Grambling IV had requested. "Requested" as in "assigned", since Tan was editor and publisher of *The Rambler*. Tan wanted her to revisit the homeless encampment that she and Jody and Marjorie had written about last summer. "People want to know how these folks survive in the winter," he said; "what they do for Christmas. What are the agencies doing? The churches? Is there any coordination?"

Branigan planned to start with Liam, her old high school friend and former newspaper colleague, who was pastor of Jericho Road. His church had eighteen beds for homeless men, as well as a soup kitchen, social worker/mental health counselor, art room, music program and growing worship services. She knew a lot about Grambling's homeless community from her stories the previous summer, but she was hoping that Liam could fast-track her to the best sources for an update.

Only now he was really late, and she was starving. She signaled the waitress and ordered Marshall's famous vegetable soup and cornbread. She was just scraping her bowl clean when her cell phone rang.

She saw it was from Liam, and answered, "Where are you?"

"The ER. It's Charlie."

"What happened?"

"She's been in a bad accident. On her way home from school."

Branigan remembered Jody's police scanner. "Not the one on I-85?"

"On 441, close to it."

"Is she…?" Branigan couldn't finish the sentence. Her mind spun wildly. They wouldn't take a fatality to the emergency room, would they?

"We don't know anything yet," Liam said. "Her Jeep flipped. The girl in the passenger seat was killed."

"Oh, Liam, no! Who was it?"

"A friend from UGA. Janie Rose Carlton. You know her?"

"I know her mother. She teaches at Rutherford Lee. Oh, man. Janie Rose is her only child. Are the Carltons with you?"

"No, and I don't know much of anything at this point. Liz is on her way. The doctors kicked me out temporarily and I remembered I was supposed to be meeting you."

"I'll be there in a few minutes. Oh, wait! Liam!"

"Yeah?"

"Which hospital? Athens or here?"

"Here," he said. "St Joe's. The paramedics were able to reach me in time to ask."

Branigan threw more money than was necessary on the table and ran out.

CHAPTER THREE

The chaplain intern, a fluttery young woman who seemed intimidated by the fact that Liam was a pastor, placed Liam, his wife Liz and Branigan in a room for families of trauma patients. Technically, Branigan wasn't family, but no one was checking IDs. She was the biological aunt of Charlie's adopted brother, Chan; to both teens, she had always been Aunt Brani.

Liz looked unnerved to find Ina Rose and Harry Carlton already in the waiting room. Harry Carlton stared blankly, and Ina Rose said, "They brought Janie Rose to the hospital morgue. We're waiting to see her."

The intern moved a box of tissues closer to Ina Rose, but spoke to Liz and Liam. "We're waiting for a doctor to take them."

Liam nodded. He'd been in the intern's place during his own Clinical Pastoral Education rotation. Clearly the couple were in shock, so he gently took over. "Is there anyone I can call for you? A pastor? Janie Rose's grandparents?"

Harry Carlton looked at him as if he were speaking Hebrew.

"Why was she riding with your daughter?" He turned to his wife. "Why wasn't she in her own car?"

Liz stiffened, hearing the unspoken accusation. Ina Rose spoke to the Delaneys as well as to her husband. "She told me she asked Charlie for a ride, but I really don't know why. She said she would drive our Subaru over Christmas." She looked around helplessly. "We have an extra car. Two now, I guess."

Realizing what she'd said, she clamped a hand over her mouth to strangle a sob.

"Was she speeding?" Harry Carlton demanded. "Did your daughter speed?"

Liz started to speak, but Liam put a hand on her arm. "Mr Carlton, we have no way of knowing yet. The state patrol is on the scene. But Charlie is a good driver, a safe driver. It could've been a deer or a dog, or anything. We just don't know yet."

"We are very sorry for your loss," Liz said, standing and heading for the door. "I'm going to see about Charlie."

Darkness had fallen by the time Charlie was stabilized and moved from the trauma unit to a private room at St Joseph Medical Center. Since both her parents and, eventually, all four of her grandparents were on hand, Branigan was careful to remain in the background, fetching coffee, finding powdery creamers, and driving to the Delaneys' to pack an overnight bag for Liz. In a call from the newsroom, Jody had also given her the unpleasant task of approaching the Carltons to see if they wanted to comment for *The Rambler*'s story. They didn't.

Harry Carlton glared at her, but Ina Rose, with whom she was acquainted through previous stories at the college, attempted a smile.

"Whenever you're ready," Branigan told her as they left the hospital. "Some families like people to know who their loved one was. But it's totally up to you."

"Maybe later," Ina Rose said.

The couple climbed into a gleaming black Mercedes and drove away. Branigan made her way back to the fourth floor, where Charlie lay with her right arm and leg broken, three ribs cracked. Both eyes were blackened and her pretty face was swollen. Two lower teeth were missing.

Branigan was about to leave as Charlie woke up. Liam and Liz and their parents crowded around her bed. Branigan hung back, giving them privacy.

After a few minutes, she heard Charlie ask, "Dad, is… Aunt Brani here?"

"She sure is." Liz's and Liam's parents, looking relieved, stepped away to give Branigan room. Liz's mom squeezed her arm, and her dad gave her a quick hug.

Charlie's blue eyes, hardly recognizable in her battered face, sought Branigan's. "Aunt... Brani," she said, her voice thick and raspy. "It wasn't... accident."

"What?" Liz and Liam exclaimed at the same time. Charlie's eyes flitted to them, closed briefly. "I need... to tell... Aunt Brani..." She was fighting the pain meds the doctors had given her, struggling to stay awake.

Liz and Liam remained rooted to her bedside. "What, baby girl?" Branigan whispered.

"The... police," she said. "Tell... police." Her eyelids flickered.

Branigan leaned closer. "Tell the police what?"

Charlie whispered one more phrase, then fell asleep again.

"It was whose?" Branigan said. "Janie Rose's?"

"What'd she say?" Liam asked.

"'It was hers,' I think she said."

"What was hers?" asked Liz.

Chapter Four

Malachi Ezekiel Martin scrunched against a wall in the emergency waiting room, as far from the entrance and its blasts of cold air as he could get. From his place there, next to Roger the Dodger who sounded like he was hacking up a lung, he watched Pastor Liam, then Miz Liz, then Miz Branigan race in. A little later, Miz Branigan rushed out, only to return with a suitcase.

Hours later, he saw Miz Branigan, looking mighty uncomfortable, walk out with a slumped couple, the woman all crying, the man like he had a broomstick up his butt. Miz Branigan watched, arms folded, as they got into a big black car.

Something was up with Pastor Liam's family. He could stop Miz Branigan and ask. They were friends. Yeah, he'd say they were friends. But everyone looked so serious and so sad he didn't want to bother them. After he'd gotten Roger the Dodger seen to, he'd bike over to Jericho Road and ask what was up. The dudes there would know.

Roger the Dodger wasn't getting the attention Pastor Liam's family had got. But then the homeless usually didn't – unless it was a heart attack or stroke or car versus bicycle situation. For casual homeless diseases – Malachi suspected bronchitis from the way Roger was wheezing – a man might die of boredom before the disease got him.

The bad part was they'd wasted a warm day inside the waiting room. Now that the sun was down, it'd turned cold. Malachi could feel it every time that door whooshed open. Now was the time you wanted to hit the emergency room. Malachi had spent many a winter's night in these chairs coughing dramatically when a security guard walked by.

Malachi looked over at Roger, slumped and coughing for real.

Malachi didn't like Roger much. For one thing, Roger was a thief. Hence his name, as in the Artful Dodger. Malachi didn't hold with thieving, or with begging, for that matter.

The only reason he was with Roger was that Roger had brought a bottle to his tent last night. So when Roger woke up with a hangover and a hacking cough and a tight chest, he asked Malachi to take him to the hospital.

Malachi balanced the smaller man on his handlebars as best he could and wobbled him all the way to St Joe's. And here they'd sat since late morning, the waiting room filled with people coughing and sneezing and even vomiting. Lord, if he weren't sick coming in, he'd be sick going out.

"Roger Louis Tompkins," called a nurse.

Malachi stood abruptly. "Thas you," he said. "I'm headin' back to my tent." A cold night there sounded better than a warm one in this germ-infested place.

Malachi slid into the dark night. Within moments, no one could have described the ebony-skinned man in faded camo pants and gray sweatshirt, a black do-rag covering blacker dreadlocks.

CHAPTER FIVE

Charlie woke with a start, brought to wakefulness by the pain of simply breathing. She saw her leg raised in some kind of trapeze, but she couldn't feel it. Neither could she feel her right arm lying like a dead weight in the cast beside her.

She took a deep breath, and shuddered at the knife in her side. She turned her head slowly, cautiously, and saw Liz asleep on a cot.

"Mom?" she whispered, careful not to expand her lungs more than necessary. Liz was on her feet in an instant.

"Charlotte? Are you hurting?"

"Did Aunt Brani… call the police?" she croaked.

"I'm sorry, sweetie, but she couldn't figure out what you were trying to say. She'll be back in the morning."

Charlie winced. She wanted pain medicine, but more than that she wanted to pass on information before the blackness overtook her. She licked her lips and tried to swallow. "Water?"

Liz flipped on the light above the bed, and reached for the filled Styrofoam cup on the bedside table, guiding the straw to her daughter's mouth. Charlie gulped. Liz flinched as she watched the pain pass over her face.

"Mom? It was a… hearse."

Liz looked at her, uncomprehending. "What was?"

Charlie swallowed again, nodded to indicate she wanted another sip.

Liz gave it to her, her eyes never leaving Charlie's blackened ones. "A hearse… ran me off the road."

"Oh," said Liz, understanding finally dawning. "A hearse. We thought you were saying 'hers'. As in Janie Rose's."

"Janie Rose," Charlie said the name flatly. Panic came into her eyes as she looked around the room. "Where is… Janie Rose?"

Liz hesitated, not knowing how much Charlie could absorb. In the end she said nothing, for Charlie began to fade out. "Tell them," she said groggily, "Janie Rose… is scared. Tell them… no one… was driving… the hearse…."

Liz looked at her watch, saw that it would be light in another hour. She'd let Branigan, out at her farmhouse, sleep a little longer. This latest pronouncement from Charlie made no more sense than her first.

Liam was the first one in Charlie's room after dawn, bringing coffee to Liz.

"Did you call Chandler?" she asked, taking the cup gratefully.

"No, his last exam is this morning, then he's headed home. There wasn't anything he could do except get upset and flunk it. He'll know soon enough."

She nodded. "You're right."

"Doctors been in yet?"

"No, but she woke up…" Liz checked her watch, "two hours ago. She said a hearse ran her off the road. Hearse. That's what she was trying to say yesterday."

"A hearse? That's crazy."

At that moment, two Georgia state patrol officers knocked on the open door. Liam, who'd met them briefly in the emergency room the previous afternoon, greeted them. "Have you found out anything?"

"All we found was the Jeep," said the muscular one he remembered as Officer Langreen, his blue shirt straining against massive arms and chest. "No skid marks. No witnesses. Miss Carlton's side hit a tree. She died instantly."

Both Liz and Liam's eyes went to their sleeping daughter, instinctively wanting to protect her from this news.

"But there was something odd." The Delaneys' attention swung back to the officer. "The Jeep's hatchback door was up and the girls' luggage had been thrown out. A large black suitcase was open, with clothes all over the site. We've seen this before with an impact like that." He hesitated.

"So what was odd?" asked Liam.

"There was also a duffel bag, like maybe for a softball or soccer player."

"I'm sure it was Charlie's," said Liz.

"Well, it was unzipped, and the clothes from it appeared to be scattered too. No impact did that."

The four adults were silent for a moment. Finally Liz spoke and her voice sounded hoarse to her ears. "Do you think someone came by and went through their things rather than call for help?"

Officer Langreen shrugged. "Could be. Or someone did both. We got an anonymous 911 call about the accident. But no one was there when we arrived."

The second officer, shorter and slimmer than his partner, spoke up. Officer Montrelle, Liam recalled. "Did I overhear you say that a hearse ran your daughter off the road?"

Liz nodded. "She woke up a couple of hours ago, and that's what she said. But I'm not sure she wasn't dreaming. She said no one was driving the hearse."

"We'll need to talk to her as soon as she wakes up," said Officer Montrelle.

"We understand," said Liam. "Will she be charged?"

Liz looked at her husband in horror.

Officer Montrelle shook his head. "Too early to tell. There are no signs of drinking or texting. So someone may have forced them off the road. We just can't know until we talk to her."

Liam nodded gravely, ushering the officers politely from Charlie's room. Only when he returned could Liz see his face, blanched and pale, every freckle standing out like a tiny circle of dried blood.

CHAPTER SIX

For once, Branigan rose before Cleo, the regal, tan and black German shepherd that shared her farmhouse. It wasn't that Branigan owned her exactly. She and the dog both knew better than that.

Cleo came from a line of shepherds raised on this land fifteen minutes outside of Grambling, and she and Branigan shared the brick ranch that had belonged to Branigan's grandparents. Once a working farm where Pa Rickman raised cattle and chickens, and where Gran canned the plentiful tomatoes, okra, beans and corn it produced, it was now owned by Branigan's mother and Uncle Bobby. Aunt Jeanie and Uncle Bobby owned the adjoining farm, and let their cattle roam between Pa's pastures and their own, occasionally using Pa's barn for their gorgeous Angus.

Branigan wasn't much of a farmer, but in the summer she did grow a few cantaloupes and watermelons among the flowers surrounding the house. She liked the smell of the cantaloupes as much as their taste – a smell she identified with home.

"We may not have time for a run tonight," she told Cleo, "so you get your own exercise today." She poured dog food into Cleo's bowl, cereal into her own, then brewed a four-cup pot of coffee. After eating, she showered quickly, washing and drying her hair, and dressing in slim-legged black pants, a cropped houndstooth jacket and slouchy suede boots. She grabbed her black leather satchel, letting Cleo out to roam the farm.

"Go terrorize some squirrels," she said, kissing the top of the dog's head. Then she drove to the hospital.

* * *

Branigan watched as two Georgia state patrol officers left Charlie's room. The girl was stirring as she entered, her parents hovering over her bed.

"Branigan," said Liz, as if she'd been waiting for her. "I'm glad you're here. Charlie woke up a few hours ago, asking for you. She said to tell you that a hearse ran her off the road."

Branigan stared. "A hearse? As in dead bodies?"

Liz nodded. "And she said that Janie Rose was afraid. She seemed coherent, but she wasn't making a lot of sense."

Charlie opened her eyes and looked around wildly. "Janie Rose?" She stared straight at her dad. "Where's Janie Rose?"

Liam took her good hand. "I'm sorry, Char," he said. "But Janie Rose didn't make it."

Charlie looked stricken for a moment. Then her eyes sought Branigan's. "Aunt Brani, Janie Rose knew... something. She was scared. Even before the hearse... she was scared." Charlie's eyes pleaded for understanding.

"And a hearse forced you off the road, honey? Do you know what mortuary it was from?"

Charlie looked away for a moment, as if in thought. "No... not from... a mortuary," she corrected. "An old black one. With those... curtains. Not like Dad uses."

Liam shrugged. "I guess she means when I perform funeral services."

Charlie's eyes went to him gratefully. "Yeah... not like that. Like... the Ghostbusters drive."

The three laughed at the unexpected comment. Charlie closed her eyes. She was asleep again.

"Did you tell the patrol officers?" Branigan asked the Delaneys. They nodded.

"But not about Janie Rose being scared," Liz said. "That was new. Also, the officers said that someone had gone through the girls' luggage."

"What?"

Liam nodded. "Charlie's soccer bag was unzipped, and that wouldn't have been caused by the impact." A thoughtful look came over his face. "But Liz, could she have left it unzipped? Seems like I've seen her do that."

"Yeah, when she had it too full or was in a hurry. I guess it's possible."

"So someone may or may not have gone through their luggage," Liam said.

Branigan gave Liz a hug. "I need to talk to Janie Rose's parents. 'Student killed on her way home from college.' It's a big story." She looked at her friends, guilty at the thought that it could have been them she was interviewing.

Liam was a former reporter, so he understood. Liz wasn't. She shook her head silently.

Branigan wasn't sure where the Carltons would be. Funeral home, maybe. That might be a good place to ask about a hearse as well. There was no question which funeral home she'd head to. Collier was the one for Grambling's well-to-do.

On the way, Branigan phoned the newsroom to confer with Jody and make sure he hadn't reached the Carltons yet. The reporters sure didn't want to double-team them on this part of the story. Jody assured her he wasn't anxious to talk to the parents, and gave her his blessing – with relief, she thought, as they disconnected. Branigan hated this part of her job.

She reached Collier Funeral Home far too quickly and recognized the Carltons' black Mercedes in the spot closest to the front door. She steeled herself and went in.

Well, no, wait a minute. She could concentrate on the hearse first. She relaxed a little, unsure if she was being smart or cowardly.

"I need to see Ranson, please," she told the young woman at the receptionist's desk. Fortunately, the funeral home owner was an old high school friend who was now running his family's business. There were advantages to working in the city you grew up in, and this was one of them. "Tell him it's Branigan Powers."

She'd barely had time to open a magazine in the waiting room that was more expensively furnished than most Grambling homes when Ranson Collier stuck his head out of his office. "Brani G," he whispered with a broad grin. "Come on in."

Ranson had that salt-and-pepper hair that could look either old or distinguished. On him it looked distinguished. He was better looking at forty-one than he'd been at eighteen.

He pulled Branigan close for a quick hug. "It's good to see you. This isn't about your folks, is it?"

"No, no, they're fine," she said, belatedly realizing that Ranson would never allow a reporter, even her, to question customers on his property. "I've got a question for you."

"Shoot."

"As you know, Ina Rose and Harry Carlton lost their daughter yesterday."

Ranson nodded. "They're planning her service right now."

"Well, you probably know from this morning's *Rambler* that she was riding with Liam and Liz Delaney's daughter, Charlie. Charlie is pretty banged up, but when she woke, she told us she'd been forced off the road by a hearse. An old-fashioned kind with curtains. She actually said it was one like the Ghostbusters drove. Only black."

Ranson strode to his laptop and with a few clicks brought up a picture of Ecto-1 from the popular Ghostbusters movies. Branigan recognized the long white car with guns on top and the red slashed circles indicating "no ghosts allowed".

"It was a 1959 Cadillac," Ranson read, "which sort of doubled as a hearse and ambulance."

"When's the last time you saw that model?"

Ranson shrugged. "Decades, I'd guess. A collector bought our last one when I was a boy. I remember my Uncle Jasper talking about it. But I don't remember the car itself."

"Would any funeral homes still have one?"

Ranson rubbed his jaw. "I wouldn't think so. Your best bet is going to be antique car collectors. I can call my dad and Jasper and see if they know any."

"Please do." Branigan handed him her business card. "Here's my email address if you can get that ASAP." She looked out of Ranson's window and saw the Carltons' car still in the parking lot.

She said her goodbyes and refrained from telling him she needed to catch the Carltons. No funeral director wanted to hear that.

Musing in the parking lot, Branigan decided she might have better luck with Ina Rose Carlton alone than with her husband. She called the switchboard of Rutherford Lee College and was connected to the secretary of the religion department. When she asked if Ina Rose Carlton was expected, the secretary put her on hold. Seconds later she was back.

"Apparently we do expect Dr Carlton this afternoon," she said. "I wasn't sure. Do you want to leave a message?"

Branigan hesitated. She feared Ina Rose might not return a call. "Tell her I'll drop by her office at one, please."

"I'll leave the message."

Branigan checked her watch. That gave her nearly two hours. Plenty of time to drive to the site of the accident and back.

Collier Funeral Home was two blocks off Main Street, in a former residential area. Most of the august houses and porch-wrapped cottages had been converted to law offices, with the exception of the funeral home and a stately bed and breakfast. She pointed her taupe Honda Civic toward Main, then turned left to head to the interstate. Standing on the corner, waiting for the light to change, was Malachi Martin, his black dreadlocks framing a thin face, his faded olive fatigues topped by a gray hoodie. The sweatshirt's hood was thrown back in favor of a nylon do-rag, added since last summer.

On an impulse, she lowered her car window. "Malachi!" she called. "Want to help me on a story?"

Malachi's face didn't change, as if a professional white woman offering a ride to a homeless black man happened every day in Grambling. He nodded solemnly and hopped in the passenger side. "This have anythin' to do with Miz Charlie?"

Branigan turned to stare at him. "How did you know?"

"Saw you an' Pastor Liam an' Miz Liz at the hospital."

"You're an observant man, my friend." Branigan knew from experience just how observant Malachi was. He had figured out the summer murderer of homeless people when she and the Grambling police could not. "Charlie was in an accident on her way home from the University of Georgia yesterday," she said. "The friend riding with her was killed. Charlie says a hearse forced them off the road. I'm going out to look at the wreck site, and I'd love another pair of eyes."

Malachi nodded, as if this made all the sense in the world. He had nothing more pressing to do.

Forty minutes later, Branigan eased off US 441 near an embankment where Malachi pointed out yellow Georgia state patrol tape encircling several trees.

They walked down the hill through the mild December sunshine, a car passing on the road above them only sporadically. They could see the divots the rolling Jeep had cut.

"Miz Charlie drive an old Jeep Cherokee," Malachi said. "I seen it at Jericho Road."

"It was totaled, Liam said."

Malachi pointed to a thick maple trunk, scraped and scarred. "Look like she hit this one pretty good."

"But a hearse," Branigan mused, looking around at the bare trees and the largely empty roadway. "Why would a hearse force two college girls off the road?"

Malachi didn't answer. He walked around the copse of trees cordoned off by the state patrol, and pushed further into the woods. Branigan could hear him tramping through the underbrush, but she couldn't make him out. His clothing blended in with the bark and the evergreens, the brush and cedars and pines of these northeast Georgia woods. Twenty minutes later, he emerged forty feet away, and walked, head down, back along the roadside grass.

"Maybe," he said, as if twenty minutes had not passed, "it ain't so much what we seein'."

"Meaning what?"

"I mean it looks like a hearse drove two college girls off the road. But what else was Miz Charlie and her friend?"

Branigan looked at Malachi, a possibility dawning. "Like maybe they are daughters? And maybe someone wanted to send a message to their parents?" She thought for a moment. "Probably not a message for a preacher and an interior designer," she added, referring to the Delaneys. "But maybe for a steel company CEO."

After Branigan had dropped Malachi at the Cannon County public library – at his request – it was time to head to the college. Rutherford Lee was a sprawling, beautifully landscaped campus a few miles east of downtown. Branigan was pretty sure that the founder Rutherford Lee was not in Robert E.'s family tree, but in the heart of Georgia, the Confederate general's surname didn't hurt.

The college's dorms were built around a man-made lake, complete with ducks and swans; woods surrounded it on three sides. In the century since its founding, fountains and flower beds, playing fields and state-of-the-art classroom buildings had been added. The private school was quite good, and quite expensive. Ironically, wealthy students from Atlanta and other parts of Georgia enrolled in droves, while Grambling's own students, like Charlie and Janie Rose, favored the state university in Athens.

Branigan drove through the arched brick entrance. Her paternal grandfather had taught economics here in the 1970s and 80s, so she'd visited the campus often. The religion department, she remembered, was housed in the same building as economics. She parked in a large lot near the student center, and stopped to order two coffees before walking to the classroom building next door.

Once inside, she sought out the glass-encased directory and saw that Dr Ina Rose Carlton had an office on the second floor. In previous visits, she'd met her in lecture halls. Branigan drew a deep breath and headed up the stairs holding the coffee before her, a grief offering.

Ina Rose's office door was open, and she was on the phone accepting condolences with mechanical murmurs. Her long brown hair was clipped neatly in an old-fashioned clasp at the back of her neck. Her skin was pale, paler even than the ivory blouse she wore. Her brown eyes, normally her best feature, showed broken blood vessels, and circles underneath revealed a sleepless night.

She motioned with her head for Branigan to sit down in the chair opposite her desk. Branigan breathed an inward sigh of relief: Ina Rose's Southern manners had her on automatic pilot, and she wouldn't throw the reporter out of her office.

When Ina Rose hung up, she pressed a button on her phone that Branigan assumed would send callers to voicemail. She came around her desk and took a seat in a second chair, shifting it to face Branigan. Unsmiling, seemingly braced, she faced the reporter she'd once prevailed upon to cover lectures and seminars sponsored by the religion department.

Branigan began with condolences – and an apology. Before she could finish, Ina Rose interrupted. "I appreciate that, Branigan. But I've been thinking about what you said yesterday, and I've decided you're right. I do want people to know who Janie Rose was. That's why I'm here when everybody is telling me to go home." She tried to smile, but her lips trembled. "TV is coming too. I didn't want them in our home, in Janie Rose's room." She paused for a moment, accepted a coffee, and swallowed hard. "So tell me what you need."

Branigan started with questions about Janie Rose's childhood, leading her mother through memories of the girl's gymnastics, water skiing, cheerleading. Pausing to grab a tissue to wipe her eyes, Ina Rose smiled. "You're asking the same things I'll need to tell our pastor for her eulogy." She clenched her eyes and sat silently for a moment. Branigan waited, handing her another tissue.

"Take your time."

Ina Rose told about her daughter's years at Montclair High on Grambling's Eastside, a summer job in a popular pizza restaurant, volunteer work at the Cannon County Humane Society, her love for the mixed terrier, Cash, she brought home.

"And then she went to the University of Georgia?" Branigan prompted.

"Well, no, not at first. She came here her freshman year."

"Oh, I assumed she was a freshman. Like Charlie."

"No."

Branigan waited, but Ina Rose didn't say anything more. "Dr Carlton?" She waited. "Can you tell me about Janie Rose's time at Rutherford Lee?"

Ina Rose was silent for another moment. "Can we go off the record?"

"All right."

Ina Rose drew in a deep breath. "Janie Rose wasn't happy here. In fact…" She stopped again. "In fact, she had a nervous breakdown." Now that it was out, Ina Rose seemed relieved. She hurried on. "Her father and I were never exactly sure what happened. Janie wouldn't say. Harry thought it was a boy. I'm not so sure."

Ina Rose twisted her fingers in her lap. "Her first semester was fine. She had good grades. She seemed happy during Christmas break. At the beginning of second semester, she pledged a sorority. She talked about going on spring break to Daytona with the sisters. She was dating a young man from Louisiana, I believe it was.

"Then in mid-February I got a call from our counseling center. Janie Rose was crying hysterically, and the counselor convinced her to call me. Thank goodness she did. The counselor got Janie's permission to share her concerns with me. She and I both suspected at first that Janie'd been raped. But after awhile, I didn't think so."

Branigan allowed the pause to stretch out. When Ina Rose didn't continue, she asked, "You didn't think she'd been raped because…?"

Ina Rose shook her head. "Because Janie Rose denied it, but she denied it without much interest, if you know what I mean. She wasn't upset with the question. She was just dismissive. So then I started wondering if she'd gotten hold of bad drugs." Ina Rose looked miserable, and Branigan wisely remained silent. "That's how out of touch I was. I didn't know if my own daughter was using drugs." Her voice cracked on that final statement, and she stopped talking. She closed her eyes and breathed deeply. When she spoke again, her voice was calmer.

"At any rate, Janie dropped out and came home. We put her in counseling, of course. But she never did tell us – or the counselor – what happened. I don't even know if anything did happen, or if it was some… some…" Ina Rose threw up her hands. "I don't even know what! But by May she was better and took make-up classes at Grambling Tech over the summer. She was able to enter the University of Georgia in August as a sophomore."

Ina Rose slumped. "We haven't told anyone that," she said tonelessly. "Harry would be very angry with me."

"You were off the record," Branigan said. "I won't use it unless you change your mind and tell me it's okay."

Ina Rose nodded.

"So tell me about her first semester at Georgia."

"She seemed fine." Her mother shrugged helplessly. "Good mid-term grades. She wasn't interested in pledging a sorority again. Of course, I was the anxious parent, calling every other day. She insisted that everything was fine and she was looking forward to being home for Christmas."

"Your husband seemed surprised that she didn't drive her car home from school."

"I thought it was odd too. But Janie Rose told me the night before that she planned to ride home with Charlie Delaney and drive our Subaru while she was here. I honestly didn't think much of it."

"Dr Carlton, when Charlie woke up, she told me that a car, a hearse actually, forced the girls off the road."

"What?" Ina Rose sounded bewildered. "A hearse? You mean someone speeding to a funeral?"

"No, an antique-style hearse from the 1950s, with curtains over the windows."

Ina Rose looked mystified. "Like the Kappa Eps'?"

Now it was Branigan's turn to look puzzled. "What do you mean?"

"One of the sororities here has an old hearse they use on homecoming floats and such. Kind of their shtick. Never mind. Surely it wasn't theirs. Did you tell the Georgia patrol officers what Charlie said?"

"Yes, the Delaneys did."

"I can't imagine what that means."

"Was that the sorority Janie Rose pledged?"

"Kappa Epsilon Chi? No. She pledged Gamma Delta Phi."

"Was Janie Rose…" Branigan hesitated, began again. "Charlie said something else. She said Janie Rose was jumpy, scared – even before the girls saw the hearse. Does that mean anything to you?"

"No." Ina Rose was shaking her head as if trying to clear it. "No. Not at all."

"Okay, my last question. Can you tell me about your husband's work?"

Ina Rose looked bewildered, but answered anyway. "He runs a steel company. Shaner. You probably remember they moved the headquarters here from Philadelphia seven years ago. I'm from North Carolina originally and had always wanted to get back to the South, so I was happy to come."

Branigan paused for a beat. "Would anyone want to hurt you or your husband?"

For the first time, she saw a veil drop over Ina Rose's eyes. "Of course not. No. What does that have to do with Janie Rose?"

"Probably nothing. But if things are as Charlie describes, the girls' wreck was no accident. It was deliberate."

Ina Rose's hand crept to her lips as this new horror hit her. Branigan watched as the realization dawned: there could be something worse than losing your daughter in an accident.

CHAPTER SEVEN

Malachi finished his salad, lasagna and brownie, slipping an apple into his pocket for later. You never knew when you might miss a meal, so it was good to have a back-up.

He waited until the other ragged people cleared out, most of them nodding, tipping their baseball caps, murmuring "Malachi" as they passed. Some of the younger ones even said, "Mr Malachi," before going back to their shoving and silliness.

Malachi was respected on the street. Part of it was the length of time he'd been there, and part of it was his reputation. He wasn't a big man, not at all. And he wasn't a threatening one. It was more the way he carried himself. Well, that and stories about knives snatched and guns kicked away before an attacker had a chance to use them.

Malachi was a Desert Storm vet, so the whispers went, trained in high-tech warfare. Or he was a tank gunner. Or a sniper. Rumors on the street ran pretty wild, and Malachi was credited with all manner of histories.

He tossed his sauce-smeared plate into the trash, then heaved the full bag from the container, tying off the top. He hoisted the bag into a wagon of molded blue plastic and rolled it into the Jericho Road parking lot. He passed the flower beds, cleared out for winter, heading for the dented green dumpster. Malachi believed in "paying" for his meal by emptying trash, doing chores. Staff member Dontegan Johnstone thanked him when he stepped back inside. "No problem," Malachi said, settling his backpack over his shoulders and leaving the church's dining hall.

The afternoon stretched before him. And he was thinking about Miz Charlie. He'd watched her grow up, shared pizza and Coke with her many a Friday night right here at Jericho Road. Watched her grow into a thoughtful and pretty young woman who was almost as worried about Grambling's homeless as her dad was.

He'd had Miz Branigan drop him at the library after going to the wreck site because he wanted to know what a 1950s hearse looked like exactly. He didn't have a clear picture in his head.

The thing was, he'd heard something unusual last night. He'd dismissed it at the time because most of what you heard under the Garner Bridge was worthless, untrue – or both. But the word was a black station wagon had been discovered deep in the woods, and Ralph and Maylene had grabbed it. Especially in winter, a car that could keep out water, wind and wildlife wasn't half bad.

So instead of heading down an abandoned street and across a worn path to his tent under the bridge, Malachi took the long way – through a thick patch of hardwoods and scrub brush that opened onto another vacant spot beneath the towering bridge. He found three tents, an open fire pit and a picnic table loaded with canned goods and bottled water. No one was around.

Rather than going up a hill and crossing railroad tracks to his own encampment, he turned and walked out the way he'd come, peering more intently into the woods this time, pushing aside pine limbs and overgrowth. Now he saw it. Down a gentle slope, he watched Ralph placing a circle of rocks for a fire pit beside his new quarters.

It could be called a station wagon all right. It was wide and long and low, a black faded to gray, with foot-long curtains hung inside.

But after his hour in the library, Malachi knew it had another name as well. A hearse.

CHAPTER EIGHT

B ranigan wrote a compelling story about Janie Rose to run with childhood pictures Ina Rose sent over. One, taken at age six, showed a skinny, gap-toothed girl in a gymnastics leotard. One, at thirteen and in braces, had her posed on a boat dock, a slalom ski tucked under one arm. One, at sixteen and in the Montclair High cheerleading miniskirt, showed the girl's startling development: her teeth were white and straight, her brown hair glossy, her petite legs shapely. A fourth photo had been taken for the Rutherford Lee yearbook. Shot during the girl's first semester, it showed a beautiful young woman with her mother's pale skin and long dark hair. Branigan thought Janie Rose's hazel eyes looked clear and hopeful. But maybe that was her imagination.

The pictures affected her in a way her mother's descriptions had not.

Branigan sighed and signaled to Julie Ames, the *Style* editor, that the story was ready. She glanced at her watch. She would barely have time to get to the farm and bake cookies before the staff party. Too bad she couldn't come up with an excuse to miss it altogether.

An early dusk was falling when Cleo leaped up to meet the Honda Civic, energetically lapping the car several times. "Sorry, girl," Branigan greeted her. "But we don't have time for a run."

Branigan tapped in the code to her alarm system, then flipped the oven dial to pre-heat before going to her bedroom. She shed her watch and rings, boots and jacket before returning to the kitchen to lay the ingredients for Crunchy Jumble cookies on the island. She looked at them morosely, then poured herself a glass of pinot noir.

False cheer is better than no cheer, she told herself.

By the time the cookies were done, Branigan had showered and changed into fitted jeans and a silky white sweater that set off her green eyes. She started to put her hair up, but with no humidity, it hung straight and sleek. She decided to let it hang loose.

She stacked the cookies into a plastic canister and headed for the door where Cleo moped.

"I know, girl. I promise we'll run tomorrow, okay?"

She set the code on the farmhouse's alarm and stepped into the dark night of the countryside, where no streetlights interrupted the gloom.

"Staff party" was a somewhat hopeful name for a dismal affair. When Branigan had joined *The Grambling Rambler* at twenty-two, management paid for extravagant holiday parties at the Nicholas Inn, directly across the street from the newspaper building. It was a historic hotel, rather grand even then. More recently, it had been renovated and restored to its early twentieth-century glory; unfortunately, its journalistic neighbors could no longer afford it.

The staff was going the way of most newspaper personnel, with forced retirements and layoffs siphoning nearly two-thirds of their number. For a while during the decline, holiday parties moved to the home of publisher and editor Tanenbaum Grambling IV. But then even he couldn't stomach inviting people into his home at Christmas and laying them off the next summer.

So now the parties were held in the home of whatever mid-level editor could be coerced. Tonight it fell to Bert Feldspar, the city editor.

Bert's wife answered the door, and hugged Branigan. "Food in the dining room." She pointed. "Bar in the living room."

Branigan veered first into the dining room to drop off the cookies and grab a handful of almonds, before going into the living room for a glass of red wine. She greeted several colleagues, then spotted Jody getting a beer. They plopped down together on a small sofa.

"Tell me what's new," she demanded. "Anything on your end?"

Jody was an old friend who'd stayed with *The Rambler* through the years Branigan worked in Detroit. He knew the city as well as anyone. "Actually, yes. I just read the story you posted, with Charlie Delaney saying she was run off the road by a hearse. The police got a report today about a stolen hearse."

Branigan sat up straight. "You're kidding."

He nodded. "A sorority at Rutherford Lee had an old hearse for some reason. They reported it stolen around 5 o'clock today."

"The Kappa Eps?" Branigan said.

"Now how did you know that?"

"Janie Rose's mother mentioned they had one. For homecoming floats and stuff like that."

"Apparently, someone took it from a parking lot behind the sorority house. But they don't know when. The police report said they haven't used it since Halloween, so they really haven't been keeping an eye on it. They realized today it was missing, but it could have been taken any time in November or December, right up until yesterday."

Branigan stood. "If you're ready to abandon this party, why don't we pay a visit to the Kappa Epsilon house?"

Exams at the private college ran on longer than at the state school, so most of Rutherford Lee's student parking lots remained full. Branigan and Jody found space behind the university chapel, its floodlit cross commanding the manicured campus. They hurried up a sidewalk beside the chapel gardens, huddling into their coats for warmth. They crossed the one-way road that meandered through the college, and walked to Greek Row, a street of mid-twentieth-century houses marking the school's northern border. The campus was well lit, and oversized letters on the front of each stately brick house allowed them to locate the Kappa Epsilon Chi residence easily.

A young woman in pajama pants and a Duke T-shirt answered the door. Branigan remembered her grandfather remarking on the puzzling tendency of students to wear the logos of other colleges, as if they weren't quite sure they'd made the right choice. She'd laughed because she'd done the same when she was in school. A handful of similarly dressed young women lounged in the living room. Kappa Epsilon must be one of the more laid-back sororities: Branigan had heard of some Deep South sororities that still required street clothes, or even skirts, in their public rooms.

"Can I help you?" asked the Duke girl.

Branigan introduced herself and Jody as *Rambler* reporters. "We'd like to talk to someone about the stolen hearse."

"Oh, right. Let me get Sophie for you. She's our president."

Jody murmured in Branigan's ear, "Sophie Long. That's the name on the police report."

The women made room for the reporters on one of three sofas. One introduced herself as a journalism major and asked if she could sit in on their interview.

"By all means," Branigan said. "You never know who might have information."

A slender woman with severely short raven hair came down the stairs in gray sweatpants and a purple and white Furman University sweatshirt. "In that case," she said, "we can talk in here and let everyone stay." She held out her hand. "I'm Sophie Long."

Two of the women got up, saying they had to study, but the others looked on with interest. "I'm surprised *The Rambler* wants to do a story on a stolen car," Sophie said.

"It's part of a bigger story," Branigan said. "There was a fatality involving an old hearse yesterday. Out on 441 near Athens."

"Oh my gosh! Was it ours?"

"There's no way of knowing yet. But it's quite a coincidence that yours was reported stolen the same day. Tell me about your car."

Sophie bit her lower lip. "I'm a senior, and the hearse was already here when I came as a freshman. We have scrapbooks showing it in pictures for years before that. It's sort of the Kappa Ep 'thing'. We use it on our homecoming float every September, then we pull it into our front yard and decorate it the week of Halloween. We use it to drive girls to rush functions in January." Sophie paused. "You know what rush is, right?"

Branigan nodded, remembering the squeals and fake smiles from her own university days, as sorority women and freshmen girls engaged in their strange mating dance.

Sophie continued, "Also, when a sister gets engaged, we make her lie down in the back, and we all pile in and drive around campus, honking the horn."

Seeing Jody's face, she grimaced. "Silly, I know."

"So, clearly it runs?" Branigan asked.

"Oh, yeah."

"And where do you park it?"

"Since we're on the end of Greek Row, we have a little more parking than the other houses. Our lot holds the hearse, and space for another twelve cars."

"Who keeps the key?"

"Nobody. It hangs on a hook in the kitchen."

Branigan and Jody glanced at each other. "So when did you notice it was missing?" she asked.

"That's the hard part," Sophie said. "Of course, we used it during Halloween week. The day after Halloween, I returned it to the parking lot. I've been back there two or three times since then, but I couldn't tell you if it was there or not." She turned to the other girls. "Do any of you remember seeing it for sure after Halloween?"

The journalism major sat up straighter. "Yes, I do!"

All faces turned toward her.

"I can tell you exactly when it was." She leaped to her feet and ran up the stairs, then returned seconds later with an oxblood leather journal. Branigan smiled to see it was similar to one she'd used as a teen.

Sophie spoke as the girl flipped through the pages. "This is Anna Hester, by the way. One of our sophomore sisters."

"Yeah, hi," Anna said. Then, "Here it is." She turned to her sisters. "You guys can't tell anyone. I'm going to sound like an idiot. But Mike – that's my boyfriend," she said, glancing at Branigan, "gave me his fraternity pin as an early Christmas present. I went to lie down in the back of the hearse to see what it would be like if we got engaged before graduation." Her cheeks flamed as the women laughed.

"You promised not to tell anyone," she said, and they held up their hands in surrender. "That was December 12. The hearse was here four days ago."

Branigan and Jody stayed for a while longer looking at scrapbook pictures of the old hearse. Some showed women dressed as witches and fortune tellers and ghosts hanging from its running boards. Others showed young ladies in shorts seated on the roof and hood, back doors open to highlight one woman waving happily with a ring-clad left hand. From what Branigan could see beneath all the smiling co-eds, the hearse looked like the one Charlie had described: 1950s, iron-gray, tinted windows at the front, short curtains at the back.

Jody quizzed the sisters about the key. Could anyone remember seeing its empty hook? Who had access?

Twenty young women lived in the house, Sophie told him, and their visitors were allowed in sixteen hours a day. A cook and an assistant worked five days a week and had groceries delivered. The sisters had a contract with the college maintenance staff, so those men came when called. Just about anyone could have taken the key.

Jody tried once more. "And you don't have any idea who might have taken the hearse?"

Sophie bit her lip again, and her eyes slid away from Jody's. "No."

Branigan got the impression she wanted to say more, and guessed she might not want to speak in front of the sisters. She stood and thanked everyone, then asked Sophie if she could walk them out.

Sophie grabbed a jacket from the hall closet and accompanied them into the front yard.

Branigan said softly, "You do have an idea who might have taken your hearse."

Under the streetlight, Sophie looked uncomfortable. "I have no proof at all. None."

"I understand."

"But my first thought was another sorority."

The reporters tried not to show their surprise. Branigan waited a beat, then asked, "Because?"

"Well, sometimes rush and pledge season gets a little… actually a little vicious. We start rush the week we get back from Christmas break. It crossed my mind that someone took our hearse because it had become so popular during rush." Sophie let out a sigh. "Sounds even lamer than the engagement thing, I know."

"Maybe not," Branigan assured her, remembering the competitiveness of UGA sororities in her day. "Are there any sororities that Kappa Epsilon especially competes with for pledges?"

"Two, I guess you'd say: Rho Theta Chi and Gamma Delta Phi."

The latter sounded familiar to Branigan. She stepped under the streetlight and flipped to her notes from her interview with Ina Rose Carlton.

She was right. Gamma Delta Phi. That was the sorority Janie Rose had pledged during her freshman year at Rutherford Lee.

CHAPTER NINE

As Malachi finished off a six-pack, he made up his mind. He would call Miz Branigan about the hearse in the woods. He hated to cost Ralph and Maylene their new place. That was why he hadn't called earlier. But acting as though he was admiring their find, he got a close-up look at the hearse's front bumper. Its right side was dented and flecked with red paint.

Alone in his tent under the Garner Bridge, Malachi crunched his last can. He grabbed the other empties and pushed out of his tent, feeling his way in the dark to a rolling trashcan made of molded plastic. City workers had learned their lesson after bringing in metal barrels last summer. By October, his neighbors Slick and Elise had built fires in them. So one morning in December, a city employee rolled the green plastic cart in. So far no one had lit a fire in it.

Funny how people in houses decided what the homeless needed. Not a toilet or a grill, which might've actually been useful. But clothes that grew mildew. Or soft drinks that rotted what teeth the crystal meth hadn't got to. And, to everyone's amazement, baby toys. Malachi had lived outdoors for the past fourteen years and had yet to see a baby out here. There might be some in the shelters or in Grambling's home for beat-up women, but not here.

Once he was out of the bridge's shadow, Malachi could see by moonlight. He walked past the river birch that guarded the camp's entrance. No one was around, so he unzipped his camo pants and peed. Careful to go far enough that he couldn't be overheard, he pulled out the cell phone that the government lady had given him. She'd been at Jericho Road one day, giving phones to homeless folks for emergencies and jobs. Pastor Liam let you charge them in the dining hall.

When Malachi gave Miz Branigan the news about the hearse in the woods, her voice rose and he heard her repeat it to someone. Then she was back in his ear, telling him she would come to his tent first thing in the morning.

"No," he murmured, keeping his voice low so all those nearby ears couldn't hear him. "Come to the old Randall Mill."

He knew Miz Branigan would have the po-lice with her. Homeless people spent the majority of their time staying out of the po-lice's way. He sure as heck wasn't inviting them to the camp they called Tent City.

No telling who had an outstanding warrant or an illegal weapon or a crack rock rattling around. No sense inviting trouble in.

Chapter Ten

B ranigan let Cleo out and rushed from the farmhouse at first light, her breath blowing smoky in the cold dawn. Across the cotton patch, the barn and empty chicken houses loomed dark against the sky, only barely distinct from the winter horizon. She called Detective Chester Scovoy as she pulled out of her driveway.

The detective was one of Jody's sources on the police beat, and Branigan had gotten to know him slightly last summer. She hadn't had occasion to talk to him since, as Jody handled the city's police-related stories. And if she were honest, she didn't relish being reminded of that time.

This story, however, was squarely on his turf. Branigan told him about Malachi's report of a hearse abandoned in woods near the Garner Bridge, and he agreed to meet her at the burned-out Randall Mill.

As they pulled onto the cracked concrete that was once the mill's loading area and later a makeshift skateboard park, they found Malachi, hands shoved deep in the pockets of a down jacket, cap pulled low over his ears and a gray sweatshirt hood over that. In the growing light, the mill's sole remaining smokestack loomed, a tower of blackened brick.

Once the pride of Grambling's mill villages, Randall had burned in the 1980s. Now its surrounding four-room mill houses were home to drug dealers, prostitutes and bootleggers, and under the nearby Michael Garner Bridge was a homeless encampment.

Malachi greeted Branigan with the slightest of nods, and looked warily at Detective Scovoy. The officer stuck his hand out.

"Mr Martin? Good to see you again." When he got no reaction, he added, "I was at Miss Powers' barn last summer when you helped us solve the murders? Chester Scovoy."

"I know who you is," Malachi said. Branigan saw the faintest frown cross his face. "Ralph and Maylene and the hearse down that way," he pointed. "Prob'ly best if I don't go wit' you."

"That's fine," Branigan said. "Can you show us the way in?"

Silently, Malachi led them across the road and into the woods. Branigan recognized the place from the previous summer, though the trees were bare now. With the sun up, they could make out a path the width of a car that led from the road to an encampment under the bridge. Malachi stopped.

"Go 'bout another thirty feet, then go right down a little hill and you see it," he told Branigan. "Be careful when you wake Ralph up. He sleep with a cutter."

"A cutter?"

"Y'know. A box cutter."

Malachi left them, and Branigan and Detective Scovoy made their way through the quiet woods. Sure enough, after going thirty feet, they could see a break where something had cracked limbs and cut tracks in the loamy dirt. They pushed in a few feet further, and saw the back of a faded hearse.

Scovoy whistled. "You were right," he said. "When the patrol boys first started talking about a hearse, we thought their witness was hallucinating. Guess we were wrong."

"That witness was Charlie Delaney," said Branigan. "She's solid."

Scovoy rapped on the hearse's rear window and raised his voice. "Ralph? Maylene? Grambling Police. Can you come out, please?"

The hearse swayed as someone stirred inside. Scovoy called more loudly. "Ralph? Grambling PD. We need to speak with you."

The hearse's back door swung open, and a stocky man of medium height, thirty-ish, his bare arms and torso sporting rudimentary tattoos of barbed wire and Confederate flags, looked out. His eyes swept from Branigan to the detective. He spat on the ground, barely missing the officer's shoes. "Yeah?"

"Detective Chester Scovoy. I'm here about a hearse that was reported stolen. This looks like it could be it."

Ralph's face relaxed. "Don't know nuthin' about that, Officer.

Me and my woman found it yesterday morning right here. We don't know nuthin' about it being stolen."

"What will I find if I run a warrant check on you? Anything to take you in for?"

"No, Officer, not a thing. Got off parole last summer. Clean as a baby's butt."

"A baby's butt isn't always clean," the detective said mildly. "Before I run it, tell me about this vehicle."

"Ain't nuthin' to tell. Me and Maylene was living up under the bridge there." He waved an arm toward the encampment. "We was walking yesterday to eat breakfast at Jericho Road and saw where this car done run down the bank a ways. Thought it'd make a warmer cat hole than that leaky tent. And it did." He looked forlorn. "You gonna take it in?"

"I'm sorry, but it may have been involved in a crime. So yeah."

A surprisingly young girl stuck her tousled auburn head out of a pile of blankets. Branigan felt Detective Scovoy stiffen. "Are you Maylene?"

"Yeah." She yawned.

"Do you have some ID, miss?"

"I'm nineteen, if that's what you're worried about."

"I'd still like to see some ID."

"Ralph, where's my backpack?" She crawled on hands and knees through the sleeping quarters and pulled a faded maroon backpack from the front seat. She fumbled inside until she found a zip-lock bag and produced a laminated card. Branigan was startled to see that it was a real driver's license, one that showed Maylene with clean flowing hair and a bright smile. According to Liam, almost all homeless folks had an inexpensive picture ID issued by the Department of Driver Services, but they didn't have a driver's license. Those were usually cancelled, suspended or carried heavy reinstatement fees.

"See?" the girl said. "Nineteen."

Detective Scovoy studied the license, then handed it back reluctantly. "Do your folks know where you are, miss?"

Maylene's pretty face darkened, and she pulled a blanket tighter around her shoulders. "They don't know and sure as hell don't care. Ralph here is the only one who cares about me."

Branigan groaned inwardly. Detective Scovoy kept his face neutral. "Well, if you change your mind, Pastor Liam at Jericho Road can help you get home or into a women's shelter. Meanwhile, a tow truck will be here in half an hour to haul this vehicle to the Law Enforcement Center. Leave everything inside and we'll return your possessions to you later."

"What?" Ralph protested. "You can't do that."

"Can and will. I'm sorry, but this vehicle was used in a crime. Your coats and backpacks may have picked up fibers or other evidence. You can take your papers and ID, but leave everything else."

"The hell we will!"

Chester reached for the walkie-talkie on his shoulder. "Scovoy here. Send a uni to Ricky's Quick Mart on Estonia Street," he told a dispatcher, using cop-speak to direct a uniformed officer to a shabby convenience store nearby. "I'll guide him in to where I need him under the Garner Bridge."

Turning to Ralph, he said, "Your choice. Your stuff gets impounded or you do."

Ralph didn't say another word – simply slammed the hearse's back door.

Detective Scovoy rapped on the window again, and Ralph shoved the door back open. His face was red as he fought to control his anger.

"One more thing," said the detective. "We'll need to get your fingerprints so we can eliminate them when we dust the car. I can drive you down now or you can walk over. But I need you at the Law Enforcement Center before noon."

"We'll walk," said Ralph, pulling the door closed.

Branigan turned to Detective Scovoy. "I guess you have to wait for your officer?"

He nodded. "Yeah, I don't want Ralph pulling evidence out of the car. I'll treat you to coffee in fifteen minutes if you want to wait."

Branigan's face showed her surprise. "I would," she answered, looking at her watch. "But I need to get to Rutherford Lee before exams start. Rain check?"

"Sure. Is it about the sorority who reported the missing hearse?"

"No, we talked to them last night. I want to follow up on something one of the girls said."

"Which was?"

Branigan paused. "Nothing concrete. The Kappa Epsilon Chi president thought another sorority might have taken the hearse."

Detective Scovoy studied her for a moment. "As a prank?"

"Or to keep them from getting a head start on rush."

The detective snorted, and Branigan could see him mentally dismissing the lead. "Let me know if you find something," he said. "Meanwhile, we'll run the prints and see if we get a hit."

The Gamma Delta Phi house was three houses away from that of Kappa Ep. Branigan's knock was answered by a middle-aged housekeeper. When Branigan told her she wanted to see the sorority president, rush chair and pledge chair, the woman responded that it might be a while: the young ladies would have to get showered and dressed before entering the living area.

Branigan tried not to let her amusement show, and thought she saw a flicker behind the woman's eyes as well.

"You are welcome to sit down and have some coffee," she offered.

"That would be great," said Branigan. "And I have my newspaper with me."

The woman wasn't kidding. It was a full forty-five minutes before three young ladies entered the living room in skirts, blouses, tights and jewelry. *What? No white gloves?* Branigan thought.

She introduced herself. She was going to have to find something to tell these three apart. The Gamma Delts, it seemed, definitely had a type. All three women were thin and brunette and had straight white teeth. All three wore skirts that came to three inches above the knee. Their differences, as far as Branigan could tell, came in their eyes, noses and blouse colors.

The president was Marianne Thurman, brown eyes, straight nose, severe gray blouse with white pearls at her throat. The rush chair was Emma Ratcliffe, vivid blue eyes, pug nose, white blouse, a cross necklace. The pledge chair was Catherine Reisman, hazel eyes, a slight bump in her nose that Branigan suspected would have a future date with a surgeon's knife, tailored coral blouse, matching beaded necklace.

The girls accepted coffee in cups and saucers from the housekeeper, thanking her in well-modulated voices.

"I can't imagine what this is about," Marianne began. "What could *The Grambling Rambler* want to know about our sisterhood?"

Branigan took a sip of coffee to hide her desire to laugh. *What was the old Southern saying? A proper lady was in the paper only at her birth, marriage and death.*

"I'm here about a pledge you had during spring semester. Janie Rose Carlton. She was killed on her way home from the University of Georgia two days ago."

"Yes, we saw that. Such a tragedy."

Branigan let the silence stretch, knowing that most people would rush to fill it. After a moment, Marianne continued. "We really liked Janie Rose. We were sorry when she left school. But I don't think any of us have seen her since last winter. I know I haven't."

"The thing is, we're not sure the wreck was an accident." Branigan watched as shock swept over the girls' faces.

"What do you mean?" asked Emma.

"The driver, another UGA student, said that a hearse forced them off the road. The police have found the hearse. It belonged to your neighbors, the Kappa Epsilon Chis."

Catherine's mouth formed a perfect O. "Oh my gosh, we see that nasty thing all the time. They seem to think that getting engaged is a campus-wide sport."

Emma nodded. "I didn't know they took it on the open road though."

"I don't know that *they* did," Branigan said. "Do you happen to know where they kept the key?"

All three girls shook their heads. Finally Marianne hazarded a guess. "I suppose Sophie kept it."

"No, they kept it on a hook in the kitchen. Just about anyone had access." Branigan let her comment hang, but the girls didn't respond.

She tried again. "I was wondering if someone from the college took it as a prank, maybe to keep the hearse from being used during rush. And then things got out of hand."

Marianne took charge. "I can't imagine such a thing. We thought that hearse was ridiculous. Any rushee who thought it was impressive wouldn't have been interested in Gamma Delta Phi and vice versa." Emma and Catherine nodded solemnly.

Okay, thought Branigan. *No sense of humor here.*

"On another subject, I want to ask you about people who may have been interested in Janie Rose during the time you knew her."

The girls looked mystified. Again Marianne took the lead. "Interested? How do you mean?"

"Well, Janie Rose was the only child of a wealthy father. Sometimes wealthy fathers make enemies."

Emma sat up straighter. "That man!" she said to Marianne and Catherine. "Remember the man who came? And we made so much fun of his accent?" She turned to Branigan. "After he left, of course. Not to his face."

Marianne looked dubious. "Yeah, I guess so. But that was what? January? February? That's almost a year ago."

"Tell me."

"Well," said Emma, warming to the memory, "rush started in early January, the day we got back from Christmas break. In fact, some of us – me, Catherine and other rush event chairs – came back even earlier to get ready. Pledge Day was February 1. That's the day the bids went out. Janie Rose joined. Normally, the house is reserved for upperclassmen. Catherine and Marianne and I were juniors then. A couple of sophomores lived here. But that Christmas, one of our junior sisters got engaged and transferred to her fiancé's school. So that left a vacancy.

"Janie Rose came to us and said she and her roommate had had a falling out, and could she have the empty room? With her dad, we knew she had the rent money, so we moved her right in."

The other girls were looking at Emma.

"Why are you telling her all this?" asked Catherine.

"I'm getting there. So a couple of days later, this man showed up at the door asking for Janie Rose. Mrs Rochester answered the door." Emma indicated the kitchen where the housekeeper was working. "But Marianne and I were here in the parlor. He had a real strong Yankee accent. We weren't trying to listen," Emma said primly. "We really weren't. But his accent was so strong, and Janie Rose got kind of wound up. So we couldn't help hearing."

"What did he say?"

Emma frowned. "That's just it. That's why I didn't think of it until you mentioned her father. All the man said was, 'Tell your father Roy said hello.'"

"That was it?"

"Well, actually more like, 'Tell yo' faddah Roy sed 'ello.'"

Branigan choked on her coffee, and it threatened to come out of her nose. After taking a moment to gather herself, she coughed and said, "He was from New Jersey?"

"New Jersey, New York, Long Island... who knows? I can't tell those people apart. But Janie Rose got upset. She asked why he didn't go and see her father himself. But the man didn't say anything else."

Emma shrugged. "Finally Janie Rose slammed the door and ran upstairs. When we asked her about it later, she said it was nothing to worry about. We never saw him again."

"Can you describe him?"

Emma closed her eyes. "Medium tall, maybe five foot ten or eleven. Thinning brown hair, kind of Brylcreemed back. A gray suit, I can't remember the tie. Oh, and his face was pockmarked, like from acne."

Marianne and Catherine looked at Emma in wonder. "You've got a better memory than me," Catherine told her.

"Does that help?" Marianne asked Branigan.

Branigan clicked off her digital recorder. "Maybe. You never know."

She closed her notebook and gathered up her coat. Then she posed the question she always asked at the termination of an interview: "Is there anything I've forgotten to ask that you think might be important?"

The girls shook their heads.

Branigan had another thought, remembering Charlie's comment about Janie Rose's anxiety. "Did you ever get the feeling that Janie Rose was scared of something?"

"Well, maybe," said Marianne slowly, "though I didn't think of it at the time. She had this habit of looking out of the parlor window before she left the house. She'd go to that curtain and peek out before leaving. I assumed she was checking the weather."

"Did that happen before or after Roy came?"

Marianne thought for a moment, fingering her pearls. "I don't know. She'd only lived with us for a day or so before he showed up."

"You ladies have been very helpful," Branigan said.

She walked out of their parlor feeling as if she were leaving a time warp.

CHAPTER ELEVEN

Malachi Martin watched as Ralph and Maylene slouched through the sliding electric door of Jericho Road. No matter how they fixed the place up, that door gave it away as a former grocery store.

And Pastor Liam was constantly fixing it up. His newest addition was a Good Samaritan mural done in three parts. The first showed two men – a priest and a Levite, Malachi knew from his granny's teaching – passing a bleeding man lying in the road. The second showed the Samaritan holding the hurt man's head in his lap. The third showed the hurt man, thrown over a donkey, as the Samaritan handed coins to an innkeeper. What Malachi liked about the painting was that the colors went from dull grays and browns in the first panel to brighter golds and tans in the second, to happy reds and oranges in the third.

Tiffany Lynn, a homeless artist who worked in Jericho's art room, had unveiled it during church last Sunday. *A triptych*, she had said proudly more than once. *It's a triptych*.

Tiffany Lynn didn't stay in the shelter; its eighteen beds were for men. But Pastor welcomed women at meals, church, the art room, all the stuff he had going on. If Malachi were a betting man, he'd bet on Pastor Liam building the women a shelter sooner or later.

For now, Malachi was glad Pastor had got what he called his "biblically correct" painting. Malachi knew the one on the other wall, the one done by high school students, drove Pastor crazy with its mishmash of characters. As near as Malachi could figure, Adam and Eve, Daniel and his lions, Joshua, David and Goliath were all mixed up in one Old Testament mess. His Bible-loving granny would've whipped somebody's butt. Pastor Liam sighed every time he passed it.

Ralph and Maylene didn't so much as glance at Tiffany Lynn's new piece. They grabbed plates and coffee, heads down. Malachi speared his eggs while keeping an eye on the two, hoping they didn't know it was him who told the po-lice about their hearse.

Maylene slid into a seat directly across the table, and Malachi saw why she had been holding her face down: an angry red mark spread across one cheek, already purpling at the edges. He averted his eyes. That was the kind of thing you didn't ask about on the street. Pastor could, and did. But not other street dwellers.

After a moment, Maylene sought out his eyes and attempted a smile. "I walked right into the back door of that stupid hearse," she said.

"Yeah," Ralph agreed, taking the seat next to her, "we had to get out fast when the police took it."

"Uh-huh," Malachi replied.

Ralph wanted to talk. "We gotta see the police after breakfast. They seem to think that ol' car we found was dumped after a bank robbery or something."

Malachi didn't correct him, and Ralph needed no response. "I hope nobody got our tent while we was away. You ain't seen no Mexicans nosin' round it, have you, Malachi?"

Malachi didn't bother to answer, for Pastor Liam walked up. He clapped Ralph on the shoulder. "Ralph, can you help us mop up after breakfast? And Maylene, can you help me in the kitchen?"

Ralph wasn't one to help. But no one turned Pastor down – not to his face anyway. "Sure," he mumbled, looking none too happy.

After breakfast, Malachi took his broom to the hallway just outside the kitchen. From there, he could hear Pastor Liam asking Maylene about her face. She insisted she'd walked into the hearse's door, but Pastor wasn't buying it. "I can all but see knuckle prints on your cheek," he told her. "You know about The Anchor, don't you?"

Maylene nodded. Yeah, plenty of people would've told her about the city's shelter for beat-up women by now.

"But I don't need that, Pastor," she said. "I walked into the car door. I swear."

Pastor talked to her for a few more minutes, then gave up. "You are way too smart and way too young to get caught up in this, Maylene. Call me, or The Anchor, when you're ready."

As he passed Malachi, the men shared a look, wondering how the Ralphs of the world got away with it.

CHAPTER TWELVE

Branigan was going to have to interview Harry Carlton about Roy, the man who had visited Janie Rose at the Gamma Delta Phi house. It was possible that Janie Rose had got caught in the crossfire from some of her father's ugly dealings.

But since she was on campus, she decided to first swing by her grandparents' house.

Their home was in an area abutting the college that had once been part of a large horse farm. Even cut into smaller lots, the neighborhood intentionally kept its horsey feel, with wide grassy areas between houses and deep back yards bordering a small lake. Branigan pulled into her grandparents' meandering driveway lined with the white slat fencing that defined many of the properties.

She found her paternal grandfather, Ira Powers, right where she expected to – on his back porch with a blanket over his knees and a mug of strong black coffee. With the trees bare this time of year, he could see the lake. His view wasn't that different from her own backyard view over a cotton patch and pastures that ended in a pond surrounded by blackberry bushes. The difference, she supposed, was in the owners. While Gran and Pa Rickman had farmed their land, Ira and Rudelle Powers were simply visitors.

"Hi, Granddaddy," she greeted him through the screened porch.

Her grandfather expressed no surprise at her sudden appearance. "Branigan, how good to see you. Did you come to fill up your grandmother's car?"

"No, but I can." She opened the porch door, and bent to kiss her grandfather's cheek. "Got any more of that coffee first?"

"I'm sure there is. Help yourself."

Branigan let herself into the kitchen with its stained pine cabinets and white appliances kept shiny by a once-a-week housekeeper. Her grandmother, white hair twisted into a bun, sat at the kitchen table reading the newspaper.

"Good morning, Grandmother."

"Darling, how are you?" She tilted a rouged cheek for Branigan to kiss.

"Coffee-deprived. Okay if I steal some?"

"Of course."

"Granddaddy said you need gas?"

"Yes, would you be a dear?"

Rudelle Powers refused to pump her own gas. Ever since Grambling's stations had gone to self-service – years after the rest of the country – she had demanded that her husband, sons and grandchildren fill her tank. Branigan was so used to it that she no longer found it unusual.

"Let me just talk to Granddaddy for two minutes, then I'll get it." She found a mug and poured coffee, then joined her grandfather on the porch.

"I need to know about Shaner Steel," she began.

"Came down from Pennsylvania four or five years ago," he said.

"Seven."

"Has it been that long? Mercy." He thought for a moment. "It was during the recession of 2008–2009, so I guess you're right. From what I heard, they had already made the land purchase and committed to the move when the ground fell out from under them."

He placed his coffee on a tiled table next to his chair, and tugged the blanket to cover his thin shoulders. "They were in a classic pickle. They probably wanted to back out of the move, but they had too much invested. So they came anyway."

"Did they move south to escape the unions?"

"That would've been part of it. Big savings on labor and personnel. But there just wasn't much business in steel for a while. Neither in cars nor in commercial construction. I'm sure they had to borrow – and borrow big – to stay afloat."

Branigan thought for a moment. "Did they borrow from local banks?"

"Couldn't say. That sounds like a question for your father."

Branigan's dad was president of Grambling First Bank, a multi-merged institution that had clung to its local name. Even newcomers wanted a bank with deep local roots. She mused out loud. "Even if they did borrow locally, I guess it's possible they also had loans from up north. Some less than mainstream loans."

"No way of knowing that," said her grandfather.

"Oh, you'd be surprised," she said with a smile. "Business writers in that area may know some gossip."

Rudelle Powers opened the kitchen door and stuck her head out. "Goodness, what are you two doing in the cold? Won't you come in for a muffin, Branigan? Marisol baked this week."

"What kind?"

"Cranberry with walnuts."

"Oooh, you bet. How 'bout you, Granddaddy?"

"I've already had one. But I'll come in with you."

Rudelle bypassed the kitchen table and set out a cloth napkin, plate and matching coffee cup and saucer on the dining room table. Branigan knew it was useless to protest, and allowed her grandmother to pour a fresh cup in the good china. She bit into the muffin.

"Fabulous," she said. "Marisol hasn't lost her touch." She turned back to her grandfather. "On a completely different subject, tell me about the college's Greek life. Weren't you chairman of some court or disciplinary council back in the day?"

"After I retired. As you know, I still hold the professor emeritus title. So I dabble."

"But what was it, exactly?"

"I was chairman of the Greek Honor Council, 'honor' being wishful thinking. We dealt with incidents involving underage drinking, hazing, sexual assault and so forth. Not pretty stuff."

"Even at hoity-toity Rutherford Lee?"

"Even at hoity-toity Rutherford Lee. From what I hear from colleagues at other schools, no college is immune."

"Did you close down any sororities or fraternities?"

"Yes. There was a bad incident that made the news about a fraternity, Kappa Rho Epsilon. A freshman died from alcohol poisoning during their pledge period. The college kicked them out and the national fraternity pulled the charter."

"I don't remember that."

"You may have been in Detroit. It got a good amount of coverage in *The Rambler* and on TV. Horrible for the school, of course. The organizations straightened up for a while. But I've been hearing rumors that they've gotten worse lately."

"Do you know who runs the Honor Council now?"

"Sylvia Eckhart in political science. She's good. No nonsense. Why are you interested?"

"I'm not, really. I've just been visiting Greek Row and it got me wondering. Apparently the Kappa Epsilon Chi hearse was stolen and involved in a wreck that killed Ina Rose Carlton's daughter."

Her grandmother drew in a sharp breath. "I just read your story about Janie Rose Carlton. It didn't say the hearse belonged to our college girls."

"That part is just developing," Branigan said. "So you've seen the Kappa Ep hearse?"

"Lord, yes! Those girls come whooping through the neighborhood every few months to announce an engagement. Which reminds me…"

"It doesn't take anything to remind you," Branigan said. "And no, I'm not dating anyone."

Her grandfather laughed. "Leave the girl alone, Rudelle. Branigan, go back to the hearse. You say it was stolen?"

"Yeah. I guess you saw in the story that Charlie Delaney and Janie Rose Carlton were returning from Athens for Christmas break. Charlie is injured pretty badly: broken leg, arm, ribs, lost some teeth. She told us that a hearse ran them off the road. The Kappa Eps reported their hearse stolen about the same time. The police found it this morning."

"My goodness!" said her grandmother. "Who would do such a thing?"

"That's what I'm trying to find out." Branigan stood and stretched. "In fact, I need to get back to it. Let me fill up the royal Buick before I head to the office."

"You know where the credit card is." Her grandmother returned to the kitchen to reread Branigan's front page story.

CHAPTER THIRTEEN

As soon as she had returned her grandmother's Buick to its garage, Branigan phoned Jody and asked if he would join her at Shaner Steel to confront Harry Carlton.

"Nervous about facing him alone?" Jody asked.

"You better believe it. But my cowardice aside, I think it'd be good to have a witness. He seems like the kind to deny something later if he doesn't like it."

"Okay. I can leave now. Where are you?"

"Ten minutes away. Let's meet in the parking lot."

Harry Carlton's offices were in a building of tinted glass and burnished steel, unusual in a part of the state where businesses built headquarters to look like colonial mansions. But here alongside Interstate 85, it wasn't as out of place as it would have been in Grambling's downtown.

Branigan and Jody took an elevator to the fourth floor, and were directed by a receptionist to Mr Carlton's private secretary. Her boss kept them waiting thirty minutes, during which time she nervously offered the reporters coffee and water.

When he finally flung open his office door to usher them inside, there was no smile, no greeting. He returned to the chair behind his desk and motioned for them to take the two hunter green armchairs facing it. It was an obvious statement of the power differential in the room.

Jody started with condolences, which Carlton angrily waved aside. "Just tell me what you want," he said.

"As you know, Charlie Delaney said the girls were forced off 441 by a hearse," Jody said. "Police have found the hearse, with red paint on the bumper, just as Charlie described."

"They've called me," he said in a cold voice. "They asked if I knew anyone who would want to hurt me by hurting Janie Rose."

"Do you?" Branigan asked softly.

"No. As I told them, that's preposterous." Harry Carlton looked like a man fighting to hold his temper.

Branigan kept her voice intentionally soft, trying not to antagonize him more than necessary. "The girls who lived with Janie Rose at Rutherford Lee last year said a colleague of yours had visited her. Someone named Roy."

Harry Carlton stared at Branigan. *Was that surprise on his face? Or contempt?*

"Roy?" he barked. He narrowed his eyes for a moment. Branigan could tell it pained him to ask, "When last year?"

"I mean the last school year. So the first week or so in February of this year. Ten months ago." Branigan's nervousness was making her babble, and she forced herself to stop.

He spun to his computer screen and tapped at his keyboard. Craning her neck, Branigan could see he was looking at a calendar. His back stiffened. He swung back to face the reporters. "Roy and his associates had no need to hurt me," he said. "Nor the brass."

His words carried the same bark as before. But something had changed. His tone was different, icier. His mind was no longer on the reporters.

"Are we finished?" he said dismissively.

Branigan figured she had nothing to lose. "I know the steel industry has had some rough years. Probably debt. If not Roy, is there anyone who would try to hurt you through your family?"

Harry Carlton's face froze. "Young lady, you have crossed the line," he said softly. "I won't forget that." He stood abruptly. "This interview is over."

Branigan and Jody left without a word. They didn't speak until they entered the elevator. Jody leaned against the back wall. "Jeez, he's got two moods – hacked off and outraged," he said. "Did you notice how something shifted when he saw his calendar? I wonder if he realized someone *was* in Grambling that day who might have threatened Janie Rose."

Branigan shivered, unnerved by Mr Carlton's attitude despite Jody's presence. "I don't know. I couldn't tell if he's a horribly grieving father or a world-class jerk."

Jody shrugged. "Probably both."

As they exited Shaner Steel headquarters, Branigan was surprised to see that it was only minutes past noon. Her day had started so early that it felt like 5 o'clock. She followed Jody to the newspaper office only to be ambushed at the elevator by Tanenbaum Grambling IV.

"How's that homeless story going?" he demanded.

"It isn't. I got sidetracked by the death of the college girl."

"Well, get un-sidetracked. I want that for Christmas Eve. The idea of Jesus' family being homeless in a stable alongside the homeless today."

"Ah, so you're going to write my lead?"

"Don't get sassy." He pushed the elevator button, effectively dismissing her. She sighed and walked to her desk, lonely now in the cavernous newsroom. In what Branigan called the "old days" – when she'd come to *The Rambler* at twenty-two right out of the University of Georgia – she frequently had the luxury to pursue stories such as the one on Janie Rose Carlton. She had routinely spent one to three weeks on a single story when it was complicated and required both research and a dozen or more interviews.

Those days were gone. At some papers, reporters were now called content providers. At least that indignity hadn't been visited upon *The Rambler* staff yet. They were still called reporters. It's just that they had to provide content for the *Metro* and *Style* sections in addition to any real stories they might be working on.

Julie was waiting by her desk, but before she could speak, Branigan held up both hands. "I know. I know. Homeless for Christmas for the *Style* front. Eggs and Christmas baking weren't enough for you."

Julie looked puzzled, and nervously tucked her blonde hair behind one ear. "I thought you wanted the homeless story."

"I did. Sorry. It's just that I really want to investigate this Carlton girl's death too."

City editor Bert Feldspar spun around in his chair. "There's more than what you wrote this morning?"

"Yeah. Can you meet with Jody and me for a minute? You too, Julie."

The four of them gathered in the smallest conference room, which could have held three times their number. They bunched at one end of a mahogany conference table, one of many relics of the paper's more prosperous days.

"Whatcha got?" asked Bert. He was thirty-five and sported the ubiquitous shaved head of so many of his peers who didn't want to deal with thinning hair.

Branigan reiterated Charlie's claim that a hearse had deliberately run her and Janie Rose off the road, and that the police had apparently found the stolen hearse abandoned in the woods.

Bert looked from her to Jody. "I read your quote from Charlie Delaney, but not the rest of it. Are you saying it could be murder? Of a college kid?"

Jody took up the story. "We don't know yet. The police are interested now they know Charlie was telling the truth. Branigan and I just got back from talking to the dead girl's father, Harry Carlton. Piece of work. There's a possibility somebody was trying to hurt him. He's just not talking. At least not to us."

"Branigan?"

"That about covers it. Obviously, I'd love some time to work on it."

Bert turned to Julie. "You got any wiggle room?"

Julie held her hands out, palms up. "I really don't on the homeless story. Tan-4 wants it. But I can try to keep Branigan off anything else until after Christmas."

"That's next week," said Jody.

"Best I can do." She looked apologetic. "You guys know the pressure we're under."

"Okay," Branigan said, gathering her notebooks. "Homeless at Christmas it is."

"Jody can keep an eye on what the police dig up," Bert said. "We're not dropping the wreck story."

Back at her desk, Branigan placed two calls: one to Liam Delaney to set up a mid-afternoon interview for the homeless story, one to Detective Chester Scovoy.

When the detective answered his cell, she didn't waste time. "I'd like to collect on that offer of coffee. But can we make it a drink this evening?"

"Sure," he said. "Cop bar or lawyer bar?"

Branigan laughed. The city's lawyers congregated in the lounge of the Nicholas Inn with its rich dark woods, stained-glass lamps and baby grand piano. Police officers preferred Leigh Ann's, a casual bar a block off Main Street that featured pool tables, dart boards and a juke box with beach music.

"Zorina's," she said.

"Hell, no."

She laughed again. Zorina's was the reporters' bar: a dark room with a sticky floor in a strip mall several blocks past the gentrified portion of Grambling's South Main Street. Journalists liked it because it was open until 4 a.m., long past closing time for most bars, and necessary for reporters and copy-editors with midnight deadlines.

"What have you got against Zorina's?"

"Besides food poisoning, warm beer and reporters? Do I need more?"

"All right. Leigh Ann's it is. See you at seven."

Branigan grabbed her coat and left the newsroom before Julie could forget her pledge and assign her another story. She had an hour before meeting Liam, and her energy was flagging. Leaving *The Grambling Rambler* office with its distinctive gold logo of an intertwined G and R, she turned right to walk the six blocks up Main Street to Bea's. She grabbed a table by the window and ordered a turkey and Swiss on a wheat bagel, and a cup of hot chocolate.

While she waited, she stared out of the window. Grambling's downtown was an eclectic mix of small-town drugstores and home-cooking restaurants and bigger city fare such as vintage clothing stores, trendy bars and art galleries. She idly watched a man of indeterminate age sit down on a sidewalk bench. His quilted black jacket was worn and dirty, and the soles of his tennis shoes appeared to be separating from the shoe tops. His face wore gray stubble, and even from here she could see the swollen nose of a longtime drinker. He pulled a ring-tab can of ravioli and a plastic fork from his backpack, along with a bottle of water with the blue and white label of Jericho Road.

The waitress brought her sandwich and hot chocolate. "Don't move this," Branigan told her. "I'll be right back."

She took out a business card and approached the man. Even up close, she couldn't tell his age, but could see that his nose was bumpy with burst blood vessels and his eyes were red.

"Excuse me," she said softly. He looked up without speaking. "I'm Branigan Powers with *The Grambling Rambler*." When she got no reaction, she added, "Our local newspaper."

"Yeah, I know." His voice was reedier than she'd expected.

"I'm working on a story on homelessness in Grambling, and what that means at Christmas. I'm on my way to Jericho Road." She nodded at his water bottle.

"Yeah, I know Pastor Liam," he said.

"Are you staying there?"

"Nah."

"Well, I'd love to include you in the article." She handed him her card. "It's got my phone number at the office. I could meet you here at Bea's or Jericho Road or at my office, or anywhere you like."

He handed it back. "Don't have a phone."

"Oh. Well, I could interview you right now." He wouldn't meet her eyes. She thought about her hot chocolate waiting for her and shivered in the chilly air. He ignored her and stuck his fork into his ravioli can.

She tried one last time. "I'd ask things like how you became homeless, what it's like in the winter, whether it's worse at Christmas, what help is available, what you'd need to not be homeless. Things like that."

He looked at her directly now, irritated. "Lady, it's bad enough being homeless without telling the whole world about it." He went back to his food.

"Oh, okay," she said, feeling her face flush. "Sorry to have bothered you."

She went back to her turkey sandwich and hot chocolate, but for the first time at Bea's had trouble finishing her meal.

Half an hour later, she entered the familiar parking lot at Jericho Road. The flower beds were filled with winter pansies planted and tended by the homeless men who lived at the shelter. Inside, Dontegan sat at the receptionist's desk. Branigan waved, and he called out, "Make sure you sees the Samarian paintin'!"

She stopped and looked around. Dontegan, smiling broadly, waved her into the dining hall.

"Oh my!" she called back to him. "This is extraordinary." She stood in front of the three-paneled painting that took up almost an entire wall of the dining room. She felt Liam come up beside her.

"I come in five times a day to make sure I didn't imagine it," he said.

"Liam, it's your crowning achievement," she said, jabbing him with an elbow. "This is glorious."

"Well, I didn't paint it, you know."

"It was Tiffany Lynn, right?"

"Yep. What a talent."

"And living on the street." Branigan shook her head. "Hard to believe." She caught herself. "Oh, and how is Charlie? And did Chan get home?"

"Charlie is sore. Sleeping a lot, which the doctors say is good. They think she can come home by Christmas. Chan made it home and spent last night at the hospital. He and Liz are taking turns." He shrugged. "We're doing pretty well, considering. We're very lucky."

"So Charlie can't come to Janie Rose's funeral tomorrow?"

He shook his head. "I'll come. I'm not sure about Liz and Chan, but at least I'll represent the family."

"I'll come with you."

He nodded and changed the subject. "Come on in. I believe you wanted to talk about homelessness in the winter?"

"Yeah, being homeless at Christmas, what you professional types are doing, how the community can help, et cetera."

"Okay, but I have a favor to ask in return."

"Of course you do."

"You've done stories on The Anchor, right?"

Branigan nodded at mention of the city's domestic violence shelter.

"I have a young girl who needs to be there. Her boyfriend is working day labor today, so I told her she could use our computer room to stay warm. I want to get her away from him, but she won't listen to me."

"Liam, she's not going to listen to me. I'm no counselor."

"Our social worker hasn't had any better luck than me. I'm hoping that since you know so much about The Anchor's operation, you can tell her more."

She looked doubtful. "I can try, but don't get your hopes up."

"Let me put you two together before she bolts. Then I can talk as long as you need me to afterwards."

Liam led her to the shelter's computer room, which was empty except for a young girl with long auburn hair. When she turned, Branigan was surprised to see the girl who'd been sleeping in the hearse. She was not surprised to see a huge bruise covering one cheek, with black and purple reaching up to one swollen eyelid.

"Maylene?" she said.

Liam looked from one woman to the other. "You know each other?"

"Not really," Branigan answered. "We met this morning."

Maylene gave her a weary smile. "So you're going to have a run at me now?"

"Well, I'm working on a story about being homeless at Christmas," Branigan said truthfully. "I can use your help. I'm guessing this could be your first Christmas on the street?"

Maylene was silent, and Liam left them, quietly closing the door.

Branigan waited. When Maylene didn't fill the silence, Branigan tried the chatty approach.

"Last Christmas I did a story on The Anchor. I talked to a lot of women who had finally left their abusers. And they told me amazing stories of how many times they'd tried – for some it was their third, fourth, fifth try. Only one woman was in there for the first time."

Maylene was looking at her with mild interest, so Branigan continued.

"They talked a lot about how holidays always seemed to bring on a crisis. Whether it was more drinking or more disappointment or more noise from the kids, it was hard to say. But they all had stories of previous Christmases when they'd had dinners thrown on the floor, or black eyes they'd had to hide from their families, or kids thrown against the wall on Christmas morning."

Maylene finally spoke. "And you think I've been there?" Her tone was mocking. "You think you know me?"

"No, I don't think I know you at all. In fact, you look way too young to have been through much of that yet – unless your family of origin was violent."

"It wasn't," Maylene snapped.

Branigan shrugged. "There has to be some reason you'd put up with Ralph."

"And it couldn't simply be that I love him?"

"I suppose it could. But you're attractive and articulate. I don't understand why loving someone has to include homelessness. I'm guessing one or both of you are addicts?"

"I wouldn't say we're addicts. We like to smoke a little crack."

"And I guess Liam has talked to you about rehab?"

Maylene tossed her head in irritation. "I thought you wanted to know about being homeless at Christmas?"

"I do," Branigan said, pulling out a notebook. "What can you tell me?"

"It sucks." Maylene pulled out cigarettes and a lighter.

Branigan knew that smoking wasn't allowed in Jericho Road,

but she didn't want to stop Maylene from talking. She watched the young woman light up.

"It sucks because you know your family are talking about you and how badly you've screwed up, and you want to go home, but if you do…" She trailed off.

"If you do, what?"

Maylene blew a blast of smoke. "Nothing," she said flatly.

"Look, I'm no counselor," said Branigan. "And you're right – I have no idea what you've been through. All I'm saying is that letting someone beat you up isn't going to help anything. It's going to make things worse. And there are people to help you. That's all."

"I'm not stupid."

"I'm sure you're not."

"I went to college."

"That doesn't surprise me," Branigan said, though it did. "But smart people make bad decisions all the time. You've got too much going for you to keep making this particular bad decision."

Maylene was silent, stubbornly so. Branigan could see her face had closed to further conversation. She laid a hand on the girl's jeans-clad knee. "If you change your mind, Liam is here. The Anchor is open 24/7. And here's my number." She handed her a business card, and walked toward the door.

Maylene stopped her before she reached it. "There is one thing I'd like to ask you."

"Shoot."

"This morning, when you came with the police to get that car we were sleeping in, the detective said it had been used in a crime. What happened?"

"Two college girls from UGA were run off the road. One was killed."

The unbruised side of Maylene's face paled. "Who were they?"

"Two girls from Grambling. Janie Rose Carlton was killed. Charlie Delaney was driving, and she got banged up pretty bad."

Maylene swallowed hard. Branigan thought her face paled further, if that were possible.

Finally the girl spoke. "Pastor Liam's daughter? I heard she was in a wreck, but nothing about that hearse."

"Do you know Charlie?"

Maylene shook her head. "I'm not from here."

"Where are you from?"

"Gainesville."

"You haven't come far then." Gainesville was only forty-five minutes from Grambling.

"We have a farm outside town," Maylene said. "My parents raise cattle."

"That's what my grandparents did." Branigan watched the girl for a moment. A little color had come back into her face, and she thought she saw a trace of wistfulness there. "You know, The Anchor's not your only option. I bet Liam would buy you a bus ticket if you wanted to go home."

This time Maylene didn't argue. She just hung her head. "Yeah, maybe."

Branigan left the room in search of Liam.

She flopped into the green-upholstered rocking chair in Liam's office. "I think I failed," she said.

"Could you figure out why she's so resistant to leaving him?"

Branigan hesitated. "You know, I'm not so sure it's Ralph in particular. She doesn't sound like she's madly in love with him. It sounded more like she's painted herself into a corner with her family, or something like that. But I'm guessing. She said almost nothing."

"Well, we tried."

"At the very end, she did seem to open the door to going home. There's an outside chance she could ask you for a bus ticket to Gainesville."

Liam's face lit up. "You think? That'd be even better than The Anchor. Good work, Brani G."

"Don't get too excited. I said 'an outside chance'."

"Better than I've done. Now how can I help you?"

For the next hour, Branigan questioned Liam about homelessness during the holidays, about the churches and individuals who called

Jericho Road wanting to serve a meal, give away turkeys, adopt a family. He told how he tried to channel the outburst of giving into more helpful avenues – storing up blankets and sweatshirts to last through early spring, designating money to hire another mental health counselor, mentoring a family throughout the year rather than piling on gifts at Christmas.

He told about the Christmas Eve service his gospel choir was putting on. It would showcase the talent of homeless singers while raising an offering for the church's ministries.

"And, thank goodness, Christmas Day is on a Friday this year," he added. "So I'm off. With Charlie's situation, that will help."

"And the staff can run the shelter?"

"Oh, sure. We'll have two churches in to prepare lunch and dinner that day. Our guys will cook their own breakfast. And we'll have volunteers in to sing carols. We try to keep it simple."

Branigan shut her notebook, stood and stretched. "Okay. I thank you, my friend. Tell Chan I'm looking forward to seeing him. How did his finals go?"

"All right, I think. He didn't know anything about Charlie then, so he should've been able to concentrate."

"I'll try to get by the hospital again before you take Charlie home."

"Thanks. I know she'll be glad to see you. I guess I'll see you at the funeral tomorrow."

"You're not taking part, are you?"

"Heck, no. I imagine I'm the last minister in Georgia the Carltons would ask."

"Yeah, I suppose so." She smiled sadly and slipped an arm around his waist for a quick hug. "I'm so glad Charlie's okay," she whispered.

CHAPTER FOURTEEN

Branigan spent the rest of the afternoon at her desk, checking in with the Salvation Army and the Grambling Rescue Mission about their Christmas plans. She assigned a photographer to get pictures of the encampment under the Michael Garner Memorial Bridge and at the evening's pizza dinner at Jericho Road, cautioning him to ask before photographing anyone's face. Liam had impressed upon her the need to respect the privacy of those who might not want to be labeled homeless.

She then returned to Jericho Road. She went from table to table, interviewing some of the people she remembered from last summer and meeting new ones. She looked around for Malachi Martin, but didn't see him. Nevertheless, within an hour, she had plenty of material for her Christmas Eve story.

She visited Liam's restroom to brush her teeth and freshen her make-up before meeting Detective Scovoy. She arrived at Leigh Ann's well-lit parking lot just as he pulled up in his navy blue Crown Victoria, the car of choice for the Grambling Police Department. He greeted her with an open smile. She wouldn't call Chester Scovoy handsome exactly. But with brown hair graying at the temples, hazel eyes and the weight-lifter's physique of so many of the force's officers, he was quite appealing.

"Detective," she said.

"Oh, no. Tonight it's Chester."

"Then I'm Branigan, not Miss Powers."

"Fair enough."

They walked into Leigh Ann's, Chester's hand resting lightly in the small of her back. Branigan was surprised to find she liked it. Chester spoke to several fellow cops, who made no attempt to disguise their curiosity. Branigan knew some of them, and nodded as the pair made their way to a relatively quiet booth near the back. Chester ordered a beer, and Branigan a pinot noir.

When it came, she took a sip and laid her head back against the cushioned booth. "This may put me to sleep. I feel like this is the first time I've stopped all day."

"Long day for sure," he said. "Did you find out anything at Rutherford Lee?"

"Seems like a week ago. Let's see. Yes, in fact." She gathered her thoughts. "Janie Rose moved into the Gamma Delta Phi house shortly after pledging last winter. Within a couple of days, a man visited her, asking about her father. The girls said he seemed to upset Janie Rose, and she slammed the door in his face."

Chester listened closely.

"They also said she always looked out of a window before she left the house. But they couldn't remember if she started that before or after his visit."

"Did they say why she left school?"

"No, they claimed they didn't know."

"'Claimed'? Meaning you doubt them?"

"No, it's not that," she said slowly. "It's more that they struck me as kind of self-absorbed. Like maybe if they'd been looking out for her, they would have noticed. Do you know what I mean?"

"I think so."

"And how about you? Any luck with fingerprints in the hearse?"

"Are we off the record?"

"Sure."

"There were tons of prints, most of them belonging to Ralph Batson and Maylene Ayers. I ran them both through GBI." The Georgia Bureau of Investigation was a statewide agency that provided assistance on forensics, databases and major crime investigations. "Ralph has DUIs and a domestic violence conviction from a former marriage. He did two years in prison. No surprise there. Maylene was clean, but do you know who she is?"

"She said her people were cattle farmers in Gainesville."

"That's one way to put it. Ever hear of Ayers Arena?"

"Sure. Horse shows. Livestock shows. Huge farm."

"That's her family. Maylene Ayers."

Branigan sat back, shocked. "Wow. What in the world is she doing here?"

Chester shook his head. "It was all I could do not to call her folks. But there's no missing persons report and she's an adult." He shrugged. "But she needs to get away from Ralphie."

"She's got a shiner now."

"Yeah, I saw it when they came in to be fingerprinted. She swore she hit her face on the car door. A story I've heard a time or two."

"On a slightly different subject, did you talk to the state patrol about what they found at the crash scene?"

"They said no witnesses."

"I mean about the luggage."

"Oh, yeah. They said the impact lifted the Jeep's back door and threw the luggage out. The latches sprung – or is it sprang? I can never remember – and the girls' clothes went everywhere. They also mentioned a duffel bag that was unzipped. At first they thought that meant something. But they mentioned it to the Delaneys and they said it was possible their daughter had left it unzipped." He shrugged. "So it's interesting, but inconclusive."

"Yeah, but if someone did force those girls off the road and then rifle through their luggage, that makes it very intentional, very deliberate."

"It does."

"But what could two college girls have that's worth all that?" Branigan mused. She shook her head as if to clear it. "Let's talk about something else. Tell me all about you and what brought you to Grambling, and the best and worst things about your job."

Chester laughed. "How long you got?"

"All night."

So Chester told her about growing up in Charleston, South Carolina, going to the state university in Columbia, then the South Carolina Criminal Justice Academy, becoming a cop back home in

Charleston, then making detective. He told her about moving to Atlanta, because it was the most challenging Southern city he could imagine for a homicide detective.

After eight years, however, Chester had lost the stomach for the senseless gang-style shootings, the drug-related killings, the grim domestic abuse that underlay so many of his cases. So ten years previously he had gladly allowed himself to be recruited by Grambling's first black police chief, Marcus Warren. At the time, Warren had been on the job only a year, brought in to professionalize the growing city's force as Grambling navigated the change from a small farming and textile town to a mid-size city.

"Best thing about the job?" Branigan repeated.

"The people of Grambling," he said promptly. "There's not a disrespect for life and for authority. Not yet anyway."

"And the worst thing?"

"Hmmm. That's harder. I guess it's having to depend on the state lab for the technology most big-city departments have. DNA, fingerprint analysis, things like that. But that's minor. Now your turn."

Branigan told him about growing up in Grambling with her twin brother Davison, about graduating from the University of Georgia, about working for *The Rambler*, then the *Detroit Free Press*, about moving back to her late grandparents' farm three years earlier.

"I'm assuming last summer was the worst part of your life," he said. "What about the best?"

"Being back on the farm, being around family, my German shepherd Cleo," she said. "And the work. I love the work. But newspapers are so uncertain right now. It's hard to know whether I'll have a job in two years."

"But you're such a good writer."

"Thank you, but that seems to matter less and less."

More than three hours passed quickly. The dinner plates that had held Leigh Ann's juicy burgers were empty, and Chester had ordered a second beer when his cell phone vibrated. "I'd better get this," he said. "They don't call after hours unless it's important."

He listened for a moment, then said loudly, "No. No. No." He slid from the booth, and stood, the phone still glued to his ear. Officers at a nearby table turned. He motioned for them to follow him, then turned to Branigan.

"Damn it to hell. It's Maylene."

He left without another word, his colleagues at his heels.

CHAPTER FIFTEEN

Malachi stood in the shadows of the depot used by Greyhound and Amtrak. The address was South Main Street, but the half-mile between the Nicholas Inn and the depot was the difference between shiny redevelopment and Southside decay.

Malachi knew both Gramblings – knew that the people who visited the Nicholas Inn never got this far south. The depot was where the city's broke-down people arrived – after being dropped off at other cities' depots by prison vans, po-lice, churches, even worn-out, broke-down families. Travelers Aid in most towns would give you a bus or train ticket if you could prove there was someone on the other end to take you in. Other towns didn't care about proof: they'd send you just to get you out of theirs.

Malachi had arrived at this very depot ten years before, when construction jobs had dried up in Hartwell. The drinking hadn't helped either, if he was honest. But the drinking did help the panic attacks, so there you go.

Malachi knew the building well – knew an exit was right behind him if he needed to make a quick escape across the railroad tracks. But for now, he stood to one side of the bus roundabout, looking through iron bars into an alley.

A uniformed po-liceman had his Tent City neighbor Ralph in cuffs, the crowbar Ralph'd been holding kicked a few feet away. Ralph was all quiet, his shoulders slumped, his mouth slack and stupid. A woman's crumpled body lay at the men's feet. Her face turned away, but Malachi knew who she was from the long brown hair that was turning black from leaking blood. Maylene. Her old backpack lay inches away, all her make-up and T-shirts and papers scattered on the ground where the officer had tossed it, looking for her ID. Her blue-jeaned legs were curled into her chest. That's what got Malachi: those legs all bent in like a baby's.

He heard sirens close by. The po-lice station was just off North Main, so it wouldn't take any time for the rest of the cops to get here. The bus dispatcher, he knew, had flagged down the officer, and was now squealing that the cops were on their way, as if the officer couldn't hear his buddies' wailing sirens.

Ralph stood strangely silent, staring down at Maylene's darkening hair, rocking on his heels. Two po-lice cars screamed into the murky light of the depot, and another two blocked the alley. The officers jumped out with guns drawn, but holstered them when they saw Ralph already in cuffs. Only then, surrounded by eight cops, several in off-duty duds, did he seem to wake up.

"Maylene!" he shrieked, staring wildly at the arresting officers. "Help her! Help Maylene!"

The first cop on the scene walked him to a car, shoving him a little harder than necessary into the back seat. "It's a little late for that, buddy. She's dead."

"But I ain't did this!" Ralph yelled. "I woulden hurt Maylene."

Malachi saw Detective Scovoy, whom he'd met at Randall Mill this morning. Scovoy squatted beside the squad car to talk to Ralph. Malachi couldn't make out the detective's question, but he could hear Ralph's answer.

"I ain't did this," he insisted again. Then a pause while Scovoy talked. Then Ralph, quieter, but still loud enough for Malachi to hear. "Yeah, okay. I did hit 'er this mornin'. But I ain't did this. Not this." He shuddered.

The detective spoke again. Ralph jerked his head from side to side. "It *is* my crowbar. I give it to her because she was goin' out alone. But I found it beside her. You gotta believe me."

Detective Scovoy stood and hit the roof of the car. "Take him," he said to the driver.

Malachi melted into the dark railroad yard behind the depot. He needed to think. Part of him felt guilty because Ralph and Maylene's tent was near his, and he knew Ralph was a violent ex-con. And part of him was mad at Maylene. Pastor Liam gave her every chance to get away. Why didn't she listen?

Lord knows he'd seen mean men and scared women on the street. But mostly, the women stayed because they didn't want to be alone, or their man held the crack supply. On the other hand, he'd seen plenty of men become unable to provide crack and start selling their women.

But Maylene hadn't seemed scared of Ralph, and she hadn't seemed overly fond of crack. Not yet anyway. That would've come later. More puzzling, she didn't seem as *worn* as most of the women out here. It was hard to put into words, but she'd been prettier, fresher, *unsullied*. Malachi remembered that word from an honors English class in high school, long, long ago.

So why was she putting up with such a loser?

He remembered a late night this fall when he'd left his tent to pee, and found her alone next to a fire barrel, smoking a cigarette. Steady snores came from the tent she shared with Ralph, so he stopped for a moment.

"Can't sleep?" he'd asked.

She'd shrugged and glanced at her tent. "Someone sure can."

Malachi had come right out and asked what was on his mind. "Whassa girl like you doin' out here? Seems you coul' do better."

"I could say the same for you," she'd responded.

"But I been out here years," he said. "You gotta life in front of you."

"So don't make the same mistakes you made?" Her tone softened the harshness of her words.

"Well, yeah," he said. "You got a fam'ly?"

"I do," she said.

"They know where you're at?"

"They think I'm in Atlanta."

"Why they think that?"

"Because I want them to."

Malachi waited for a moment while she blew smoke into the

frosty air. "Why you don't want your fam'ly to know where you're at? They beat you?"

She sighed. "No, they didn't beat me. Let's just say I screwed up and I don't want them paying for it."

Malachi thought for a moment. "By bringing Ralph home?"

Maylene turned then, and looked him full in the face. "You're a nice man, Mr Malachi. But you don't know everything. Good night."

No, she hadn't seemed scared of Ralph. But maybe she should've been.

CHAPTER SIXTEEN

Branigan followed Chester Scovoy to the bus and train depot at a distance. Leaving her car on the street, she cinched her coat tightly and entered the bus depot. The cavernous place was creepy enough during daylight hours. At night, its dim interior was positively eerie.

She approached the iron bars that separated the concrete structure from the grassy alley, normally an unexpected shock of green between the bus station and office building next door. Only now, Maylene's curled body lay on the grass, her face invisible beneath a mass of dark, wet hair. Branigan felt her stomach lurch.

Things had changed so rapidly over the course of the evening. She had very much enjoyed her time with Detective Scovoy and didn't want to impose on his friendship. She waited until an officer had covered Maylene's body, and the crime scene was taped and secured, before calling softly to him. He walked over.

"I don't want to bother you," she said, "so can I just ask a couple of questions, then get going?"

"Sure." His tone was clipped, businesslike, all trace of their earlier camaraderie dissipated.

"Was that Ralph I saw leaving in the back seat?"

"Yes."

"Full name? And what's he charged with?"

"Ralph Lemay Batson. He will be charged with murder."

"Any witnesses?"

"Don't know yet." Chester looked around and assured himself that his fellow officers weren't paying attention. He seemed to relax a bit. "We've got one officer talking to the dispatcher and other officers talking to everyone in the bus station. No one's come forward yet to say they actually saw it happen. The dispatcher called it in after a lady saw Maylene's body and screamed. But with the murder weapon and Ralph's history of domestic violence, it shouldn't be a problem." He ran a hand through his hair. "I'm just sorry it came to this."

"You and me both," she said. "Good night."

He had already turned back to the crime scene.

Branigan hurried to her car and locked the doors. Her teeth began to chatter, whether from the cold or from seeing Maylene's battered head, she couldn't say. Was it just this afternoon that she'd talked to the girl, urged her to get help? And was it her imagination or had the girl considered going home to Gainesville? Chief Warren would probably send an officer to the Ayers home. Pity the officer who got that assignment.

Branigan called the newspaper office and dictated a few paragraphs to Bert, alerting him to Maylene's identity as a member of the Ayers Arena clan. It was forty-five minutes before the last deadline, so he could get it in the paper and online. He thanked her and told her that Jody would follow up in the morning.

Wearily, Branigan turned her Civic toward the farm, jumpy and unsettled. She thought she would fall asleep minutes after crossing her threshold, but for most of the night she kept jerking awake, her mind returning instantly to the alley and Maylene's broken body. She finally patted her bed to invite Cleo to leap up beside her. Only when she buried her face in the thick fur of the dog's neck was she finally able to sleep.

Janie Rose Carlton's funeral was at ten on Saturday morning at Covenant United Methodist Church, a large, affluent campus near the courthouse on North Main Street. Branigan met Liam and Chan in the narthex. Her heart constricted when she looked at her nephew, lean and blond and slightly gawky, so like her brother Davison had looked at eighteen. Like his father, Chan towered over Branigan as he grabbed her in a bear hug.

Aware of their somber surroundings, she stifled her delight. "How was Furman?" she whispered. "I want to hear everything."

"Mom asked if you can come to dinner tonight," Chan said. "I'll tell all."

"Who'll be with Charlie?"

"Grandma and Grandpa Delaney. Can you come?"

"Sure, but tell Liz I'll bring the bread and salad and wine. She can't be messing with all that while she's running back and forth to the hospital."

"I'm sure that'll be fine," said Liam. He nodded toward the church sanctuary where organ music could be heard. "But we need to go in."

The three of them signed the register, then took a pew near the back, not wanting their presence to make things more difficult for the Carltons.

The church was filled with friends and neighbors of the Carltons, employees of Shaner Steel, a good portion of the faculty of Rutherford Lee, and friends of Janie Rose home from college. Branigan noted that two rows held what had to be Gamma Delta Phi sisters, dressed nearly identically in black sweater sets, black skirts and white pearls, with only an occasional blonde or redhead breaking the march of smooth brown heads. She saw Ranson Collier standing at the back, the funeral so important that he was working it himself. She waved discreetly, and he responded with a tight smile and a nod.

The congregation stood as four of Ranson's somber-suited employees rolled the casket to the front of the church, followed by Harry and Ina Rose Carlton and a dozen wet-eyed people Branigan took to be extended family members. Ina Rose was rubber-legged and leaned heavily on her husband, looking as though she might pass out at any moment. Harry Carlton walked stiffly, awkwardly, his body rigid with a barely contained anger.

While she was standing, Branigan looked around for police detectives, and spotted two in plain clothes. She couldn't find Chester, and didn't know if he was simply out of her sight line or tied up with Maylene's murder.

The congregation were invited to sing "A Mighty Fortress is Our God" and then to recite the Lord's Prayer. When they were seated, the church's youth minister rose to speak. She talked with warmth and first-hand knowledge about Janie Rose.

After another hymn and a Scripture reading, the senior pastor stood. Clearly, he knew the family, including Janie Rose, which always made a huge difference in funeral services, Branigan thought. This pastor too generated warmth and sincerity, and acknowledged that it was all right to experience doubt and confusion and even anger over the death of someone as young as Janie Rose. Branigan thought of Harry Carlton and wondered if the minister had been on the receiving end of his heated tirades.

Near the end of his talk, the pastor extended an open invitation to friends and family members who'd like to speak. A woman who introduced herself as Janie Rose's aunt did so, as did two members of the church youth group.

Branigan saw movement among the Gamma Delta Phi members, heads turning, shaking. Finally, a young woman rose, and Branigan recognized the sorority president, Marianne Thurman.

Marianne made her way to the podium, more poised than the youthful church members had been. She looked out over the congregation, and gripped the podium tightly.

"Good morning. I am Marianne Thurman, a sorority sister of Janie Rose when she attended Rutherford Lee. I just wanted to say…" She swallowed and looked at her feet. She waited a moment, appeared to regain her composure, and started again. "I just wanted to say what a great girl Janie Rose was. Kind and thoughtful and sweet." Branigan heard sniffling and looked at the Gamma Delta Phi rows. The sisters were passing Kleenex and crying openly.

Marianne told a funny story about rush, when Janie Rose was in great demand by three competing sororities. "We're not allowed to 'guarantee bids'," she continued. Her smile was self-deprecating, as if to say she recognized how silly rush and bids sounded out in the real world of death and funerals. "But Janie had three guarantees. Wink. Wink." The congregation laughed politely. "She was the kind of girl everyone wanted to be around. Our loss was UGA's gain."

Chan stirred next to Branigan. She turned to find him rolling his eyes. The minister helped Marianne off the podium, and she walked back to her pew. Another brunette stood, as if to make room for Marianne to pass. But then she took a step toward the front of the church. Branigan saw Marianne's arm snake out and grab the other girl's arm. The girl staggered, then slid back into the pew row and landed heavily. Marianne placed an arm around her shoulders, and even from a distance Branigan could see the girl's shoulders quaking. She wished she could see her face, but all those Gamma Delts looked alike from this angle.

The service concluded with a final hymn. The crowd stood as the coffin was wheeled out and the family passed by. Ina Rose kept her eyes on the carpeted aisle, but Harry Carlton's eyes darted over the funeral-goers. They landed on Liam and Branigan, and remained for a moment, hard, furious. Then his wife stumbled. He caught her and moved on.

CHAPTER SEVENTEEN

B ranigan decided not to accompany the funeral procession to the cemetery. It would be a much smaller affair, and she didn't want to set Harry Carlton off.

Alone in the church parking lot, she reached for the newspaper she'd grabbed from her driveway that morning. Removing its protective plastic bag, she was surprised to see a picture of Maylene at the bottom of the front page alongside her abbreviated story. Bert must have made a prodigious effort to find the photo before deadline. She looked at the credit line: *Courtesy of The Times, Gainesville, GA.* Okay, he'd followed up on her information that Maylene was from Gainesville. Given the prominence of the Ayers family, Branigan knew it'd be an even bigger story there – especially when reporters figured out the girl had been living on the street in Grambling. They'd probably be swarming in today.

She looked out of the Civic's window onto North Main, half expecting to see unfamiliar reporters prowling, notebooks in hand. All she saw was Christmas shoppers. She needed to do some Christmas shopping herself and get groceries and wine for tonight's dinner with Liam, Liz and Chan. She wanted to get in a run with Cleo. But first she'd swing by the hospital to see Charlie.

When she arrived at St Joe's, she met Liz coming out of Charlie's room. They hugged. "I'm going for coffee," Liz said. "Can I bring you some?"

"Sure. Take your time if you need a break. I'll stay until you get back."

Liz hesitated. "I do need to run to the grocery store. You're coming for dinner, right?"

"Yeah, but I told Chan I'll bring the salad, bread and wine."

"That'd be great. I'll make pasta and we'll call it dinner. I'll be back in half an hour."

"Take your time," Branigan said again. "Don't worry about us."

Branigan entered the hospital room to find all the lights on and Charlie sitting up in bed, her leg in a cast, but out of traction. She was working on a yogurt topped with granola, her red-gold hair pinned on top of her head – by her mother, no doubt. The swelling was beginning to recede from her face. She attempted a smile, and her missing teeth reminded Branigan of the snaggle-toothed grin she'd had as a first-grader. "It's hard to eat with one hand," Charlie said, by way of greeting. "The carton keeps sliding."

Branigan tossed the newspaper on the bed. "Your left hand at that. I can hold it steady for you."

But Charlie's attention had shifted to the newspaper. "Ah, civilization," she said. With her good hand she lifted the paper. When her eyes fell on Maylene's picture, they widened. "What happened to Maylene?" She scanned the brief story and looked at Branigan in disbelief. "Maylene is dead?"

Branigan hardly knew what to say. "How could you know her?"

Charlie's face was flushed, and she looked near tears. "She came up here yesterday."

"To your hospital room? When?"

"Late afternoon? My mind is foggy on time. She said you told her about my accident, and she wanted to meet me." Charlie reread the story, shaking her head, her bruised face crumpling. "I can't believe this, Aunt Branigan."

Branigan sat down on the recliner beside Charlie's bed, trying to remember her conversation with Maylene. Charlie interrupted her thoughts, her voice choked. "She was *beaten to death*? Is that right?"

"Yes," Branigan said softly. "Honey, the reason your dad had me talk to her was to try to help her, to get her away from that boyfriend, Ralph. But she wouldn't listen."

"And he *killed* her?"

"That's what it looks like." Branigan waited a moment. Charlie's tears remained unshed, though her face kept its shocked expression. "Charlie? Can you tell me what Maylene said?"

Charlie nodded. "She told me she knew Dad. And you. And how she was sorry for my accident. Then she asked me questions about the wreck."

"What sort of questions?"

"Mainly if I'd been able to see who was driving the hearse."

Branigan sat back. "How odd."

"She said she'd lived in that hearse for a day or two, and the windows were tinted real dark. But she could see the woods and trees through the windows. She wanted to know if I could see *in* the windows – from my car."

"What'd you tell her?"

"Same thing I told those patrolmen – that I couldn't see anyone inside."

"Why did she want to know?"

"I don't know." Charlie paused. "But she asked if Janie Rose knew who was driving."

Branigan was more confused than ever. "Did she know Janie Rose?"

"I don't know. I don't think she ever said, exactly."

"Try to remember her exact words," Branigan said.

Charlie closed her swollen eyes. "She said, 'Think, Charlie. When you were driving, did Janie Rose call out a name?'" Charlie's eyes flew open. "Aunt Brani, could Maylene's boyfriend have been driving the hearse, then brought it to the woods for them to live in?"

Branigan thought for a moment, then spoke slowly. "I suppose so."

"So maybe she was trying to find out if I could identify him?"

Branigan stiffened, her mind reeling at the possibilities Charlie's question opened. Before she could answer, a nurse in St Joe's green scrubs walked in wheeling a cart to check blood pressure. She placed the cuff on Charlie's arm, a thermometer under her tongue. "How's Miss Charlotte today?" she said with practiced cheer. Her eyes fell on the open newspaper in Charlie's lap, and her cheeriness dropped abruptly. "Oh, no. Isn't that your visitor from yesterday?"

Charlie nodded, the tears finally beginning to spill.

The nurse took the paper and read it quickly.

Branigan spoke up. "Do you remember what time she was here?"

"Which time?"

"What do you mean?"

The nurse checked her computer screen, then turned to Branigan. "Well, I saw her the first time when the aide brought Charlie's supper around 5 o'clock. But then I saw her leaving again maybe two hours before my shift ended at midnight."

Charlie took the thermometer out of her mouth. "Maylene didn't come back," she said. "Or I was asleep if she did."

The nurse looked thoughtful. "Ask your mom. Wasn't she here? I'm sure it was the same girl I saw out by the elevators."

Branigan was puzzled. *Why was Maylene at the hospital thirty minutes before she died? And did she confront Ralph about driving the hearse that killed Janie Rose?*

Then Branigan had a thought that drove everything else from her mind. *Or did Ralph send her to find out if Charlie could identify him?*

CHAPTER EIGHTEEN

B ranigan made an excuse to leave Charlie's hospital room and wait in the hallway for Liz. When Liz arrived, Branigan pulled her further down the hall, keeping the doorway in view.

She relayed what the nurse had said about Maylene coming back around 10 o'clock the night before. Liz shook her head emphatically. "I met that poor girl around suppertime," she said. "Her face looked nearly as bad as Charlie's. But no one came in after Liam left at nine."

"That's so strange," mused Branigan. "The nurse is sure she saw her by the elevators and assumed she'd been back in Charlie's room."

"No," Liz repeated. She made a move to return to the room. Branigan laid a hand on her arm.

"Wait a minute. I don't want Charlie to hear this. But it sounded like Maylene might have suspected her boyfriend, Ralph Batson, of driving the hearse when it hit Charlie's Jeep."

Liz's eyes widened, then darted to her daughter's doorway. "And then he killed her?"

Branigan nodded.

"Oh, my goodness," Liz breathed. "You think Maylene came back to hurt Charlie?"

"I don't know. Hurt her or warn her. We may never know. What I wanted to tell you, though, is it never occurred to me that Charlie might be in danger. You guys have somebody with her at all times, right?"

Liz nodded, her face tight. "But Chan and I have gone down to the cafeteria and left her when the nurses came in."

"You might not want to do that any more."

"But Ralph is in jail."

"Yeah. But Maylene could've had the right idea, just the wrong guy."

Liz turned abruptly and strode back into her daughter's room.

Branigan gave up on the idea of Christmas shopping, and headed home. On the way, she called Chester Scovoy and left a message on his voicemail about Maylene's visit to Charlie. "I'm not sure, but it sounded like she suspected Ralph was driving the hearse when it hit the girls' Jeep. You might question him on that while you've got him." She cringed as she disconnected. He didn't need her telling him how to do his job. She started to call back, then decided that would be worse.

Jody would be working on Maylene's murder today, and presumably probing into Ralph's background as well. Meanwhile, she needed a run to clear her head.

Cleo bounded out of the dormant cotton field when the Civic pulled into the driveway. Branigan patted her head. "Run?" she said. Cleo barked excitedly and ran to the side door. "You've been awfully patient. Let's get you some exercise."

Branigan pulled off her skirt, sweater and tights, and exchanged them for mismatched sweatpants and T-shirt. She pulled a UGA sweatshirt over her head, planning to shed it halfway through the run. It was a little too cold to start without it. Grabbing a hair tie, she pulled her hair into a high ponytail and locked the side door, a habit she'd gotten into last summer.

Cleo raced ahead on the well-worn path that traversed the cotton patch and emptied into the barnyard. Branigan walked between the barn and empty chicken houses, then rolled under a barbed wire fence and into the pastures her grandfather's farm shared with Uncle Bobby's. She held up the slack lowest wire for Cleo, and the shepherd obediently dropped to her stomach and shimmied under it. Branigan set out at a fast walk, crossing the broad expanse of pasture grass until she reached the fence and treeline that bounded the far side. Then she broke into a run.

Usually she lost herself in this landscape, the blue-green lake and gray-brown woods, the vine-covered cabin where her grandfather's poker buddies had once gathered. The land was now reclaiming the old shack. Another summer, and a green mound would be all that remained. But today, appreciation for northeast Georgia's ceaselessly moving topography was crowded out by worry. Worry about bruised and cracked Charlie, lying defenseless in a hospital bed. It wouldn't matter that Charlie hadn't seen the hearse's driver. It mattered only what the driver thought she saw.

But Ralph was in jail. That should take care of it, right?

She remembered Harry Carlton's hard eyes as he left the funeral service. What if it weren't Ralph after all, but the original thought she and Malachi had had: an angry associate of Janie Rose's father? Then Charlie could still be in danger.

Branigan stopped abruptly, and Cleo ran back to check on her. She took a moment to catch her breath and allow her sides to stop heaving, then pulled her cell phone out of the deep pocket of her sweatpants. She dialed Chester Scovoy's number. This time he answered.

"I'm sorry to keep bothering you," she began. "Did you get my earlier message?"

"Branigan?"

"Oh, sorry, yes. It's Branigan Powers." She didn't know what was sillier: giving her last name or expecting him to know her voice.

"Yeah, we'll be questioning Ralph again in a few minutes," Detective Scovoy said. "I'll ask about him taking the hearse to begin with."

"There's something else," Branigan said. "I'm not sure it's going to make sense. It's about Charlie Delaney."

"You want a guard on her?"

"How'd you know? Ralph can't get to her. But what if we're wrong about Maylene and Ralph, and somebody else suspects she saw something?"

"I sent a uni over as soon as I got your message," he said.

Branigan breathed a sigh of relief. "Gosh, that's great. I didn't know if I was letting my imagination run wild."

He laughed. "I can't speak to that. But I had the same thought."

"Okay. Thank you, Detective."

"You're welcome, Miss Powers."

Cleo barked and Branigan raced to catch up.

Branigan could sense the tension as soon as she walked into the Delaneys' home in a gentrified neighborhood west of downtown. She unloaded her bread and salad in their fashionable red, black and white kitchen, and poured a glass of the cabernet sauvignon she'd brought. Then she and Chan tiptoed to the living room, leaving Liam and Liz to their argument.

"It's about that homeless guy who killed the girl," Chan whispered. "He wants Dad to visit him in jail, and Mom says he might be the one who hit Charlie."

Branigan nodded. "Got it. We'll talk about it over dinner. But for now, I want to hear all about Furman."

For the next fifteen minutes, Chan told her about his classes, his roommate from Savannah, his decision to play intramural soccer rather than try out as a walk-on for the varsity. "Man, Furman's hard. I don't see how those varsity guys practice that much and stay in school. Finals about did me in."

"When will you know your grades?" she asked.

"They'll be posted by early next week."

"But you do like it? It's the right place for you?"

"Oh, yeah. I really do like it. I'm already looking at study abroad semesters. Maybe Spain. Maybe Australia."

"Wow."

"The funny thing is, when people find out where I live, they ask why I'm not at Rutherford Lee. Apparently everybody who looks at Furman also looks at Rutherford."

"And you tell them, 'Duh, because it's in Grambling.'"

He laughed. "Exactly."

"And... the other?" Branigan scarcely knew how to ask about the trauma her nephew had suffered the previous summer.

He shrugged. "It still sucks. Obviously. A few people picked up on the name when I said I was from Grambling. But it hasn't been an issue. Getting out of the state was a good idea."

Branigan didn't realize she'd been holding her breath. "I'm so glad." She reached over and squeezed his knee, adopted her best German accent. "Yousa a goot kid."

Gathered around the dining room table, Branigan, Liz, Liam and Chan held hands as Liam prayed a blessing over the meal. While they passed the pasta, bread and salad, Liam said, "So tell me about this police guard at Charlie's door. Thank you for that, by the way."

"Well, as I'm sure you know, Maylene visited Charlie yesterday and asked about what she saw on the day of the wreck – if she could see who was driving the hearse."

Liam nodded.

"Then a nurse said Maylene was back a couple of hours before midnight, but Liz and Charlie said she didn't return to the room. It started me thinking that she might be spying for Ralph. Maybe he was the driver."

Liam stopped his fork halfway to his mouth. "But you must suspect someone else if you asked the police to put a guard at the hospital."

"Actually, I didn't have to ask. Detective Scovoy put that guard on her room as soon as he heard about Maylene's visit. I think he and I both had a bad feeling, you know? It could be Ralph. But what if it was somebody else – somebody who doesn't know what Charlie saw?"

Liz spoke up. "Well, whatever, we're glad. And grateful." She paused. "Liam, tell her your news."

"Ralph called me today."

Branigan looked up from her plate. "What's he want?"

"A visit."

"Like a pastoral visit?"

Liam nodded. "Yeah, I do that a lot. Obviously." Branigan smiled to herself at how much Liam and Chan sounded alike.

Liz jumped in. "But I think if there's even a chance he ran Charlie off the road, Liam shouldn't go. Won't that confuse things if Ralph goes to trial?"

"I have no idea about the legalities," Liam said. "But as the pastor of Jericho Road, I feel I have to go."

"We'll let you be the tie-breaker, Branigan," Liz said.

"Oh, no! I'm not getting in the middle of that. But…"

"What?" they asked simultaneously.

"What if you were able to ask Ralph questions? See what he knows." Another thought occurred to her. "And maybe something else."

The other three waited, knowing that Branigan often worked out her thoughts aloud.

"Maybe see if he was working for someone."

Liz was the first to grasp her line of thought. "Like someone out to get Harry Carlton."

Liam thought for a moment. "There you go," he said to Liz. "You can't object to that."

She nodded. "How soon can you see him?"

CHAPTER NINETEEN

Malachi planned his Sunday carefully. First stop, church at Jericho Road.

Pastor Liam stood and said he wasn't a stickler for Advent. Malachi was a little fuzzy on that, but it had something to do with Pastor letting the choir sing Christmas carols before Christmas. Whatever, the singers sounded good on "Mary, Did You Know", "What Child Is This" and "God Rest Ye, Merry Gentlemen". It was the first time all season that Malachi missed his granny and pop.

After the service, he helped drag the tables back into the dining hall to set up for a lunch of meat loaf, green beans, mashed potatoes and rolls. He wrapped his roll for later. He had a long day ahead and wasn't sure he'd get supper.

At 1 o'clock, Jericho Road's clothes closet opened. It was a single room, way smaller than when Pastor Liam had arrived five years ago. Pastor talked a lot about helping people out of homelessness rather than making them good at being homeless. So in his first year, he gave most of the clothes to thrift stores. Those stores were creating jobs, he told the complainers. Now, the closet held two racks of coats, three racks of jeans and work uniforms, and a floor-to-ceiling shelf of work boots. The coats were because Pastor didn't want anybody freezing to death. The work clothes and boots, he said, were for "helping a man to fish". You had to have a job or a job interview to get them.

Malachi usually went along with Pastor's thinking. He'd seen enough drunks and addicts out there who used the do-gooders to support their habits. But today he needed something and he needed it quick. He might have to stretch the truth a bit.

He peered into the clothes closet, located next to the prayer room. Luckily, Pastor wasn't around, and it was being run by two old white ladies. Malachi didn't recognize them, which meant they were probably from a partner church.

He took off his stocking cap as he entered the room, his dreadlocks dangling to his shoulders. The ladies looked up, glad to have a customer. Malachi smiled shyly and explained that he had a job interview on Monday and wanted to dress to show the employer he was serious.

"What's the job?" asked one of the women, a grandmotherly sort with white hair and kind brown eyes.

"Subcontractin' for Shaner Steel," Malachi answered, hoping it was vague enough to prevent further questions. It was.

"So what do you need?"

"Just a plain work shirt and pants. Navy or gray."

The other woman, *pleasingly plump* his granny would've said, jumped up to help him.

"I think you'd take the smallest size we have," she said, eyeing Malachi's frame. "Try this."

She handed him an appropriately forgettable shirt, but the stitching above the pocket read "Earl". Malachi laughed to himself. He hoped no one would get close enough to read the shirt, but if they did, he was no Earl.

"Lemme see the next size, please," he said politely. The woman held out a short-sleeved navy shirt. "John" said the name above the pocket.

"That one'll do," Malachi said. The pants and shirt would be big on him, but that wouldn't matter.

"Do you need boots?" the first lady asked.

Malachi looked down at his black tennis shoes. "No, thank you, ma'am. Mine'll do fine."

Malachi slipped out of Jericho Road without running into Pastor Liam. He headed southeast toward the bus station, stopping in the back yard of a law office to change clothes. His gray hoodie, jeans and backpack were fine for disappearing in downtown Grambling. People looked away if they thought you were homeless. But where he was going, a homeless man would attract attention. So he stuffed his old clothes into his backpack, cushioning the tools he'd borrowed from Slick. He emerged into the alley beside the bus depot. All that remained of Maylene was a small circle of matted grass. If you didn't know those blackened blades were bloodstained, you'd think a car had dripped oil in the alley.

He paid for a ticket to Athens with money he'd squirreled away doing day labor, and was on his way by mid-afternoon.

The Greyhound stopped a mile short of the university. Malachi pulled out a city map he'd printed at the library, and figured out where he was. It'd been more than a decade since the summer he worked maintenance at an apartment complex filled with students. He'd thought the job would last longer, but bourbon got in the way.

The *Rambler* story had quoted a next-door neighbor of Janie Rose from Stone Hearth Apartments, a rich-ass complex that hadn't existed back then. Miz Branigan had vouched for Malachi to Jody Manson, who'd given him the young man's apartment number.

Now he had only to figure out which "next door" was Janie Rose's.

Malachi sat on a bench that allowed him to see three separate entrances to Stone Hearth's C Building. Then he waited. On the Sunday afternoon before Christmas, there wasn't much foot traffic. He grew chilled sitting in his work uniform, and wished he'd grabbed a coat too.

Two girls went in the front entrance, but they were too quick for him. An older woman entered a side door, but he barely made it to the stoop before the door closed and locked behind her. After an hour, he saw what he was looking for: a man in paint-spattered clothes carrying a ladder out of a side entrance. He'd gambled that Christmas break was a time for repairs and painting, and he was right. Malachi gave the painter time to get the ladder halfway out before helpfully holding the door. The man gave him a nod, and propped the door open while he returned to get his paint cans.

Malachi entered the ground floor hallway and then walked up the stairwell to the fourth floor. There was 405 C, the apartment of the young man. Malachi knocked on 406. No answer. Then 404. No answer.

Every door on the hallway was closed, so Malachi knelt and pulled out his laminated ID card. With these interior doors, he wouldn't need Slick's tools.

Sliding the card into a crack in the doorway of 404, he grabbed the doorknob to twist. To his surprise the knob turned easily. It wasn't even locked.

He eased the door open.

The living room was a mess, but not the kind of mess a young lady would leave. Couch cushions were on the floor, and the shelves were swept bare. He glanced into the kitchen, but it looked untouched except for a pile of framed pictures on the table – most likely the contents of those shelves. He picked up one and saw a mother, father and teenage girl, the same girl as in the newspaper who rode home with Miz Charlie. Bingo.

Malachi walked back across the gray carpet and into the bedroom. The mattress had been thrown off its box springs. Every book was tossed onto the floor, every drawer flung open and emptied, every under-the-bed storage box rifled.

Someone had the same idea as Malachi. Only someone had beaten him to it.

CHAPTER TWENTY

B ranigan slept in on Sunday morning. She stayed in her pajamas, built a fire in the den fireplace, and made hot chocolate, alternating between reading a mystery and watching reruns of *Law and Order: SVU.*

She and Cleo went for an abbreviated run late afternoon. It was long past dusk when she finally turned on her laptop and brought up the Gainesville newspaper's website. Maylene Ayers' death was the subject of the top two stories. Branigan skimmed the one about Ralph's arrest, written largely from Grambling sources. Then she read more carefully the one that quoted Maylene's aunt, who had apparently been appointed family spokesperson. It was fairly well fleshed out, with interviews from Maylene's middle school principal and several high school teachers. Sweet girl. Lacrosse player. Star of the high school's production of *Oklahoma!* and *Grease.* A volunteer for her church's soup kitchen. Huh?

And then there was something that made Branigan go back and read again. Freshman at Rutherford Lee College. Maylene had entered Rutherford Lee sixteen months previously. The story was unclear as to whether she completed her freshman year. It was equally unclear as to when and why she was living on the streets of Grambling. Her aunt expressed horror to learn that Maylene had been living in a homeless encampment. The last her family had heard, Maylene was in Atlanta. Though they were upset and confused by her dropping out of school and the subsequent lapse in contact, they never suspected she was homeless, and in fact questioned whether the Grambling police were mistaken.

Branigan was still puzzling over the story when her phone rang. It was Bert Feldspar.

"I guess you saw the stories from Gainesville?" he said. "That Maylene Ayers had gone to Rutherford Lee?"

"I did. But did you also see that she'd volunteered in the soup kitchen at her home church?"

"Yeah, but I didn't think anything of it. Why?"

"It's just strange that she went from helping the homeless to living with the homeless."

"Either way," Bert said, "we've got the death of two affluent college girls in the same week. Janie Rose's death is still unsolved. Maylene's death looks pretty cut and dried, but why in the world was she living on the streets of Grambling? Lots of questions."

"I'll say."

"So anyway, it's all hands on deck tomorrow. Wanted you to know in case there's anything you need to get out of the way tonight."

"Right. I'll hammer out that homeless story."

"Okay. See you in the morning."

Branigan sat back for a moment, mind reeling. Then she called Liam's cell. He assured her that he was taking a turn sleeping in Charlie's room, and there was a cop at the door.

She returned to her laptop, retrieved her notes and started writing.

Being homeless at Christmas was horrible, she thought as she assembled her story. But for Maylene, it had been only the beginning.

CHAPTER TWENTY-ONE

The hearse was inches from Charlie's car door, flying down the road beside her Jeep. To her right, Janie Rose was plastered to the seat, her face a mask of fright.

Charlie was trying to scream, but nothing was coming out. She wanted to scream for her father, to tell him she'd tried the twenty-second rule for looking in her rearview mirror, but the hearse had come out of nowhere. Charlie peered into the blackness of the hearse's window. She could see nothing. But wait… there was a shadow, a face turned toward her, no features visible. But the face was topped by some kind of fabric. A hat, maybe? A stocking cap with a ball on top?

The scream she attempted came out as a whimper. Charlie struggled to open her eyes. Finally, they opened, and she saw a face topped by a Santa hat. This time she did scream.

Maggie Fielding yanked the hat off with a yelp. "Charlie?" she cried. "What's wrong?"

Liam shook Charlie's uninjured shoulder gently. "Charlie, it's all right. Wake up, honey. You're having a bad dream."

Charlie's frantic eyes took in the room, her father, her old high school friend, and finally she relaxed.

"Magpie," she murmured. "What are you doing here?"

"Well, the idea was to cheer you up. But I think I'm failing." Maggie Fielding had been Charlie's "big sister" on the Grambling High East soccer team, two years ahead of her. Now Maggie played varsity for Rutherford Lee. "How you feeling, girl?"

Charlie groaned. "About as bad as I look, I imagine." She was having trouble sweeping away the cobwebs of the dream.

"I'm so sorry," said Maggie. "But I brought someone to meet you."

For the first time, Charlie's eyes went to the far wall and noticed a handsome young man with black curls and electric blue eyes. "Hi, Charlie," he said softly. "I was trying not to startle you."

"This is Jones Rinehart," said Maggie, rather proudly it seemed to Charlie. "My boyfriend."

"Oh," said Charlie. "Well, it's nice to meet you. Sorry to look so ratty."

Liam stuck out his hand. "I'm Liam Delaney, Charlie's dad."

"Sir." Jones nodded politely and shook Liam's hand. "I'm so sorry about the accident."

"Yeah, us too."

"Charlie, can you tell us what happened?" Maggie asked. "I read *The Rambler*, but it makes no sense. Someone stole our hearse to run you off the road?"

Liam looked puzzled. "*Our* hearse?"

"Maggie's a Kappa Ep at Rutherford Lee," Charlie told her dad.

"Yes, sir, we held a big meeting right after we found out our hearse had been used. The police have been by to ask questions, but they seem to think anybody and everybody could have gotten hold of that key. It was on a wall in the kitchen.

"Anyway, a few of the girls knew Janie Rose, but I was the only one who knew Charlie. So I said I'd come by and ask if there's anything we can do."

Charlie shook her head gingerly. "Not unless you're orthopedic surgeons. Or dentists." She pulled her lower lip back to show Maggie her missing teeth.

"Ouch."

"Or," Charlie added, "you can find out who took your hearse."

"We'll keep trying, but none of us paid much attention to that old wreck. It just sat out back unless we were using it for rush or homecoming or Halloween."

"Or engagements," said Liam.

Maggie and Jones exchanged a glance, and Maggie blushed slightly. "Yeah, that too."

The four chatted for a few minutes. Charlie asked Maggie and Jones how they'd met.

"At a party," he answered. "The Robies and Kappa Eps had a Bloody Mary party one Friday morning."

"The Robies?" said Liam.

"Rho Beta Iota. It's easier to say Robies. Anyway, that was two years ago, but we didn't start dating until this fall. We've been together all semester."

Maggie smiled. Her friend was smitten, Charlie realized.

They talked for a while longer about Charlie's physical therapy and Christmas plans, until Charlie began to tire. Maggie noticed and stood to leave, kissing her young friend on the cheek. "You have a good Christmas with your family," she whispered.

"Don't forget your Santa hat," said Liam, tossing the red and white fur to Jones.

CHAPTER TWENTY-TWO

I t was dark by the time Malachi got back to the Grambling bus depot, plumb worn out. But since he had to walk back to his tent anyway, he figured he'd stop by St Joe's.

He passed a seedy convenience store, trash blowing across the parking lot in cold gusts. Inside the hot and crowded store, he bought a snack cake shaped like a Christmas tree. He figured Miz Charlie'd be tired of hospital food, and how stale could it be?

When he reached the hallway outside her room, he saw a cop leaning back in a chair. He could hear voices through the open door. He held back, and the cop eyed his maintenance uniform and his dreadlocks.

"You a friend of Pastor Liam?" he asked.

Malachi nodded, and held up the snack cake. "Brought Miz Charlie a present. But I'll wait."

He could hear most of the talk inside the room. He knew Charlie's voice, and Pastor's. Then there was a woman's voice he'd never heard. Then a second man's voice. He felt his stomach clench when he heard it, but he couldn't place it. Who *was* that? Malachi trusted his instincts enough to know the recoil of his body meant something, but for the life of him he couldn't remember where he'd heard that voice. And the men weren't talking much. The women were carrying the conversation.

Malachi waited a few more minutes, then heard the scraping of chairs and murmurs of goodbye. He crossed the hall and stood in front of a utility closet so it looked like he was coming out of it.

The man walking out of Charlie's room was from the right side of the tracks, Malachi knew at once. But he'd seen him on the wrong side. It took but one look at those black curls and blue eyes, and Malachi knew exactly where he'd seen him before.

And Malachi didn't want him anywhere near Miz Charlie.

The young man looked directly at Malachi, but Malachi knew there was no danger of recognition. His kind did not pay attention to Malachi's kind. And indeed, the young man's eyes flicked away as he put his arm around a woman. They walked to the elevators without looking back.

The cop knocked on Charlie's door to let Pastor Liam know they had another visitor. But when he turned around, Malachi was sliding the Christmas tree cake onto the nurse's station and leaving by the stairs.

CHAPTER TWENTY-THREE

B ranigan was well rested when she arrived at work on Monday
morning. She knew she'd made the right decision to take Sunday
off. Well, at least until she had to spend the evening writing the
homelessness story for Christmas Eve. But when she wrote in her
pajamas, it didn't feel so much like work.

Despite the damp chill from an early morning fog, she felt
energized, as she always did when a challenging story presented
itself. She'd never voice this, but she couldn't wait to delve further
into the deaths of Janie Rose and Maylene. Somehow their deaths
seemed more personal than usual. Presumably that was because of
Charlie's proximity to Janie Rose. As for Maylene, Branigan wasn't
sure why she cared so much. Maybe it was that she suspected the
girl's bravado had hidden fear and loneliness.

She put her hand out to push the heavy glass door at *The Rambler*
entrance, when she heard someone say her name. She turned, but
all she could see was unrelenting gray mist. She shivered. A man's
figure emerged near the corner of the building.

"Malachi," she said, shifting her satchel in order to shake his
hand. "What brings you here?"

"It's Miz Charlie," he said. "Someone in Miz Charlie's room last
night."

Branigan was instantly alert. "Who?"

"She's all right," Malachi said hastily, sensing Branigan's anxiety.
"Pastor Liam, he was there too."

Branigan relaxed, and waited for Malachi to continue.

"I stopped in last night to see Miz Charlie and Pastor Liam, to
take her a cake I know she like. But I heard voices in the room, so
I din go in. I thought I heard the man's voice before, but I coulden
figure out where. Then he walked out."

Branigan waited, unspeaking, knowing there would be a point; Malachi rarely talked this much.

"I seen him last winter. He was with a bunch of college boys out rehabbing."

Branigan looked at him blankly. "Rehabbing?"

"You know, when a gang come in and beat up a homeless dude. Like they be 'rehabbing' a crack head."

Branigan stared at him in horror. "*What?* Does that really happen?"

"Yeah. It be all over the Internet sometime. It jump up in Gramblin' ever' few years… Last winter," Malachi continued, "sometime after Christmas is all I 'member – about twelve or fifteen college boys came under the bridge where Max Brody stay. You 'member his tent?"

"How could I not?" Max Brody had been involved in the ugliness of last summer.

"Well, they found him passed out and beat the crap outta him."

"How did I not know this?" Branigan asked.

Malachi shrugged. "Ain't nobody reporting it to the po-lice, thas for sure."

"But did Max go to the hospital?"

"Don' know. Even if he did, he prob'bly din say what happen."

"How do you know they were college boys?"

"They use'ly aren't," Malachi said. "They use'ly be gang members gettin' 'nitiated, or cracker high school kids. But on this night, we heard noise on the side of the tracks where Max stay."

Branigan nodded. Malachi's Tent City was separated from Max's former encampment by a large hill topped by railroad tracks.

"Slick and Vesuvius and me and a couple of the womens run over to see what the noise was. We had flashlights. That's how I seen this dude who come to Charlie's room. He was waving a likker bottle and yellin', 'Rehab him, gentlemen! Rehab him! Make him a ornery robby.' Or somethin' like that."

"What's an 'ornery robby'?"

"Don' know."

"That still doesn't make them college kids."

115

"Some of 'em had on sweatshirts from Rutherford Lee and other schools. And some of 'em had on shirts with those Greek letters. Miz Branigan, I worked 'roun colleges. They were college kids."

Branigan drew in a deep breath. "I don't even know what to say. This is horrifying."

Malachi shrugged. "It happens. I want you to know 'cause this guy hanging round Miz Charlie."

"You didn't get a name?"

"No, but Pastor Liam know."

"It's okay if I tell him, right?"

"Yeah."

"All right. Well, Malachi, thank you for telling me."

"And, Miz Branigan. Somethin' else."

She waited.

"Somebody broke in Miz Janie Rose apartment down at Athens."

Branigan's eyes widened. "How do you know that? Police scanner?"

"Nah. I rode down to take a look. Thought there might be somethin' in her place somebody was after. If they was, somebody done took it."

"You could tell someone had been in her apartment?"

"Yeah, it was all tore up."

"Surely the police have searched it. It was probably them."

"Ain't no po-lice tear up a place like that."

Branigan had more questions, but Malachi was already walking away, disappearing into the gray of early morning.

It was indeed all hands on deck in the newsroom. Branigan walked in to find publisher and executive editor Tan Grambling already there, along with city editor Bert Feldspar and *Style* editor Julie Ames, reporters Jody Manson, Marjorie Gulledge, Harley Barnett and Lou Ann Gillespie. Even business writer Art Whittaker.

Bert was passing around a box of bagels and cream cheese, while Julie poured coffee. One good thing about all the layoffs was that it meant room for a coffee bar and dorm-size refrigerator in the newsroom – something that wasn't possible in years past.

"I can't be the last one in," said Branigan. "The sun's not even up."

"Yep," said Bert. "You are. Six reporters. Full court press." He glanced at Tan. "You wanna start?"

Everyone was gathered around Bert's desk in rolling chairs or perched on nearby desks, not bothering with a conference room. No phones rang this early.

"No, I want you to quarterback this," Tan answered. *Sheesh*, thought Branigan, catching Marjorie's eye. *Can you guys trot out any more sports clichés?* She wisely stayed silent.

"Okay, then." Bert rubbed his hands together, a gesture Branigan had seen Tan-4 make numerous times. "Two college girls killed within a week. Different MOs, obviously. But there are similarities. Both came from wealthy families. Both attended Rutherford Lee."

The reporters looked up expectantly. They respected Bert's organizational skills.

"Jody, you camp out with law enforcement – state patrol on the wreck and Grambling police here in town. Update online with everything they have. Nothing is too small.

"Lou Ann, you take Gainesville. Who was Maylene Ayers? Why was she living on the street? What went wrong? That may be the strangest part of all this. Call Branigan if you need back-up.

"Harley, you take Ralph Batson. Who is he? Hometown, education, prison records, the works. How did he meet Maylene? See if Jody can help you get inside the jail for an interview.

"Marjorie, I want you to use your contacts from last summer to talk to people in that homeless camp about Ralph and Maylene. Did they fight? Was she frequently beat up? What did people hear?

"Branigan, hammer Charlie Delaney about that wreck. Does she remember anything more? And stay on the Rutherford Lee angle. Did the victims' paths cross while they were there? Why did they leave school?

"Art, can you check into the Carltons' background in Philadelphia? Look into the finances of Shaner Steel. Is it possible Janie Rose was targeted because of her dad? Maybe it was a kidnap attempt gone bad.

"Lou Ann, ask the financial questions about Maylene too, though it seems pretty remote. But the Ayerses do have money."

He swiveled back to Art. "Are there any connections – financially, business-wise – between the Ayers and Carlton families? Probably not, but let's rule it out."

Bert stopped for a moment, jotted down a few notes. He rubbed a hand over his freshly shaved head. "Actually, now that I'm saying it out loud, *was* that wreck a kidnapping attempt gone bad?"

Branigan glanced at her colleagues and saw them pondering the possibility. She hadn't considered it, but it made sense.

Bert continued, "Was the driver trying to force the girls off the road to grab one of them? Then one of them died and he fled?"

Marjorie spoke up in her raspy smoker's voice. "Kidnapping points to the Carlton girl because of her family's money. But since we don't know that for sure, should we look at Charlie Delaney as a potential victim too? There was no way of knowing that someone would survive that wreck."

Bert turned to Tan-4. "What do you think?"

"Branigan, you're closest to the Delaneys," Tan-4 responded. "Is that possible?"

"Well, the police have a guard on Charlie's hospital room," she said, not adding that she'd had a hand in it. "I think that's more in case someone thought she saw something. But yeah, I guess anything is possible."

Bert nodded. "So yes, Marjorie. Keep an open mind. Could one of the Delaneys have angered someone enough to make their daughter a target?" He looked at his watch. "Any more questions? Comments? Concerns?"

"Is everybody writing?" Jody asked. "Or are we feeding someone?"

Bert glanced around. "I want Marjorie and Branigan taking the lead on the profiles, you on the police angle. But it'll depend on what everyone comes up with. If Lou Ann or Harley comes up with something especially good on Maylene or Ralph, we may have them write it. We'll see."

Hearing nothing more, Bert dismissed them with final

instructions. "Let's meet or call in at three and see what everybody's got for tomorrow's paper. Meantime, call or email me when you're ready to post. I'll coordinate all the online stuff. Julie will be handling all other stories, at least for today. Are we good? I want a slam dunk."

Branigan stopped by Art Whittaker's desk. With his khaki slacks and bow tie, he was the best dressed man in the newsroom – which wasn't saying much. She motioned for Jody to join them, then relayed Malachi's claim that Janie Rose Carlton's apartment had been ransacked.

Art looked puzzled. "What could a nineteen-year-old have that's worth killing over? This doesn't make a lick of sense."

"I don't know either," Branigan admitted. She filled the men in about the luggage at the crash scene that might have been searched as well. "If the hearse driver was looking for something in their luggage, that takes kidnapping off the table."

She then told Art about a colleague of Janie Rose's father who had visited her at Rutherford Lee the previous winter. "Finding him might be a place to start."

"Got a name? A description?"

"First name is Roy. No last name, but a pretty distinctive description. It's in my notes. I'll email it to you to make sure I don't leave anything out."

Jody jumped in. "I'm thinking we need to share the information about Janie Rose's apartment with the cops. Any problem with that?"

Branigan shook her head. "Fine with me. In fact, it might help to know if someone searched it before or after the crash."

Art turned to his laptop to begin a search on Shaner Steel. "I'll let you know if I find anything," he promised.

Branigan walked to her desk, flipped through her notes and emailed Emma Ratcliffe's description of Roy to Art. She sat for a moment, drinking coffee and planning her calls. The first one went to Liam. He sounded groggy.

"Did I wake you?"

"Yeah, but it's okay. The doctor will be by in a minute anyway."

"You're with Charlie?"

"Yes."

"Who was the young man who visited her last night?"

"The boyfriend of her old soccer buddy, Maggie Fielding. Jones Rinehart, I think his name was. Yeah, that sounds right."

"Malachi came to my office this morning and told me that Jones fellow was involved in beating a homeless man last year. He called it 'rehabbing'."

"My Lord! Was Malachi up here? I didn't see him."

"Yeah, he was. But have you ever heard of that? Rehabbing?"

"Yeah. But not by college boys."

"I've never heard you mention it."

"Well, it comes in spurts. Two summers ago there was a bunch of stuff on the Internet about homeless people in other cities being paid to fight each other. Then videos of masked teenagers rolling homeless men, sometimes as gang initiations. Then sure enough, it happened here. Some of the guys told me about it, but they wouldn't report it to the police. So I invited the police to Jericho Road, and they sat down with our guys. They assured them they'd take any reports seriously."

"Did they make an arrest?"

"Not that I know of. Everything kind of quieted down after that. But Brani, go back to this Jones fellow. You're saying he was involved in rehabbing?"

"According to Malachi. Not two summers ago, but more recently."

"Tell me what Malachi said exactly."

"He said it was sometime last winter, after Christmas. That twelve or fifteen college boys – and he was adamant they were college boys – beat up Max Brody in the camp under the Garner Bridge. Malachi and some people from his side of the railroad tracks heard the commotion and witnessed it. Malachi said that guy in Charlie's room was waving around a liquor bottle and yelling, 'Rehab him, rehab him!' And something I didn't understand: something about being an 'ornery robby'?"

Liam's voice rose an octave. "Malachi said *that*?" There was silence on his end for a moment. "Could he have been trying to say 'an honorary Robie'?"

"Yeah, I guess. What's it mean?"

"It's Jones's fraternity. Rho Beta Iota. They call themselves the Robies."

Now Branigan and Liam were both silent. Finally she spoke. "Liam, it *was* a gang initiation, wasn't it? Only an upscale gang."

Liam sighed. "Yeah, sounds like it."

Branigan's next call would have surprised her editors. But over the years, she'd found that her sometimes offbeat way of looking at things paid off. Ira Powers picked up on the fourth ring. He might be slow getting to the phone, but Branigan knew he'd be awake.

"Granddaddy, I need a huge favor."

"And what's that?"

"Can you invite Sylvia Eckhart to your house? Today?"

"I suppose so." He didn't ask why, which was one of the many reasons Branigan adored him. "Do you want Rudelle and Marisol to rustle up lunch?"

"No, I don't want them to go to that much trouble. Coffee and Marisol's muffins would be great. I'd like to pick both of your brains about the Honor Council. It'll save me time if I can get you together."

"You know we can't speak about specific cases for the paper?"

"I know. This will be background."

"Very well. What time do you want me to invite her?"

"As soon as possible. I imagine she's grading exams this week, right? See if she can take a break."

"She lives two streets over. She could probably do that. I'll call you back as soon as I've got a time."

"Thank you so much, Granddaddy. I think some of those frat kids of yours may be worse than you suspect."

Chapter Twenty-four

Tears leaked out of Charlie's blackened eye, which was only now fading to a yellowish green. At least the swelling was down. But her back was aching from the enforced bed rest, and the leg inside the cast itched. In a word, she was miserable.

Plus, there were those dreams. Or rather the one dream. She wasn't really sure if she was awake or asleep – the pain meds made everything hazy – but she kept envisioning the minutes before the wreck.

In the dream, she looked from Janie Rose's frozen face to the black window of the hearse. She was trying so hard to see behind that glass. There were moments when she almost could. Not a face exactly, but something on top of the face. A fedora? A scarf? A hijab? Okay, now she was being officially silly.

But then her eyes flew open. It wasn't an answer, but it was something. Chan stirred in the chair beside her bed, put down his book and stood to stretch. "Why, Miss Charlotte, I do believe you're awake."

"Imagine yourself the subject of a withering look," she said. "And call Aunt Branigan."

He obediently stabbed his cell phone. "Remember something?" he asked while waiting for his aunt to pick up.

"Yeah."

Branigan answered from the hospital parking lot, and told Chan she'd be in Charlie's room within two minutes. Brother and sister waited silently, Charlie consciously reserving her strength, Chan nervously patting her shoulder. They could hear Branigan talking to the cop outside the door. Chan stuck his head out and told the young rookie that she was family.

Branigan burst through the door. "What is it?" she said.

"I keep having this dream that's more than a dream, if you know what I mean," said Charlie. "I mean I think it's a memory."

"Okay."

"And I'm trying hard to see through the passenger window of the hearse. I can't, but I almost can. I can't see a face, but I can almost make out something on top of the head, you know? A hat or something. That's probably not important. What's important is that it means…"

Chan looked from his sister to his aunt, mystified.

Branigan was nodding. "It means…"

Both women finished the thought: "… there was a passenger."

Branigan plopped into the chair Chan had vacated. "So we may be looking for two people, not just a driver. Wow." She looked around. "Where's your dad? I talked to him half an hour ago."

"He went home to shower, then to see Ralph Batson in jail," Chan answered.

"Did he get to talk to a doctor first?"

"Yeah. She said Charlie can come home on Christmas Eve."

Branigan turned to study Charlie. "You ready for that?"

"Oh, yeah. Dad promised me his recliner. It's got to be easier on my back than this bed." She hit the button to incline the bed, and struggled to sit up straighter.

"Charlie, I need to ask you something else. Do you remember if you zipped your duffel bag when you packed to come home for Christmas?"

"Mom and Dad asked me that already. I'm pretty sure I could only zip it halfway because my hair dryer was sticking out."

"So I guess your clothes could have spilled out when it hit the ground."

"I think so. The patrol thought someone had gone through our stuff?"

"They thought it was a possibility. They also got an anonymous 911 call, but the caller didn't stay at the wreck site with you. Which is very strange."

The three were silent for a minute. "Tell me more about this dream or memory," Branigan said. "And if you want me to pass it on to Detective Scovoy."

"Yes, definitely." Charlie closed her eyes. "Every time I'm on the edge of sleep, I'm in the Jeep again. It may be the humming of this bed. It adjusts itself or something and I can hear it hum or buzz every few minutes. It sounds a little like a car engine."

Branigan and Chan had heard it too.

She went on. "And I'm scared in the dream, but I'm also trying hard to see who's inside the hearse. It's like my mind knows and it's trying to show me. Last night, I half woke up and my friend Maggie was in here wearing one of those Santa hats, and I started screaming. I don't know if I saw the same hat in the dream, or if I somehow saw her hat as I was waking up and transposed it into the dream."

Branigan and Chan looked at each other. "Actually, Charlie, that may be important," Branigan said. "You really think the passenger in the hearse was wearing some kind of hat?"

Chan interrupted. "Wait a minute. Isn't it Maggie's sorority that had the hearse?"

Branigan wheeled on him. "What?"

Chan explained. "Charlie has this good friend from high school soccer, Maggie. She plays for Rutherford Lee now. But she's also a Kappa Ep. I've seen her in that shirt half a dozen times."

"And this Maggie showed up in a Santa hat?" Branigan asked.

Now it was Charlie's turn. "What are you saying? That Maggie ran me off the road in a Santa hat? That's ridiculous."

"No, I'm not saying that," Chan said slowly. "But weird coincidence with you dreaming about the hat."

"Well, like I said, maybe I dreamed about the hat *because* I got a glimpse of Maggie in it when I was half awake. Though I have to admit, I think I'd dreamed about it before." She grimaced. "With these pain meds, it's hard to tell."

"And Maggie's the one who brought the boyfriend?" Branigan asked. "Liam mentioned him."

"Yeah, super hot," said Charlie. "Magpie seemed really into him."

Branigan stayed for a few more minutes, chatting with the

brother and sister, but with half her mind elsewhere. She bent to kiss Charlie, and hugged Chan.

She didn't tell them what Maggie's hot boyfriend did in his spare time.

CHAPTER TWENTY-FIVE

B ranigan paused to speak to the young rookie guarding Charlie's door.

"I don't want to be alarmist," she said, "but make sure to check everyone who visits this room. Even if you're sure they're friends of Charlie or Chan."

"Detective Scovoy said the same thing. Anyone in particular I'm looking for?"

Branigan sighed in frustration. "Unfortunately, no. I guess I'm just saying even if Charlie says it's okay to let someone in, please keep an eye on what's going on."

"Sure thing."

Ira Powers called Branigan as she was en route from the hospital to the college. Sylvia Eckhart was willing to come over at 11 a.m.

"That's perfect," she said. "Granddad, thank you so much. I'll see you at eleven."

She had well over an hour before that meeting. She drove slowly through the college's archway; against the red bricks, scrolled ironwork announced Rutherford Lee College. Trying to ascertain her next move, she drove halfway around the campus loop, pulled into the chapel parking lot and called Liam.

He was leaving the Law Enforcement Center. "Can we meet?" he asked. "I think you'll want to hear this."

"Any chance you can come out to Rutherford Lee?" she said. "I'm sure the coffee shop is open, because faculty members are still around."

"Yeah, I can do that. I'll meet you there in ten."

Branigan took the time to continue the leisurely campus loop. As if the universe knew it was the first day of winter, the sun had disappeared, replaced by a grayish white sky. The plentiful hardwood trees made stark silhouettes against it, reminiscent of Asian art. She entered the lake road, where most of the dorms were located. *Imagine living on a lake as your first adult residence*, her grandfather used to say. *Our alums spend the rest of their lives trying to find a setting like this.*

Maybe outside, she thought. But inside, a dorm room was a dorm room.

There was no traffic, so she paused in the middle of the road to look over the lake. Swans and ducks floated on its placid surface, unbothered by the cold. A few students walked past her car. She supposed there were always some who stayed on campus over the holidays for jobs or internships, or because home was too far away. But it had to be bleak.

She pulled into the parking lot beside the Student Union building. She entered from the lakeside patio, empty today. The coffee shop, with its hardwood floor, navy walls and yellow accents to reflect the school colors, was comfortably warm. Not seeing Liam, she ordered two cappuccinos, and selected a booth near the floor-to-ceiling windows that faced the lake.

She grabbed a student newspaper, *The Swan Song*. She remembered her grandfather telling her about campus unrest during the 1960s. While Rutherford Lee didn't claim a Confederate rebel or general as its mascot, it did sport a vaguely medieval cavalier that came under protest. The cavalier survived, but pacifist journalism students made their statement by dropping *The Cavalier Clarion* in favor of *The Swan Song*.

She now opened it to a reprint of the *Rambler* story on Charlie's wreck and Janie Rose's death. But the focus of a sidebar was on the Kappa Epsilon hearse. Branigan checked the date – Saturday, two days earlier – and the byline: Anna Hester. That was the girl she and Jody had met when interviewing the Kappa Eps.

She read with interest the girl's story about the history of the vehicle. Clearly she'd talked to Detective Scovoy about finding the hearse in the woods. Amazingly, she'd even quoted Maylene Ayers about living in the hearse.

How did she find Maylene? Branigan wondered. She added Anna Hester to her mental list of the day's interviewees.

Liam slid onto the navy vinyl seat across from Branigan and grabbed his cappuccino. "Oooh, thanks for this. That fog this morning got into my bones."

Branigan waited for her friend to take a sip. His red hair was wild as usual, his smile tired.

"I must've just missed you at the hospital," she said. "I stopped and saw Charlie and Chan."

"Did you? Good. Doctor says we can bring her home Thursday."

"She's ready, that's for sure. So what did Ralph have to say?"

"That he didn't kill Maylene. And you know what, Brani? I'm not at all sure he did."

"I was afraid you were going to say that. Tell me why."

"Off the record, right?"

"Yeah, I'm not even writing about him. Harley Barnett is trying to get an interview."

"Well, it's not so much what he said. I'm used to hearing denials. Every damn time I'm at the jail, in fact. But this was different. Ralph was… shattered. I think in his own messed-up way he loved Maylene. He admitted he'd hit her. That was the thing. He pretty much admitted he was abusive, and that he'd done plenty in his life to be locked up for. But he hadn't done this. He hadn't killed her." Liam leaned back, took another sip. "This is good cappuccino," he said. "I guess when you pay $50,000 a year for college, you get good coffee."

Branigan's mind remained on Ralph. "So what did he say about the night Maylene died?"

"He says she left their tent several times to talk on her phone. She was being real secretive. She told him she was going to the bus station to price a ticket to Gainesville. She swore she was just going to price it, and didn't take any clothes with her. Ralph had already had a few beers and didn't want to walk her there. It was getting dark, so he gave her that crowbar to protect herself."

"What a guy." Branigan thought for a moment. "But that *does* line up with what I told you, doesn't it? Maylene could have been considering going home. And of course, now that we know she's an Ayers, she sure didn't need any clothes from their tent."

Liam held his palms up. "The problem is, who besides Ralph would want to hurt her? His motive is even stronger if she was leaving him."

Branigan nodded. "Yeah, and I guess it makes sense that he'd kill her well away from their tent too."

"But if you coulda heard him, Brani G." Liam shook his head. "I know I'm a sucker for a sad story, but I believed him."

"You think she was talking to her family on the phone?"

"I don't know. But that'd be easy to find out."

She made a note to call Lou Ann.

"Okay, for the other part of the story," she said. "Did you ask him about driving the hearse that hit Charlie?"

"Yes. I started out by asking if he knew Maylene had come to the hospital to see Charlie. He seemed genuinely surprised and asked me a lot of questions. When I got around to the hearse, he swore he'd never seen it before finding it in the woods."

"And how was your truth-o-meter then?"

Liam smiled. "Same as before. He convinced the preacher." He shrugged. "I gotta tell you though: I want whoever did this to Charlie – and Janie Rose – in prison. If it's Ralph, so be it. And Branigan, one more thing. Ralph asked if I was friends with that 'blonde reporter chick' who came to his campsite."

Branigan laughed. "I've been called worse."

"He said you needed to watch out, that you might not know what you're getting into."

"Huh. That's weird. Was it some kind of threat?"

Liam stared out of the window at the swans on the lake. "It didn't feel like a threat, exactly. He said I needed to look after you and Charlie. We have a cop at Charlie's door, but not at yours. So be careful." He shook his head. "Anyway, I know I'm an easy sell. I'd love for your Detective Scovoy to have a go at him – see what he thinks."

"*My* Detective Scovoy?"

"Oh, yeah. Liz called that six months ago."

Branigan slid out of the booth, batting her eyes in jest. "Liz and my grandmother ought to get together. Maybe between them they could get me married off."

Rather than heading for the parking lot, Branigan walked the opposite way, to the religion and econ building next door. Like most campus buildings, its three-story brick edifice was neatly set off by trimmed grass and beds flush with winter pansies, colorful even at this time of year. She doubted Ina Rose Carlton would be in her office, but thought it worth a look.

The building was quiet, and Branigan's footsteps fell unheard on a navy and gray carpet. If faculty members were around, they were grading exams in their offices. Branigan could hear a vacuum cleaner in the distance, but it was barely discernible.

Her ears picked up the sobbing before she reached the professor's office. Dr Carlton's door was slightly ajar. Branigan peered in to see Ina Rose clutching her stomach and rocking herself, tears streaking down her face, wrenching sobs emanating from her throat.

Branigan hesitated. Should she interrupt the woman's grief? Would she prefer to be left alone, or was any human contact better than none?

Finally, she knocked softly. The sounds ceased. There was the sound of a throat clearing and tissues being whipped from a box, then quiet. "Yes?" Dr Carlton's voice was scratchy.

Branigan stuck her head in, and Ina Rose attempted a smile. "Hello, Branigan."

"Are you still having to work?"

"No, just avoiding home. Come on in."

"Christmas week too hard to take?" Branigan asked.

"I'm afraid *any* week would be too hard right now. I just can't, I can't…" She waved her hands helplessly. "Janie Rose's gifts are wrapped and under the tree. I can't be there."

"Anything I can do?"

"No. I planned to write you a note." Ina Rose stood unsteadily and came around her desk to hug Branigan. "Your story on Janie Rose was lovely. Thank you for that. I'm glad you talked me into it."

"I'm glad if it helped."

"It did."

The silence stretched between them. "Do you want to sit down?" Ina Rose sat in one of the chairs in front of her desk and turned it so she was face to face with Branigan.

Branigan wanted to ask about associates of her husband who might have harmed Janie Rose, but in the face of the woman's grief, she couldn't bring herself to do it. Her husband was all she had left. She didn't want to rob her of that.

So she took another tack. "I don't know if you've been reading the news, but another Rutherford Lee student – well, a former student – was killed Friday night."

"Yes, I read about Maylene Ayers. Horrible, when all she wanted was to help those people."

Branigan was startled. "What people?"

"Homeless people."

"I'm afraid I don't know what you're talking about."

For the first time, Branigan sensed a spark of interest from Ina Rose. Maybe talking about something else would help.

"Maylene was in my freshman seminar on writing and social justice. Those are intentionally small classes with a lot of discussion. Maylene talked – a lot – about wanting to work with the homeless."

"Are you saying she was living on the streets as an experiment?" *Holy cow, this was dynamite.*

"Well, I'm not sure it was anything formal. In fact, I know no faculty members were working with her. Her name came up last year in faculty meetings. No one knew where she'd gone."

Branigan held up a hand. "Okay. Let's start at the beginning. You're telling me things I don't know."

Ina Rose stood and went to a filing cabinet, pulled out two slim research papers and handed them to Branigan. "Here's what she wrote that semester."

Branigan glanced at the titles: *Homelessness in Northeast Georgia* and *Unhelpful Remedies: Helping the Homeless Remain Homeless.*

"She was an intelligent young lady," Ina Rose continued. "The kind we see occasionally – privileged but concerned about those without privilege. Isn't this what her family is telling you?"

"I don't know. Another reporter is in Gainesville working on that angle."

"Surely, they will know what she was doing."

"I'm not so sure. The early stories out of Gainesville said they were surprised to learn she was on the streets. They thought she was in Atlanta."

"Oh, my."

Branigan repeated her request that Ina Rose start at the beginning with how she met Maylene.

"It was last school year, the same year Janie Rose started here." Ina Rose pinched her lips tautly for a moment, and swallowed before continuing. "All freshmen choose a seminar in a subject they're interested in. Each has only eight to ten students.

"Basically, it's a class designed for faculty to keep an eye on incoming freshmen, to see how they're orienting to campus, fitting in and so forth. We smaller colleges still sell that as an advantage over a larger university. So in the seminar, we have a lot of discussion. We urge the students to open up."

"And Maylene chose writing and social justice."

"Right. She talked about working in a soup kitchen during high school and how that wasn't the answer to homelessness. For an eighteen-year-old, she seemed to have a rather sophisticated view of the problem."

"So she finished the seminar?"

"Oh, yes. Made an A. Came back after Christmas break. She wasn't in my classes second semester." She paused, gathered her strength. "Then I got all tied up with Janie Rose. It was probably the end of March before I realized Maylene had dropped out. I asked about her in a faculty meeting and no one knew what had happened. Even her faculty adviser didn't know, which is unheard of. I know the administration made calls to her parents, but like I said, I got tied up with our problems and never followed up."

"So when you read she had been living with a homeless man who killed her…?"

"I assumed she'd gone to live out there to learn more. Or to live in solidarity. Or something." Ina Rose held out her palms in a gesture of bewilderment.

Branigan sat back in her chair, dumbfounded. "I had no idea. Even when I talked to her at Jericho Road, I didn't pick up on that. I mean, she was getting *hit* by this guy she was living with. I'm amazed that she'd take any project or philosophy or do-goodness that far."

"Maybe I'm wrong," Ina Rose said. "But given what I knew of her, that's where my mind immediately went."

Branigan shook her head, then rattled Maylene's seminar papers. "Anyway, thanks for these. They'll be a big help. And probably a comfort to her family."

"I hope so. Please tell them how sorry I am. She was going to make a difference."

Branigan walked a few feet down the hall from Dr Carlton's office and found a bench. She sat down and called her colleague Lou Ann, already in Gainesville. She filled her in on Ina Rose Carlton's theory of why Maylene might have been living among the homeless, and read sections of the girl's papers to her.

"And one more thing. Ralph claims Maylene was making phone calls on Friday, and went to the bus station to price a ticket home. Ask her family if she called them about coming home."

"Those two things put a different light on her, don't they?" said Lou Ann. "Man, if she was at the point of trying to 'come in from the cold', it's even sadder."

"Yeah, but it might make the family more likely to talk to you," said Branigan. "Maylene as missionary rather than crackhead."

"Got it. Thanks, Branigan."

Branigan checked her watch and saw that she still had half an hour before she was due at her grandparents' house. She wanted to talk to journalist-in-the-making Anna Hester.

When Branigan pulled her Civic in front of the Kappa Epsilon Chi house, two girls were exiting, rolling huge suitcases. She stopped to ask them when exams ended.

"Most are already done," said a redhead with no make-up. "A few poor suckers have them today. And some of us stayed for one more party night." She grinned and widened her eyes. "Nothing like heading home hungover."

"How about Anna Hester?" Branigan asked.

"Oh, she's still here," said the redhead. "I think she postponed an exam because of that story in *The Swan*."

Branigan thanked the girls and walked through the front door they'd left ajar. Finding no one in the living room, she wandered into the kitchen. Two girls were spreading preserves on wheat toast and eating while standing at the island. A pot of coffee brewed on the counter.

"Can we help you?" asked a blonde whose hair was piled messily on her head. Branigan remembered the glorious relief of finishing that last exam and heading home, no make-up, hair uncombed.

"I'm looking for Anna Hester."

"I saw her upstairs. I'll get her."

A few minutes later, the blonde returned with Anna, wearing black and white plaid pajama pants and a T-shirt with red and green Christmas cats. "Pardon the fashion statement," Anna grinned, pouring herself a cup of coffee and holding out the pot to offer Branigan one. She declined.

"Anna, I read your story in the student newspaper. Very good, by the way. I wanted to ask you about it."

"Sure. Want to sit in the living room?" She padded into the living room in bare feet and tossed some magazines off the couch. She put her feet on a leather ottoman and sipped her coffee.

"We got permission to run the *Rambler* story," she said. "Georgia state patrol wouldn't return our calls."

"But you did talk to Detective Scovoy about the hearse in the woods," Branigan said. "Nice work. What I want to know, though, is how you connected Maylene Ayers to the hearse."

"Maylene was on my hall freshman year. So when Detective Scovoy said there was a Ralph and Maylene in the hearse – it's an unusual name *and* I remembered her interest in the homeless – I put two and two together."

Branigan was pleased with this confirmation of Ina Rose Carlton's information. "But where did you see Maylene to get the quotes?"

"I went under the bridge. Detective Scovoy said she lived there in a tent before finding our hearse. I lucked out. She'd moved back there."

Branigan looked at the young woman with admiration. "You are going to make one heck of a reporter."

Anna looked down and blinked. "Thanks. But by the time the story came out, Maylene was dead."

"Tell me how she seemed to you. Why was she there? Was she planning to leave the camp? Did she say anything like that at all? It's okay if I record this, isn't it?"

Anna nodded. She told Branigan much the same story that Ina Rose Carlton had, about Maylene's passion for social justice and her determination to work in homeless services.

"During our first semester as freshmen," Anna went on, "she spent her Saturdays taking blankets and canned food down to that encampment under the Garner Bridge. Also to the bus station, places like that. Then she stopped. I asked her why one time, and she started talking about 'empowering' rather than 'enabling'. You know – giving someone the tools to help themselves rather than simply handing out stuff. She talked about that *a lot*."

"Makes sense," said Branigan. She'd heard much the same thing from Liam.

"Then the next thing we knew she was gone. Disappeared. We thought she'd moved back home or transferred to another school. I had no idea she had moved to that homeless camp until Detective Scovoy mentioned her name in connection with our hearse. I mean, she'd been gone nearly a year."

"And she didn't mind being quoted in your story?" Branigan asked.

"Oh, she minded."

Branigan looked up from her notebook.

Anna shrugged. "I told her she could talk to me or I'd make up quotes. Isn't that what reporters say when they want someone to cooperate?"

She stared at Anna in horror. "No, that isn't what reporters say at all."

"Well, she didn't want to talk, and I had to get the story."

Branigan hardly knew what to say. She regretted the praise she'd given Anna earlier. "Do you have a journalism class here? Or a course in journalistic ethics?"

"No, just a newspaper workshop."

"Well, just so you know, professional reporters do *not* make up quotes or threaten to do so." She paused for a moment. "So, *did* Maylene say the things in your story?"

"Most of them."

Branigan shook her head. "I'm a little surprised that you were willing to compromise your friendship like that."

"We were hall mates, but it's not like we were sorority sisters."

"So she wasn't a Kappa Ep."

"Nah. A do-gooder like that, she was a Gamma Delt."

Branigan paused in her note-taking. "A Gamma Delta Phi?"

"Yeah."

"The same as Janie Rose Carlton."

Anna nodded.

"In the same pledge class?"

"Um hm." Anna slurped her coffee, then noticed Branigan's face. "What? Is that important?"

"I could have sworn she said she didn't know Janie Rose."

Branigan and Anna sat in silence for a moment. Anna shifted on the couch. "Are you sure?" she asked. "Because they were pretty good friends."

"No, I'm not sure." Branigan closed her eyes and recalled her conversation with Maylene in Jericho Road's computer room. Maylene had asked what crime the hearse had been used for. Branigan had answered that the hearse had run two UGA students off the road. Maylene had asked their names, and Branigan had responded; "Two girls from Grambling. Janie Rose Carlton was killed. Charlie Delaney was driving, and she got banged up pretty bad."

Maylene had looked shocked at the news, Branigan recalled. But then she had asked only about Charlie. So no, she didn't deny knowing Janie Rose, exactly. But she didn't offer that she and the dead girl were friends. Why not?

And right afterwards, she'd gone to Charlie's hospital room.

Branigan opened her eyes. "I was wrong," she said. "She didn't say that. But she sure didn't acknowledge that she knew Janie Rose either."

"That's weird," said Anna.

"Anna, do you know when Maylene left Rutherford Lee?"

"Second semester freshman year."

"Yes, but when during second semester?"

"I have no idea. Before spring break, I think. That's late March. But I'm really not sure."

Branigan got up to leave.

"Miss Powers?"

"Hm?"

"So you think it's wrong to tell a source whatever you have to to get them to talk?"

"I certainly do. There are lines we don't cross."

Anna's eyes were trained on her coffee cup. Her voice got quieter. "When I heard that Maylene was dead, I was scared her boyfriend had gotten mad at something I wrote. But then I realized she was killed on Friday night, before *The Swan* came out. So it wasn't anything I did."

Branigan nodded. "But that's why you always want to be careful," she said. "And accurate. So if something bad does happen, at least you know you were honest with your source and that you told the truth.

"Plus, burning a source is not worth it. He – or she – will never talk to you again. In a town this size, that's a career killer."

As Branigan shoved her notebook into her purse, her eye fell on a cardboard box sitting on the fireplace hearth. A furry red and white Santa hat lay on top. "What's that?"

Anna saw where she was looking. "Leftover hats from our Christmas concert."

Branigan walked over and peered inside. The box was full of Santa hats. "What do you use them for?"

"All the Greeks compete in a Christmas concert in early December. And we all wear hats in our sorority or fraternity colors. Luckily, ours are red and white. These Santa hats are easy to find. The others buy elf hats in navy and green, or green and yellow, whatever. Some can't find their colors and have to make them."

"How many fraternities and sororities are you talking about?"

Anna looked up from her coffee cup. "All of them."

CHAPTER TWENTY-SIX

B ranigan would have liked to walk from campus to her grandparents' house to give her time to think, but she didn't want to leave the Civic in front of the Kappa Epsilon house. Her brain was churning.

Did Charlie really see some sort of hat through the passenger window of the hearse?

Most homeless men wore a baseball cap, stocking cap, do-rag or hoodie – sometimes two at once. So presumably Ralph did too.

And what about Roy? She steered with her left hand while scribbling a note to call Emma Ratcliffe. *Roy – hat??* she wrote, underlining it.

And apparently, the whole frigging student body at Rutherford Lee wore holiday hats. Or at least its Greeks did. And they did have access to that hearse. Of course, it was the hearse's passenger who wore a hat, she conceded, not necessarily the driver. Still, to find one would lead to the other.

Branigan pulled into her grandparents' winding driveway. Their rambling cedar-shingled house blended into the gray-brown vegetation. A metallic red Toyota Prius, parked where the driveway flared in front of the house, provided the only splash of color. Sylvia Eckhart must already be inside.

Branigan approached the front door figuring – correctly – that her grandmother would have Dr Eckhart in the formal living room. She hugged her grandparents, then shook Sylvia Eckhart's hand. The political science professor was an attractive woman in her mid-fifties, with stylish white hair cut into a soft bob. She wasn't in a dress, as Rudelle Powers was, but she'd no doubt changed out of her exam-grading clothes. She wore fitted black trousers and a tunic-length beige sweater, with a black and tan scarf knotted in front.

"Branigan, what a pleasure to finally meet you," she said. "I've been a fan of your writing for years."

"Ah, someone who hasn't given up on newspapers," Branigan said.

"Couldn't do without mine. Computers are for work, not for sitting down with a cup of coffee."

Branigan smiled widely. "I thank you, and the industry thanks you."

She turned to Rudelle. "Where do you want us, Grandmother?"

"Well, Marisol has baked chocolate chip muffins, and we have coffee. Shall we sit in the dining room?"

The four took places around the dining room table, already set with dessert plates and forks. A woman in white trousers, shirt and sneakers pushed through the swinging dining room door with a silver coffee service.

"Marisol!" Branigan squealed, getting up to hug the housekeeper, who was only a decade younger than her grandparents. "How are you?"

"Just fine, Miss Branigan," she said, placing the service on the table and accepting Branigan's embrace. "It's good to see you. I was sorry I missed you last week."

Marisol had worked for the Powerses for more than thirty years, and had done her share of babysitting Branigan, her brother Davison and their cousins.

"Sylvia, as you can tell from Branigan's greeting, this is Marisol Weaver," Rudelle Powers said. "Marisol, this is Dr Eckhart."

Rudelle Powers' formality-that-could-come-across-as-snobbery didn't extend to Marisol, who was more like family than employee.

"Call me Sylvia, please."

Marisol smiled a greeting, poured coffee all round and retreated to the kitchen.

"So, Branigan," said her grandfather, "we'll let you tell us what you need."

She took a deep breath. "As you might imagine, we're exploring the deaths of Janie Rose Carlton and Maylene Ayers. Turns out both were freshmen at Rutherford Lee last year, both were Gamma Delta Phis, in fact, and both left school second semester. Both of them are connected to this hearse owned by the Kappa Epsilon Chis – Janie through the wreck, and Maylene through living in it. None of which makes any sense. I can't connect the dots."

She paused and looked at Sylvia Eckhart. "I guess you and Granddaddy know as much behind-the-scenes stuff about Rutherford Lee's Greek system as anyone. So I wondered if you could tell me about it. Is it piddling? Or does some of it rise to the level of criminal behavior?"

She sat back and sipped coffee from her grandmother's china cup, and let her words sink in.

Sylvia Eckhart was the first to speak. "Ira assures me we are off the record?"

"If we need to be."

"For now, let's do that. If we say something you want to use, you can ask us specifically later."

"All right."

"That's a tough question to answer. In theory, if something is against the law, the Grambling police handle it. The campus is within the city limits. In practice, it can get muddier. Say a girl is raped at a fraternity party but absolutely refuses to report it to the police. She, or more likely the administration, may bring a case to the Honor Council against the fraternity for creating a hostile environment."

Sylvia Eckhart outlined several more scenarios handled by the Honor Council where the school wasn't anxious to bring police in, such as underage drinking, academic cheating rings, hazing.

"The teeth we have with the fraternities and sororities," she said, "is the ability to put them on probation. That cuts their January rush parties from five to one. They kick up a huge fuss over it, claiming it can ruin an entire class. They even have a name when it happens, 'probation class', meaning a class that's not quite up to their standards."

"Ouch," said Branigan.

"Tell me about it," sighed Dr Eckhart.

"What groups at Rutherford Lee give you the most trouble?"

Dr Eckhart and Ira Powers exchanged a glance. "Our problem children," she said, "are the Kappa Eps, the Robies, and the Sigma Etas."

Branigan was startled. "Really? The hearse girls? What can you tell me?"

"Well, full disclosure. I was a Kappa Ep myself. University of Michigan. But every chapter has its own personality. And they tend to keep that personality over time. The Kappa Eps at Rutherford Lee – and the Robies and the Sigma Etas, for that matter – are huge drinkers. They are in constant trouble with over-consumption and underage drinking."

"Tell her about the weekday morning party," said Ira.

"About two years ago, the Kappa Eps and the Robies held a Bloody Mary party at 7 a.m. on a Friday. Most of them had the sense to skip class afterward. But a handful stumbled into their classes absolutely blitzed. The administration locked down both of the houses by noon."

Ira Powers added, "Something like that happened just about every year I headed the council."

"What about the Gamma Delta Phis?" Branigan asked.

"Never a peep out of them," said Dr Eckhart. "Have you been in their house?"

"Yeah, I thought I was in a time warp."

Dr Eckhart laughed. "Exactly. Those girls are a throwback. Big on legacies. Their grandmothers were Gamma Delts. Their aunts and mothers. The first time I went to their faculty and wives' tea I didn't know about the heels and pearls. I was horribly underdressed." She turned to Branigan's grandmother. "You were there, Rudelle. You were the only one from our side dressed appropriately."

"What can I say? Everyone in my day dressed like them."

Branigan's mind was spinning ahead. "I'm interested in the Robies too. Any trouble besides drinking?"

Again, Dr Eckhart and Ira Powers exchanged glances. "Hazing," he said. "Some pretty serious charges. Remember I told you about another fraternity getting shut down entirely when a pledge died from alcohol poisoning? I think the Rho Beta Iota incident came in the next year or so. Sylvia, can you look it up?"

Dr Eckhart pulled a hard-backed notebook from her purse and flipped through several pages. "Let's see… that was seven years ago – Rho Beta Iota was shut down for a year. That wasn't just rush probation. That was no activity at all. Sometimes a chapter will fold after that. But they bounced back."

"What did they do, Granddaddy?"

"They made a drunk pledge walk around the ledge of his dorm roof, three stories off the ground," he said. "When he sobered up the next morning, he realized how close he came to dying. He was angry enough to bring them before the Honor Council before he transferred out."

"That was brave."

"Yes, it rarely happens like that. Usually the administration finds out or a parent complains. Hardly ever a student."

Branigan paused to eat a few bites of her muffin. "Can I tell you something in confidence? I don't have it verified yet, so it's not something I can print."

Her grandparents and Dr Eckhart nodded assent.

"It's about the Robies," she said. "A homeless man I know through Jericho Road said a boy named Jones Rinehart led an attack on a homeless man under Garner Bridge last winter. From what he described, it sounded like a pledge outing."

Dr Eckhart looked shocked. "Jones *was* pledge chairman last year, and he's president this year. But I never heard anything like that. What exactly do you mean by 'led an attack'?"

"Supposedly, they had him on the ground, kicking him."

She drew in a sharp breath. "That would definitely be a police matter. Was it reported?"

"I doubt it. Liam Delaney, the pastor at Jericho Road, says homeless people don't always report crimes. They may have warrants out on them and don't want police nosing around."

"That's awful. Is it too late to talk to the victim and get him to report it?"

Branigan forced herself to meet Dr Eckhart's eyes. "He's dead. Not from that. He was killed last summer."

Rudelle reached over and patted Branigan's arm. Dr Eckhart, presumably having read about the events of last summer, didn't inquire further.

Her grandmother's pats turned into a tap for attention. "I don't want to interrupt, Branigan," she said. "But your mention of the Gamma Delta Phis reminded me of something Arlene Samson said. You remember Arlene next door?"

Branigan nodded.

"Well, she teaches Intro to Economics and a freshman seminar. Your grandfather and I were working in the yard last spring and she mentioned one of her students, a freshman, who had left school. She had been a Gamma Delta Phi in her day, and that's why she mentioned that the girl was too."

"You're right," Ira Powers added. "I'd forgotten that."

"It had to be Janie Rose, because Maylene was in Dr Carlton's seminar," said Branigan.

"That's just it. It wasn't Janie Rose. She said another name."

Now Branigan was interested. "You're saying another freshman pledged Gamma Delta Phi and left school the same spring semester? Do you remember the name?"

"Heavens, no. I just know it wasn't Janie Rose Carlton. Knowing Ina Rose, I would've remembered that."

"How about you, Granddaddy?"

"Heck, no. I wouldn't have remembered the conversation at all if Rudelle hadn't brought it up. As I recall, we were talking about how colleges have abandoned the idea of *in loco parentis* – of serving as surrogate parents or guardians. That's why Arlene mentioned it."

Branigan turned to her grandmother. "Can you get the student's name?"

"I can call Arlene."

"I mean, can you get it right now?"

"Very well. Excuse me, Sylvia."

Branigan opened the door to the kitchen so she could hear her grandmother's side of the conversation. She heard her grandmother's preamble, asking her next-door neighbor about her holiday plans. She raised her eyebrows in exaggeration at her grandfather, who chuckled. "You're surprised?" he said.

Finally Branigan heard her grandmother get to the point of her call. She waited in silence for an extended period, presumably while the professor searched her notes. A few minutes later, Rudelle said her prolonged goodbyes and returned to the dining room with a sheet of paper.

"The girl's name is Mackenzie Broadus. Address at the time of her enrollment was 215 La Montagne Street, Columbia, South Carolina. 'Montagne', spelled like that," she said, pointing to the paper.

Branigan looked at her grandmother with admiration. "Wow. Good work, Grandmother. Is that address as ritzy as it sounds?"

"No idea. And Branigan, Arlene said that when she talked to the dean about Mackenzie's withdrawal, she was told the girl left with no exit interview. That's highly unusual. All the dean knew was that she had transferred to an all-women's college in Columbia. And he got that only after repeatedly calling the girl's parents."

"It could be nothing," said Branigan. "But it *is* a coincidence, isn't it?"

Sylvia Eckhart sipped her coffee. "What are you going to do?"

"Maybe track down this Mackenzie to see what she knows. It's probably a wild goose chase, but I always say that when you start shaking things loose, you find the most interesting things."

Dr Eckhart nodded. "It does seem rather far afield to go all the way to Columbia."

"Yep, and if I achieve nothing, it won't be the first time."

Branigan pulled a business card from her purse to leave with the professor, thanked Dr Eckhart and her grandparents profusely, then left through the kitchen so she could say goodbye to Marisol.

CHAPTER TWENTY-SEVEN

Malachi sat on his favorite bench in front of Grambling's courthouse. He had the whole square to himself today. He was trying out his full-length coveralls from the Army Navy Store, zippered and insulated, the dull green of an army Jeep. He'd saved awhile for these, given up some drinking in October and November to buy them. It was like walking around in a sleeping bag.

It really wasn't cold enough for them yet – high 40s or low 50s now that it was mid-day, he figured. But Malachi wasn't about to leave them in his tent. They'd get stolen, sure as the world. So he unzipped them to his belly button every now and then, until he got chilled in the sweatshirt underneath, then zipped them back up again. He was thinking about going to the library to read, but he'd get hot in there. So he sat on a cold bench of iron and wood.

He'd been there an hour or more, he guessed, when he heard his name called. Tiffany Lynn stood on the sidewalk, waving two lid-covered coffee cups. Like Malachi, she was bundled into a shapeless mass of bulky clothes, layer over layer, topped by a solid green cap with a green and white pompom. *Machine-made*, Malachi had heard Pastor Liam instruct his donors, who wanted to give hand-knitted caps and mittens to the homeless. They didn't realize the wind whipped right through the holes of those hand-knitted things. What you needed was the tight fit of a machine-made cap or gloves, even if they were cheap polyester.

"Look what I got!" Tiffany Lynn called again, waving the cups. "Want one?"

"Sure."

Tiffany Lynn waddled over, her clothes slowing her usual bouncy walk. Stringy blonde hair fell below the cap, past her shoulders. She handed Malachi a coffee and pointed up the street. "Church kids was handing these out," she said. "They had plenty, so I took two. And candy canes." She reached into a pocket and pulled out some small canes and tossed them on Malachi's lap.

"No san'wiches?"

"They had some, but they all gone."

"Have a seat."

Malachi held her coffee long enough for Tiffany Lynn to shed her backpack and settle on the other end of his bench. "That was a good paintin' you did at Jericho," he told her.

She grinned, showing missing front teeth, top and bottom. "Pastor was sure happy 'bout it."

"I like the way you use brighter colors as the story got brighter."

She appeared delighted. "You seen that?"

"Yeah."

"I thought Pastor and Miz Charmay in the art room was the only ones who'd get that part."

"Nah, anybody who know that Good Samaritan story would know. Even if they diden understan' the art part of how you did it, they'd know." He tapped his chest. "In here."

"Good." Tiffany Lynn sat back with a satisfied smile. After a moment, she spoke again. "That sure was bad 'bout Pastor's girl."

"Yeah, Miz Charlie a good one. I watched her grow up."

"People say Ralph tried to run her off the road, tried to kill her, 'cause Pastor was trying to get Maylene away from him."

Malachi was used to the wild rumors that flew around the street, but this was a new one. "People say a lot of things don' make no sense."

"Yeah, but that Ralph had a bad temper. You seen that yourself."

"I seen Maylene's black eyes, if thas wha' you mean."

"No, I mean that time Elise was in jail and Ralph thought Slick was being a little too nice to Maylene. He beat the crap outta him."

Malachi sat up straighter. Tiffany Lynn prattled on. "And that time before Maylene even come to Tent City. That time those boys beat up Max Brody. You 'member that?"

"Yeah."

"'Member Ralph took off after 'em? All by hisself?"

"No," said Malachi. "I don' 'member that."

"Well, he did. Most ever'body else gone back to their tents. But I stayed longer. When those boys ran back in the woods, Ralph took off after 'em. I thought maybe he gon try to catch the slowest one." She laughed.

"Did he?"

"Don' know." She shrugged. "I din see him again 'til the next mornin'. And he had a broke nose."

Malachi sat back. Ralph was violent, sure enough. If Tiffany Lynn was right, he had a run-in with those college boys from Rutherford Lee. And then the hearse was stolen from the college. And then one of the boys was in Charlie's hospital room.

Were he and Miz Branigan looking at this all wrong? They had assumed the driver of the hearse was after Janie Rose Carlton because her daddy had money. But what if he'd been after Charlie all along? After Charlie out of some misguided anger at Pastor Liam?

Malachi stood abruptly.

"Where you goin'?" asked Tiffany Lynn.

"Hospital."

If he walked, it would take an hour to get to St Joe's. So Malachi walked the six blocks to Jericho Road and got Dontegan to unlock the basement where his bike was. He hopped on it and headed to the hospital.

Malachi was glad to have the coveralls to cut the nippy wind as he rode. But by the time he arrived, he was sweating. There was nothing to be done about it but unzip to his belly button.

He walked past the information desk and took the elevator to Charlie's floor. He was relieved to see a cop reading the newspaper outside her door. Just to be sure, he stuck his head in the room.

The cop stood up. "Help you?"

Miz Liz looked up from her own newspaper. "Malachi!" she whispered, smiling and nodding at her sleeping daughter. "How nice of you to come!" She walked to the doorway and gave him a sideways hug.

"It's fine," she told the policeman. "He's a friend."

Malachi knew Miz Liz from a hundred Friday night pizza dinners. But he didn't really have anything to say to her.

"Jus' want to make sure Miz Charlie, she okay," he mumbled. He touched the peak of his ball cap and turned to leave. "You tell her I said 'hey'."

He left Miz Liz staring after him, no telling what she was thinking.

CHAPTER TWENTY-EIGHT

After the cappuccino and muffin, Branigan didn't want lunch, so she was the first of the special team reporters to arrive back at the office. She waved at Bert, then sat at her desk. With a name and address, she quickly came up with a listing for Broadus on La Montagne Street in Columbia. She dialed the number, and a woman answered – young, from the sound of her voice.

"Mackenzie Broadus, please."

"This is she."

"Hello, Mackenzie, this is Branigan Powers from *The Grambling Rambler* in Georgia," she said. "I'd like to –" She heard a click, then a dial tone.

She redialed. This time an answering machine picked up, with a man's voice announcing it was the home of Al and Cynthia Broadus. *Please leave us a message.* Branigan gently replaced the receiver without leaving one. Al and Cynthia were Mackenzie's parents, she assumed. She'd need to think about what she wanted to say.

She leaned back in her chair and studied the ceiling. Then she made a decision.

"Bert," she called. "I'm going to dump what I have from this morning, then head to South Carolina, okay?"

He swiveled in his chair. "What for?"

"You're gonna have to trust me," she said. "It's the Rutherford Lee angle you asked me to follow. It leads there."

"And what is it you're going to dump?"

"Some really good stuff on Maylene for Lou Ann's story. I've already touched base with her, so she knows it's coming. She can weave it in."

He swiveled back to his laptop. "Stay in touch."

* * *

Over the next hour, Branigan drove to the farm, packed an overnight bag, and carried food and water to the barn for Cleo. She punched up a mound of hay for the dog's bed, then took a well-worn tennis ball from a shelf and threw it into the cotton patch. Cleo bounded in to fetch it. They continued this game until the dog was panting. Branigan hugged her and propped the barn door open.

"See you tomorrow, girl," she promised.

The trip was at least four hours, probably more with all the small towns she'd hit. The alternative was to take I-85 north to Greenville, then cut back south and east. She chose the back roads; if they were too awful going down, she'd take the interstate back.

Driving through the rural winter landscape, she felt herself relax. An empty road stretched before her, and she wondered how Charlie and Janie Rose must have felt as a hearse bore down on them in just such a place.

Janie Rose and Maylene. Young women with every advantage, cut down before they had a chance to begin their adult lives. Janie Rose, according to Charlie, frightened, watchful, even before the wreck. Maylene, living in a homeless camp, getting beat on by an ex-con. Branigan didn't care how justice-minded she was, that was off the charts. Plus, she couldn't get that last picture of Maylene out of her head: the beautiful young girl curled into a fetal position in a dark alley, estranged from all those back home who surely loved her.

Was there a link between those girls and Mackenzie Broadus? Or was she on a wild goose chase?

She fumbled to get a disc from the soft-covered CD holder on the passenger seat, and popped in an oldie from the Four Tops. There was no decent radio reception out here in the hinterlands.

It was well after dark when Branigan pulled into Columbia. She used her GPS to guide her to 215 La Montagne Street, and was not surprised to find it in an expensive subdivision. There was a Christmas party in the neighborhood, so cars lined the curbed street. Parking her Civic across from the Broadus house would not raise concern.

She turned off the ignition and studied the two-story house of stucco and stone with wings on both sides. From the looks of it, some kind of plant conservatory was on one side, a three-car garage on the other. It looked like many of its elegant neighbors, landscaped with a mix of currently naked hardwoods, evergreen shrubs and the ubiquitous palmettos of the South Carolina Midlands.

Lights were on inside the house, but Branigan didn't see movement. Maybe the Broaduses were at the party. And now that she was sitting still, she grew sleepy. The effects of that pre-dawn meeting were kicking in.

After twenty minutes, Branigan shook herself and employed the GPS again – this time to locate the nearest Embassy Suites. She figured she had a fifty-fifty chance of getting reimbursed by the newspaper. If not, it would be a Christmas present to herself.

The next morning, Branigan enjoyed a rare hot breakfast of bacon, grits, toast, juice and coffee from the hotel's lavish spread. She then packed and checked out.

She was back in front of the Broadus house by 8 a.m., looking over *The State* newspaper and keeping an eye out for movement. At 8:45, the garage door rumbled up. Branigan strained to see the person backing down the driveway in a large silver van. She almost laughed when the van passed her, the driver more intent on the radio than on her driving. She had long, sleek brown hair and, if Branigan wasn't mistaken, pearls around her throat. Yep, this one was a Gamma Delt all right.

Branigan made a U-turn in the spacious street and followed the van out of the neighborhood and onto a four-lane road. Three days before Christmas, Mackenzie could be shopping, meeting friends, attending an early-morning drop-in or, from the size of her van, picking up a soccer team. With only two flashes of a turn signal as warning, the van turned into a Barnes & Noble Booksellers, and slid into a space at the front door.

Branigan parked across the lot, to the far left of the van, leaving a direct sightline. The van's side door opened, apparently by remote control, and a robotic platform emerged. Branigan blinked in amazement to see it gently set a wheelchair onto the asphalt, and the driver open her door and lower herself expertly into the chair. The girl reached back into the van and got her purse, then clicked a key ring and the doors shut automatically. She wheeled herself onto the sidewalk, and an alert store employee opened the double doors to let her in.

Branigan sat for another minute in her car. Why did her grandmother's neighbor not say that Mackenzie Broadus was in a wheelchair? It seemed like the kind of thing you'd mention.

Branigan slammed her car door and entered the store. Mackenzie had settled at a table in the coffee shop section. Branigan approached her, smiling, and Mackenzie returned the smile. With wide gray eyes and a creamy complexion, she was a beautiful young woman.

"Miss Broadus?"

Mackenzie's smile disappeared; Branigan couldn't tell whether the girl recognized her voice from yesterday's phone call or was startled by the use of her name. "I'm Branigan Powers from *The Grambling Rambler*. I tried to call you yesterday, but we were –"

Mackenzie interrupted her with a sound that was nearly a bleat. "No! I can't talk to you!"

"Please, Miss Broadus. There's nothing wrong. I just need to ask you some questions about a story I'm working on. About some friends of yours."

Mackenzie's head had been shaking the entire time Branigan was talking. But now it stopped. "What friends?"

"Janie Rose Carlton and Maylene Ayers. I'm sure you've heard."

"Heard what?"

"They were killed last week."

"*What?*" Mackenzie began to tremble. "No, no, no. That can't be."

Branigan slid into the chair across from the girl. She spoke quietly. "I'll begin at the beginning," she said. "But can I get you anything first? Water?"

Mackenzie nodded. "Yes, water," she whispered.

Branigan was grateful to have something to do while the girl collected herself. It hadn't occurred to her that Mackenzie wouldn't know the news out of Grambling. But Columbia *was* more than 200 miles away. Maybe its own universities provided enough drama that the newspaper didn't need to run stories about college students in Georgia.

She requested a cup of water from the man behind the counter. Taking her place across from Mackenzie, she placed it on the table, because the girl was still quivering.

"What about their families?" she asked.

Branigan wasn't sure what she meant. "They're devastated, of course."

"I still can't talk to you." Now Mackenzie's lips were trembling. Branigan feared she was going to cry. "But... but... can you tell me what happened?"

"Of course. Janie Rose was on her way home from the University of Georgia for Christmas break. Someone ran her and a friend off the road, and Janie Rose was killed."

Mackenzie's pupils were impossibly large, but she said nothing.

"And then Maylene Ayers was beaten to death beside the Grambling bus station. With a crowbar. A homeless man was arrested."

The girl still didn't speak, but she began breathing rapidly. Branigan was worried that she was going to hyperventilate. "Can you drink some water, Miss Broadus?"

Mackenzie obediently picked up the water. Her hand shook as she brought it to her mouth, spilling some. Branigan handed her a napkin.

"Why are you here?"

"Well, in investigating the girls' deaths – which is a huge story in Grambling – we realized both had been freshmen at Rutherford Lee, both were in the same sorority and both left school about the same time last winter. As you did. We're just trying to follow some of the oddities, I guess you could say, during the last months of their lives. See if there was any connection, overlap. I was hoping you could help."

Mackenzie was beginning to breathe a little more easily.

"You say there's been an arrest?"

"Yes. Maylene was living with a man in a homeless camp. The evidence indicates that he killed her."

"And Janie Rose?"

"No arrest yet, though it could have been the same guy."

Mackenzie sat for a long moment. "I don't like to talk about it," she said. "What happened to me."

Branigan was silent. She could hear a "but" in the girl's voice and didn't want to spook her.

"Obviously, it changed my life. For the worse." She hit the arms of her chair.

"What did?"

"You didn't talk to Janie Rose or Maylene? You don't know why I left school?"

"No, sadly none of us talked to them." Branigan didn't know how to put this delicately. "They weren't a story until they were killed."

"Well, the three of us were friends. We lived on the same hall freshman year. We went through rush together, and we all wanted to pledge Gamma Delta Phi. And we all got in. We were so looking forward to our next few years there. Then we did something stupid. Or I should say I did something stupid."

Again Branigan allowed space for the girl to talk.

"I sneaked two bottles of my parents' wine back to school after last Christmas. One night in February, Janie Rose and Maylene and I had been studying and decided to take a break. I pulled out those bottles and we pretty much finished them. Then we decided to take a walk around campus." Mackenzie's voice took on a wooden quality. Branigan recognized that she was trying to distance herself from something painful. "We ended up on the football field. I had been a gymnast in high school, and they knew it. I guess I talked about it a lot. So I wanted to show off. I took off my shoes and socks, and climbed up the goalpost. That crossbar is six inches wide, two inches wider than the balance beam I was used to. The difference,

I guess, is I'd never walked the beam drunk." Mackenzie's face reddened. "I did a few scissor leaps. Then I tried a cartwheel. I fell off the goalpost, flat on my back. Which I broke."

Branigan was bursting with questions, but she didn't want to push Mackenzie too hard. "That would've been a big story," Branigan said softly. "But we never heard it from the police. And I don't think the school knows about it."

"I know."

"So how did that happen?"

"I was hysterical. Scared and crying and probably in shock. I insisted that Janie Rose and Maylene drive me to the hospital."

Branigan gasped inadvertently. "With a back injury?"

Mackenzie's face grew redder still. "I know. I know. Stupid decision on top of stupid decision. But they carried me to the hospital, which helicoptered me to our bigger hospital in Columbia. I was there through April."

"Why didn't you let the school know?"

"They kept calling," she conceded. "But I begged my parents not to say anything. I was humiliated. I just wanted to forget I'd ever heard of Grambling, Georgia."

Now that the story was out, Mackenzie's face began to clear a little. "Don't you see?" she said. "It was all my fault." For the first time, her eyes locked with Branigan's. "Are you going to use all this? It's okay with me now. After all this time."

"I imagine so," Branigan said. "I appreciate how hard it's been for you to talk about this."

She thought for a moment – of Ina Rose Carlton's suspicion that Janie Rose had been raped; of Maylene's move into the path of Ralph's fists. Something didn't make sense.

"I understand why you left school," she said. "But that doesn't explain why Janie Rose and Maylene left. Were they *that* distraught over your accident?"

"Yeah, I guess," she said. "Survivor's guilt and all that. We never talked about it."

Branigan didn't know how to pose this next question. "Did

they think maybe you might not be paralyzed if they'd called an ambulance instead of moving you?"

Mackenzie kept her eyes on her lap. A tear plopped onto her folded hands. "Yeah, maybe. But I made them do it."

"I'm not sure an accident victim is the best one to decide," Branigan said mildly.

Again, Mackenzie's face and throat flushed. "I guess I was pretty persuasive."

"Hmm. Well, Mackenzie, I appreciate your talking to me. Can I get you anything else before I go?"

Mackenzie smiled weakly and shook her head. Branigan felt the young woman's eyes follow her out.

She sat in the Civic and drummed her fingers on the steering wheel. Mackenzie Broadus had had no intention of talking to her. Branigan had met resistance often enough to know it when she saw it. The girl had opened up only upon learning that Janie Rose and Maylene were dead.

Did learning about their deaths mitigate her fear and allow her to talk? Or did their deaths scare her further?

For there was one thing Branigan was sure of: Mackenzie Broadus was terrified.

Branigan pondered her next move. She guessed she'd learned everything she could in Columbia. She watched idly as a gleaming white Porsche Boxster pulled into one of the empty spaces still available in front of the store. A good-looking young man emerged, dipping his head to get out of the car's confined space. He glanced around, and Branigan stared: he was a male version of Mackenzie Broadus, all dark hair and square jaw and preppy clothes. As he walked into the store, she pulled her Civic into a handicapped space beside Mackenzie's van so she could see through the store's plate glass window.

Sure enough, the young man was bent over Mackenzie, giving her a quick hug around the shoulders, then rubbing a fist over her head. Branigan smiled to herself. If she wasn't sure he was her brother before, that noogie confirmed it.

But now Mackenzie was crying, and the young man looked bewildered. He leaned across the table for a moment, still standing, his weight on his hands, listening intently. Suddenly he spun and looked directly through the window, his eyes raking the parking lot. He charged for the door. Branigan swallowed, and got out of her car.

"I think you're looking for me," she called as he flung the store door wide and barreled onto the sidewalk. She held her hand out. "Branigan Powers."

His face was flushed and he ignored her hand. His anger seemed to be battling his Carolina upbringing. "You're a reporter?" he said. "From Grambling?"

"Yes."

"What do you want with my sister?"

"Did she tell you that two of her friends from Rutherford Lee have been murdered?"

He visibly sagged, and the bewildered look Branigan had seen through the window returned.

"She did. These are the girls who took her to the hospital? I'm more confused than ever."

Branigan relaxed slightly. "As are we. Obviously, the murder of two co-eds is a big story in Grambling. I was following up on the coincidence that they – and your sister – all left Rutherford Lee during their freshman year. Your sister filled in *a* missing piece. But I gotta tell you, I too may be more confused than before."

The young man stared at Branigan for another moment, then stuck out his hand. "I'm Tony Broadus. Can you tell me what happened to her friends?"

"Janie Rose Carlton was run off the road on her way home from her new college for Christmas break. Maylene Ayers was beaten to death with a crowbar outside the Grambling bus station. Her boyfriend was arrested."

He frowned. "That sounds pretty random."

Branigan looked at him closely. "How much did you know about Mackenzie's accident?"

"Just that those three had been drinking and she climbed on a goalpost in the football stadium to do balance beam routines. She fell off and broke her back." He shrugged. "It kills me – and our mom and dad – to see her in that chair."

"What did you think about what happened after the accident?"

"What do you mean?"

"Well, it sounds like Mackenzie insisted the girls drive her to the hospital rather than call paramedics trained in spinal injuries."

"Yeah, a supremely dumb move. Though we try not to say that to her face."

Branigan considered how to phrase her next question. "But you don't – didn't – blame her friends?"

Tony Broadus shrugged again. "What good would that do?" He paused. "I mean, I admit I wasn't happy about it. But they were eighteen-year-old girls. I did some pretty dumb things when I was eighteen. What are you gonna do?"

He turned his gaze toward the bookstore window. Mackenzie had stopped crying and wasn't even looking at her brother and Branigan on the sidewalk. Instead, she was staring straight ahead.

Branigan was silent for a few moments, watching Tony as he watched his sister through the glass. She couldn't quite make out the look on his face. "What are you gonna do?" he repeated softly.

CHAPTER TWENTY-NINE

Charlie and Chan called this day Christmas Eve Eve. Only this year it was something even more special. It was Going Home Eve.

Charlie had had a lot of visitors as old high school friends came home for the holidays and heard about her wreck. Even her former soccer coach came, along with three high school seniors who'd played on teams with Charlie.

Now it was nearing dusk, and Maggie Fielding and Jones Rinehart were back. Maggie had brought Christmas cookies her mom had made. When she handed over the tin container, she tapped it deliberately with her left hand. "Oh, what was that noise?" she said.

Charlie shrieked. "Oh my gosh! Got your rock, did you? Congratulations. You too, Jones."

She pushed herself a little higher in the bed. She was happy for her friend. But there was something about the fiancé she wasn't sure about. He was handsome all right. And friendly. But maybe just a bit too… what? Smooth, maybe?

"Is Jones spending Christmas with your family?"

He answered. "Nah, I'm heading to Alexandria tomorrow. But I've been at the Fieldings' a few days."

Maggie looked at him adoringly. *Maybe that's it*, Charlie thought. *Maggie acts different around him. Less assertive. More simpering. Ah well, none of my business.*

Maggie chatted easily for half an hour, asking Chan and Charlie about their freshman semesters. As she and Jones prepared to leave, they invited Chan to join them for the free hot chocolate in the lobby.

"No, I'd better stay with Charlie," he said.

"Go on," she told him. "I'm fine by myself."

"Are you sure?"

"Absolutely. I'm going to take a nap. And there *is* a cop at the door."

"Well, okay. I'll go down for a few minutes."

With the room finally quiet, Charlie groped for the remote console and turned off the lights, then snuggled as far into the blankets as she could get. Her side was still sore, but there were positions she could manage that were relatively pain-free.

She drowsed, thinking, or maybe dreaming, about sleeping in her own bed tomorrow night. She could feel the other dream starting, the movement of the Jeep beneath her, when the scrape of a chair beside the hospital bed woke her. Her eyes flew open. Jones Rinehart stood over her.

"I forgot my phone," he said, holding it up. But he remained standing by her bed.

Charlie cleared her throat, hoping it wouldn't squeak. "Where are Chan and Maggie?"

"Drinking hot chocolate. It's a mob down there. Oh, and your policeman got called away. Some traffic pile-up at the mall."

Charlie's heart started pounding.

"Your pillow looks like it could use a little help," he said, reaching for it.

"No, no, it's fine," she said, but he ignored her, grasping the pillow on either side of her head.

"It looks bunched up. You'll sleep better if it's smooth."

Charlie's uninjured hand frantically sought the console under the blankets. Unseeing, she punched every button. A buzzer sounded.

Jones jumped back. "What was that?"

"You must've hit the Call Nurse button with your elbow. She'll be right in."

His eyes flicked to the bedside rail. "Well, sorry about that. I'd better be going." He smiled. "You guys have a merry Christmas." He slipped quickly into the hallway.

Charlie's heart continued to pound. A nurse poked her head round the door. "You called, Charlotte?"

"Yes," she said weakly. "Can you stay with me just a minute until my brother gets back?"

PART TWO

CHAPTER ONE

Marjorie raised her beer bottle for a toast: "To Christmas and New Year's and MLK Day being over for one more damn year!"

"Here! Here!" the reporters shouted and clinked bottles.

It was close to midnight on a Friday, the first week of February, and the crew from *The Rambler* were at Zorina's. No reporter liked holidays, or the obligatory stories that came with them. This year Branigan was more relieved than usual to be past them. The Christmas egg story and the New Year's champagne story and the Martin Luther King Day panel discussions were the least of it. Christmas with her family had been cheerless. Oh, they'd tried. She and Mom and Dad had gone to family dinners with both the Powers and Rickman sides. The most normal was Aunt Jeanie and Uncle Bobby's annual brunch – complete with sausage rolls from their own hog slaughter, Aunt Jeanie's cream cheese braid, and three of their five children, Branigan's favorite cousins, home for a few days. The Delaneys had come to that, Charlie in a wheelchair with her leg straight out in front, her arm in a sling, her teeth not yet ready for dental work.

Branigan's mom had overdone it on the gifts, especially for her grandson Chan and his sister Charlie, trying to make up for the fact that Davison, Branigan's twin, was gone and wouldn't be coming back. Branigan was grateful when December 26 arrived, and she and Cleo could huddle by the fire without seeing anyone.

The Christmas week stories on the murders of Janie Rose Carlton and Maylene Ayers got a lot of attention. Tan-4 planned to enter them in the Georgia Press Association contests, maybe even some national competitions. Unlike police officers, who wanted only to solve a case, journalists could produce compelling crime stories, whether they were solved or not. In fact, Branigan thought secretly, sometimes the unsolved mystery made a better story.

That would certainly seem to have been the case as Marjorie, Jody, Branigan and Lou Ann spun their narratives about the girls. Reporters had circled back to the Carlton and Ayers families with the explanation Mackenzie Broadus gave about why their daughters left Rutherford Lee. The parents were stunned to hear it, but it was hardly a blip in the horror they were living. And the fact that Maylene's family confirmed she was headed home for Christmas made their grief all the more piercing.

Harley had assembled a portrait of Ralph as a longtime low-life, locating a former wife who talked freely about his abuse and a former co-worker who talked about his temper.

The Grambling police located Roy Browoski of Philadelphia and sent Detective Scovoy to question him. It didn't make the story, but the detective shared with Branigan that Roy was never without his blue Phillies baseball cap with a red peak. There wasn't enough to make an arrest, but Browoski remained a person of interest in the case.

Business writer Art Whittaker uncovered some interesting buzz from his counterparts in Pennsylvania. Nothing that made the *Rambler* stories, mostly gossip, but detectives were interested to learn that Harry Carlton had borrowed money from some questionable sources. Scovoy met with colleagues from the Philadelphia Police Department who were acquainted with these sources, who, in turn, sometimes used the services of one Roy Browoski. But killing a college student over her father's debts? The scenario had the Northern police officers shaking their heads in doubt.

Chan had returned to Furman, but Charlie chose to stay at home for spring semester while undergoing extensive dental surgery. She'd arranged to take two online classes, which was all she could handle. Her plan was to take two more classes at Grambling Tech over the summer and return to the University of Georgia in the fall, ready for her sophomore year.

Suddenly, a cry went up from the reporters' two tables pulled together in a corner of the dark bar. "*Bert!*" It was the customary greeting for those working the desk on a weekend night.

Bert gave a wave and stopped at the bar to order a beer. He slid into a chair that Jody and Branigan pulled from a neighboring table.

"The Rutherford Lee Greeks are at it again," he said.

Branigan and Jody leaned in to hear him over the din.

"A girl came into St Joe's to have her stomach pumped. Pledge party."

"Which sorority?" Branigan asked.

"Kappa Epsilon Chi."

"That may be it for them," she said, remembering Sylvia Eckhart's stories of their accumulating offenses.

"Where's the girl from?" Jody asked.

"Atlanta. The parents weren't there yet when Harley left the hospital. But the college dean was. I think he was shaken by our Christmas stories and wanted to get out in front of this one."

Another roar went up from the adjoining tables. "*Harley!*"

Harley grinned, and Bert waved a waitress over. "I'm buying for him. He's had a rough night."

Jody got another chair and Harley plopped tiredly onto it, accepting a beer from the waitress.

"Tell," Branigan commanded.

"The Kappa Eps had a pledge party at that new Marlin Hotel on I-85. Guess the hotel wasn't aware of these girls' reputation. They were playing drinking games, and this chick couldn't hold it. She passed out right there in the ballroom. Fortunately, two girls took her to the ER. Doctor said she could've died if they hadn't."

"Boy, they don't learn, do they?" Bert said.

Branigan sat back. "What did the dean say?"

"He didn't say he was closing them down, and I asked that specifically," Harley said. "But he said he personally would bring them up on charges before the Honor Council, because this girl was only eighteen."

Jody turned to Bert. "Playing it on 1A?" he asked.

Bert nodded. "Bottom. Wouldn't have normally, but after the interest in those murders, yeah."

Branigan sipped from her glass of white zinfandel, the only wine Zorina's carried. The story about Janie Rose and Maylene was over as far as *The Rambler* was concerned. Well, at least until the police solved it. Then it'd flare up again. But it was hard for Branigan to let go, especially since she'd never been completely satisfied that the intended victim of the wreck was Janie Rose and not Charlie. Hard to let go after seeing Maylene's body in the alley, blood seeping into her tangle of hair. A reporter was rarely on the scene in time to see things like that.

So the story had lain under the surface this winter, surging, shifting, never entirely leaving her mind.

CHAPTER TWO

B ranigan slept late on Saturday, and Cleo remained lazily on her own pillow beside the bed until she got up. Branigan pulled on warm socks and padded into the kitchen to make coffee. When she stepped out to get the morning *Rambler* from the driveway, she was delighted to find it was sunny and 64 degrees. Patting Cleo, she said, "This, my friend, is why we live in Georgia." She stood for a moment with her face raised to the sun, enjoying its spring-like feel. Georgia had plenty of cold weather, that was for sure. But every February you got a sprinkling of days that portended spring.

Branigan fed Cleo, then sat at her kitchen island with a bowl of Raisin Nut Bran, and coffee in a handmade pottery mug Chan had given her for Christmas. She read Harley's story twice, pondering the fate of these sorority women who'd provided alcohol to an underage girl and wondering if they'd told her everything they knew about their hearse. The vehicle was still in the police compound as far as she knew.

After a third cup of coffee, Branigan went into the guest bedroom, the one she'd slept in as a child visiting Gran and Pa, and rummaged through drawers containing her summer clothes. She pulled out striped running shorts and a worn sleeveless T-shirt. Calling to Cleo, she trotted across the driveway and through the cotton patch, past the barn and empty chicken houses to the pasture, luxuriating in the warm day she hadn't anticipated.

They ran past the lake into a second pasture, where Uncle Bobby's cows raised their heads to look at them. But the cows were so accustomed to Cleo that they resumed their grazing, knowing the pair posed no danger. Branigan's feet pounded across a dike between two additional lakes and into an open field. Here the grass was a little high for running, so she turned back to the second pasture and circled twice, the cows scarcely noticing. After thirty minutes, she began a cool-down walk that took her back to the pasture closest to the house.

Halfway through the cotton patch, she was startled to see a white SUV parked in her driveway, but almost instantly recognized the muscular figure leaning against it. She'd been out with Chester Scovoy twice more since the night Maylene died – not nearly as often as they would've liked. He raised an arm, and Cleo bounded over to leap on him. That was another plus as far as Branigan was concerned. Cleo had bonded instantly with the detective when they met downtown one Saturday.

"Whatcha doing way out here?" she asked when she reached the driveway, her breathing returned to normal.

"Such a pretty day, it made me think of you."

"Ah, smooth talker. Can I get you some coffee?"

"I'd love some. What've you got planned today?"

"I told Liam and Liz I'd stay with Charlie for awhile this afternoon. Liz is with her mom, and Liam needed to go to the jail."

"Want some company?"

"Sure. Charlie would love to see you. Let me get you some coffee, and I'll get a shower."

Chester followed her into the house. "Nice place, Branigan."

"Feel free to look around. There's also cereal and Pop-Tarts if you haven't eaten. I spare no expense in the realm of breakfast."

She quickly showered, and dressed in jeans and a lightweight sweater. She pulled her hair into a ponytail and applied sunscreen, face powder, mascara and lipstick, not bothering with foundation. She located her summer flip-flops in the back of her closet, and came into the kitchen to find Chester perched at the island with coffee and the newspaper.

"You look right at home," she said.

"You've got so much room to spread out. You make me think I'm right in wanting to buy a house."

"Really?"

"Absolutely. I've been living in an apartment for ten years. Not much bigger than your kitchen, and nothing to show for ten years' rent."

"It makes sense if you're staying in Grambling. But why now?"

"I've known for years I wanted to stay. I just never took the time to get a real estate agent, look around, get approved by the bank, all that stuff."

"I'd be glad to help you look."

"Oh, right. You have so much spare time. Like me."

She smiled. "Good point. But sometimes you have to carve out time for yourself."

He looked around again. "Mind giving me a tour? I need to start getting ideas."

"Sure," she said, pouring herself another cup of coffee. "As I've told you, Pa Rickman – that was my grandfather – built this house after he and Gran worked in the mills. At the time, it was the most modern thing any of Gran's sisters had seen. Their old home place literally had an outhouse. So Gran and Pa were quite *la-de-da* there for awhile."

"You're talking to a man from South Carolina. I get it."

Branigan pointed to the adjoining den. "Pa added the den later. That whole room was originally the garage. He brought it up level to the kitchen, and made it living space. That's why its windows are so much larger than the ones in the rest of the house. It was a chance to bring in more light. And the tile floor is great for Cleo's shedding."

She nodded her head toward the kitchen cabinets. "When I moved back, Mom and I renovated the kitchen, adding the island, granite countertops and new cabinets. Luckily, we were able to keep the tile floor."

Chester walked into the den and stood in front of a painting of a lake at night, woods crowding in, the lake surface lit by a single moonbeam. "This looks like the Vesuvius Hightower piece that Malachi was so taken with." Vesuvius was a homeless artist, killed last summer in a hit-and-run.

"It's very similar," she agreed. "But I bought this one from

Jericho Road before his paintings started to be worth so much. You know, an Atlanta gallery is carrying his remaining inventory. I couldn't afford one now."

Chester looked at the rest of the artwork that hung above the green and rose florals and stripes of Branigan's furniture. "A lot of these look familiar," he said. "Maybe from those street fairs in the spring?"

"Yep. I like to collect local art. There's more in my office."

She led the way, Cleo following, into the formal dining room and living room that ran across the front of the house. Her grandparents' furniture was still in place on beige carpet – a dining room table for eight, a handsome china cabinet filled with gold-rimmed dishes, an adjoining living room with a couch and two armchairs in white brocade. There was very little of the vibrant color found in the den and kitchen.

"This part looks like a different house," Chester said.

"Yeah, I hardly ever come in here. The family just left Gran and Pa's furniture." She pointed at the bay window that looked out over the front yard and empty country road. "At Christmas, Pa used to put painted wooden cutouts of carolers in the yard, with a spotlight. And Santa and his sleigh on the roof. And they always put the tree in front of that window. I spent weeks of my childhood lying under a Christmas tree. Always a real one, always smelling wonderful." She forced a smile. "That's the hard part of living here," she said. "Remembering those Christmases, and having so many of the people gone."

Chester put his arm around her shoulders and squeezed, saying nothing.

Branigan led him from the living room into a small hallway, pointing out the guest bedroom that faced the roadway, and her bedroom that looked out over the cotton patch.

"One bath?" he asked.

"Two. There's one off my bedroom, and another larger one down the hall. Look around all you want."

Chester stuck his head into the guest bedroom, then wandered into Branigan's, where a queen-sized bed took up most of the floor space. Cleo went to her pillow and flopped onto it with a sigh. Branigan showed Chester the small bathroom with its dated miniature tiles of black and white, and cramped shower stall.

"This will be my next remodeling project," she said, "if I decide to buy from Mom and Uncle Bobby. Maybe bump out the entire bedroom and bathroom for more space. Mom and I went ahead and did the kitchen because it would increase the value no matter what. But I'm still renting, so..." She trailed off. "Come see the bigger bathroom."

They walked down the hall. "Oh, wow," Chester laughed. The fixtures were turquoise, and the wall and floor tiles bright pink. "Someone was making a color statement here."

"This will be renovation No. 3," Branigan said. "Nothing big. Just getting the color off the Pepto-Bismol spectrum."

The hallway led into the house's original den, which now served as Branigan's office. Her desk faced sliding glass doors that opened onto a porch. They could see all the way past the cotton patch and down to the pastures and lake, the sun glinting off its blue waters.

"So you can work with that view?"

She laughed. "Some days."

Chester looked around. The walls were paneled in stained pine, and Branigan had filled them with colorful canvases, mostly watercolors, but with a hand-colored photograph as well. Chester's eye went immediately to the photograph, which showed a weathered two-story house being reclaimed by wildly growing vines and encroaching undergrowth. The photo was black and white except for the peach color of the old house's chimney and hurricane shutters. The picture frame was made of distressed wood that looked as if it could have been taken off the house itself.

"What's this?" he asked.

"That's by Jamie Wardlaw. She's a photographer in town. I bought it because it reminds me of a shack down in my pasture." She pointed toward the lake. "You can't quite see it from here because of the trees, but it's a place where Pa and his buddies played poker.

Gran wouldn't allow cards in the house, so they played down there. It's being taken over by vines. Not kudzu, thank goodness. But stuff just about as aggressive. It's beautiful in a wild kind of way."

"That picture is haunting," Chester said.

"I know." She led him out of the opposite side of the office, and they found themselves back in the kitchen.

"This is a really nice sized house," Chester said enthusiastically. "Plenty big enough, but not crazy big like some of those new subdivisions. I like it, Branigan."

"Me too. Obviously." She poured the rest of her coffee into the sink. "Ready to head to Liam's?"

"Let's do it. I'll follow you."

Branigan let Cleo out, locked the door and led the way to the Delaneys' house.

It was hard to tell who was more surprised – Liam, to see Branigan arrive with Detective Scovoy in her wake, or Branigan, to find Malachi Martin standing in Liam's yard.

"So Charlie's getting a babysitter from the Grambling PD?" Liam smiled knowingly at Branigan. "You haven't heard something, have you, Detective?"

"No, no, nothing like that," Chester assured him. "I'm off today. I just happened to go by Branigan's farm this morning, and she was headed here. So I'm tagging along."

Liam raised an eyebrow at Branigan, who blushed and turned to Malachi. "And Mr Malachi? Are you going to the jail with Liam?"

"Yes'm. Ralph call Pastor Liam and ax him to bring me. Don' know what it's about."

The pairs split – Branigan and Chester walking into the Delaneys' house to stay with Charlie, Liam and Malachi heading for the Law Enforcement Center.

CHAPTER THREE

I f you didn't already know you were in the Deep South, thought Malachi, the Grambling jail would sure tell you. Visitors talked to inmates by phone (in the jail's old section) or by hollering through a metal screen (in the new section). And "new" meant the part built thirty years ago.

At least coming in with Pastor Liam, Malachi got seated across a table from Ralph Batson in a private room. No phones. No barriers. No guard even.

"Buzz us when you want out," said the guard who'd hustled Ralph in.

Apparently, the po-lice had decided that preachers – especially Pastor Liam and the town's black preachers and those with old mill village churches – could be a help in keeping crime down. So they made sure the prisoners saw their preachers as quickly as their lawyers.

Pastor Liam had been in here plenty, Malachi could tell. While Malachi didn't like those clanging metal doors one little bit – he'd been on the wrong side more times than he could count – Pastor was leaning back in his chair as though he was in his church office.

"You wanted to see us, Ralph?"

Ralph was a lot whiter than when Malachi saw him last. His tattoos stood out more, and he didn't look as broad or as solid. With the alcohol and drugs out of his system, he was quieter too. Not the know-it-all Malachi had known in Tent City.

"Yeah," he answered. "It's 'bout my cell phone."

"The police have it?" asked Pastor Liam.

"No, it warn't in my pants when I got arrested." He looked at Malachi. "Anybody in my tent?"

Malachi nodded. "Somebody done stole Slick and Elise's tent while they in jail. They moved into yours when they got out."

"Who done stole a whole tent?"

Malachi shrugged. He had an idea, but he didn't want Ralph going after him.

"Malachi, I need you to find my phone."

"Where you put it?"

"I buried it in one of them lunchboxes, then pitch the tent on top of it."

"Why you do that?"

"There's somethin' on it that might show the po-lice I ain't kilt Maylene."

Pastor Liam and Malachi looked at each other, and Liam spoke up. "Like a voicemail?"

"A video," Ralph said.

"What kinda video?" asked Malachi. "Them gov'ment phones don't got video."

"I bought me a phone. Worked a lot of day labor last year."

Malachi and Liam waited for him to continue.

Ralph breathed noisily through his nose. "You 'member last winter when them college boys come under the bridge and beat up Max?"

Malachi nodded. "Well, I caught 'em on my phone. I followed the boys and saw what frat house they went to. The Robies, they call theirselves. I tried to talk to one of 'em, but he was roarin' drunk. Threw a wild punch and busted my nose.

"I went back to my tent and thought 'bout it and thought 'bout it. Ol' Max was so drunk he didn' wanna report it and couldna told the po-lice nothin' noway. But I had their faces on my phone.

"A few days later, I went back to the frat house and found the guy who was the ringleader. He was sobered up, and when I played the tape for him, he 'bout peed his pants. He said he'd pay me not to report it to the po-lice. So I let 'im."

"What was his name?" asked Liam.

"Jones Rinehart."

Malachi saw Pastor's mouth stretch into a thin line. "How much he pay you?" Malachi asked.

Ralph's face reddened. "A hunnerd at first. Then I realized that warn't nothin' for this rich boy. So 'nother two hunnerd. That's when I got the idea."

Malachi and Liam looked up.

"If this frat boy was willing to pay three hunnerd – and who knew how high he'd go? – what 'bout the other frats? And whatta 'bout the girls? The sor-rah-ri-ties. I mean that fancy-ass school costs fifty grand a year." Ralph looked down at the table. "So I started hangin' 'round."

Malachi glanced at Pastor Liam to see how he was taking this news. He looked disgusted. "And?" he said.

"I got a lot of kids throwin' up," Ralph said, "and makin' out. Didn' think nobody gonna pay for that. But then I shot a video at one of them girls' parties durin' rush or pledge or whatever they call it. That's the one I think the po-lice might be inter'sted in."

"Why?" Liam asked.

Ralph leaned back with a look more haunted than satisfied. Malachi could barely hear his next words.

"'Cause it's got them dead girls in it."

Chapter Four

Branigan, Malachi and Detective Scovoy stood outside Slick and Elise's tent under the Michael Garner Memorial Bridge. It was cooler now that they were out of the sun, and Branigan pulled her thin sweater around her.

Detective Scovoy grabbed the tent flap and shook it. "Grambling Police," he called.

Elise's head, her patchy brown hair covered with a red scarf, popped out. "Whatchu want?" she said irritably.

"We have a tip that something's buried under this tent, ma'am." He showed his badge. "We need to move your tent just a few feet."

When Elise continued to stare at him, he added, "We'll be glad to help you set it back up, ma'am."

She ignored him. "Whatchu doin' wit' the po-lice, Mal'chi?"

Malachi shrugged. Branigan knew they were placing him in a difficult position with his Tent City neighbors, but he answered anyway. "When Ralph be livin' in this tent, he bury somethin' under it we gotta see. Where Slick?" Not for the first time, Branigan marveled at how Malachi's speech pattern changed to match whomever he was speaking to.

Elise flounced back into her tent, shouting over her shoulder, "He diden come home las' night. Good riddance."

The three of them quickly emptied Elise's tent, carefully clearing a space on a nearby picnic table for her sleeping bag, blankets and belongings. By the time they had finished, the only other Tent City occupants around at mid-day on a Saturday appeared from a shack atop the concrete incline. The two men crab-walked down the slope, then stood silently beside a cold fire pit to watch.

"We may not even have to move the tent," said Detective Scovoy. "If we can lift the stakes on one side and hold up the floor, one of us can dig."

Branigan and Malachi held up the canvas floor while Scovoy worked with the shovel they'd brought from Liam's house. It wasn't hard to see where the red dirt had been disturbed.

After just a few inches, the shovel struck metal, and Scovoy shimmied the tool around until he pulled out a *Star Wars* lunchbox. He brushed the dirt off the latch and popped it open. Inside was an empty plastic lunch bag.

"Damn it!" the detective exclaimed.

He turned to Malachi. "You're our best hope," he said. "Who could've gotten to it?"

Malachi shook his head, which Branigan took to mean he'd prefer to move the conversation elsewhere. So the trio quickly re-staked Elise's tent. "Do you want us to move your things back in?" Branigan asked.

"Yeah, but jus' mine," Elise said. "We gonna leave Slick's out here where he gon' be stayin'." Elise found a box of cereal bars a church group had left on the picnic table, and unwrapped one. As the three left Tent City, she sat at the table's attached bench, eating and balefully watching them go.

"Ralph ain't coming back, iz he?" she called to Detective Scovoy.

"No way of knowing yet," he answered as they rounded the river birch at the encampment's opening. "Thank you for your cooperation, ma'am."

Branigan, Malachi and Detective Scovoy walked to Branigan's Civic, parked at Ricky's Quick Mart.

"Okay if we go back to Liam's," she asked as they piled in, "since he was the one who got Ralph talking?"

They were silent as she pulled into the Delaneys' driveway, and knocked on the side door to the kitchen. Liam met them and led them to the living room, where Charlie sat on a sofa upholstered in yellow and white striped chintz, a bowl of tomato soup on a tray in front of her.

"Can I get anyone anything?" Liam offered. "Soup? Iced tea, Malachi?"

They waved him off. "The phone was gone," Branigan blurted.

Liam sank into a recliner. "You're kidding."

Detective Scovoy held up the *Star Wars* lunchbox. "Everything was exactly as Ralph described to you, but there was only an empty plastic bag inside." He turned to Malachi. "Like I said, you're our best bet on who would have it."

"You saw there ain't no privacy in Tent City," Malachi said. "'Most anybody coulda seen Ralph bury it. Most likely people, though, would be Slick or Elise. They coulda felt somethin' bumpy under their sleeping bags. Or Maylene coulda taken it."

"Maylene," Branigan said. The others looked at her. "Liam, tell us again what Ralph said was on the video."

"He'd been talking about his intention of filming rush or pledge parties in order to blackmail people. Then he said this video's 'got them dead girls in it'."

"Well, Janie Rose and Maylene went through rush," said Branigan, "so I guess they could've been at any sorority party. And they pledged Gamma Delta Phi, but those girls are so goody-goody, it's hard to imagine him getting any blackmail material on them."

Detective Scovoy stood and turned to Liam and Malachi. "And you two can't remember anything else Ralph said?"

When they shook their heads, he said, "Guess it's time to question him myself."

After Detective Scovoy and Malachi had gone, Branigan stayed for awhile with Charlie and Liam. "How you doing, girlie?" Branigan asked, pulling up a footstool near Charlie's seat on the sofa.

"Much better. Now that I'm getting work on my teeth, I feel a lot more positive."

"Casts coming off soon?"

"Yeah, Monday, I hope."

"Any more dreams?"

"Yeah, a new one that tops all the others. Mrs Santa Claus is chasing me in a sleigh."

Branigan laughed. "Not Mr Claus?"

"No, it's definitely Mrs Claus, which is bizarre because I've never even thought of her driving the sleigh. And there are all these evil, giggling elves sliding around and riding the reindeer." Charlie laughed and held up her hands. "I know it sounds ridiculous in the light of day. But when I have it in the middle of the night, I wake up terrified. Poor Mom's had to come to my room more than once."

Branigan frowned. "Are you still having the dream about being in the Jeep right before the wreck?"

"Not in a few weeks. I think the hospital bed was driving that – with all the engine noise it was making."

"Well, I'm a big believer in our subconscious trying to tell us things," Branigan said. "Though I think we can safely dismiss Mrs Claus and the elves." She stood. "I think I want some of your mama's iced tea," she said. "You two want any?"

"I'll have some," said Charlie.

"You know where everything is," Liam said, waving Branigan to the kitchen to help herself. "I need to work some more on tomorrow's sermon if you don't mind. I'll leave you two to it." He went into his study and closed the door.

Branigan rummaged in the kitchen's lacquered red cabinets for two glasses, filled them with crushed ice from the refrigerator door, then tea from a cut glass pitcher inside. After handing a glass to Charlie, she sat on the small sofa across from the girl.

"You've got to be feeling like you're about to get your life back," Branigan said.

"I do. And I want to find out what happened to Janie Rose."

Branigan cocked her head. "How so?"

"That's what I want to talk to you about."

Branigan raised her eyebrows. "Okay."

"Tell me everything you learned that wasn't in your stories. Was there anything you heard that you wanted to go back to and didn't have time?"

"Well, yeah, Nancy Drew, now that you mention it." Branigan hesitated. "But what do you intend to do? We're not entirely sure you're out of danger yourself."

"Well, assuming I can drive after Monday, I'd like to visit Janie Rose's apartment in Athens. Just look around and see if anything hits me."

"Funny you should say that. Malachi had the same thought and said someone beat him to it. He said it looked like the apartment had been ransacked. We told the police that."

"So Malachi didn't find her journal?"

"I didn't know there *was* a journal."

"Yeah, we used to have lunch together after class. She mentioned that she journaled."

Branigan sat back. "Wow. I wonder if it did have something in it. And if the hearse driver found it – in her apartment or at the crash site. The police don't have it, so there's still the possibility that the driver went through your luggage before they arrived." She thought for a minute. "Tell me about those lunches. What else did she say?"

"I've been racking my brain trying to remember," Charlie admitted. "We mostly talked about classes, homework, boys we were dating. Nothing stands out. There were usually another one or two people there too, so nothing really personal."

"No sense of the nervousness you saw in the Jeep that last morning?"

"Not that I was aware of. I've been trying to think back over our conversations to see if I missed something. But I was so involved with my own settling in, you know? I'm not sure I would've noticed even if something was off."

"Well, I'm interested in her time at Rutherford Lee," Branigan said. "That seems to be where everything converges. So it might be worthwhile to circle back and check out some of the things we've been told. Like her mom said she dated a boy from Louisiana. And the Gamma Delts said she had a falling out with her freshman roommate. Stuff like that."

"Wait a minute," Charlie said. "She talked about some boy visiting her at Georgia whom she'd dated at Rutherford Lee. He came down every month or so. But then around Thanksgiving she found out he was pretty serious about another girl from Rutherford Lee, and told him not to come back."

"You don't know if he was from Louisiana?"

"No idea."

"That might be worth looking into. Did she say anything about the freshman roommate?"

"Yeah, that's why she wanted to live off-campus at UGA. By herself. She said she'd grown up as an only child and found out she didn't particularly like having a roomie. But that's all she said about it. To me, anyway."

Branigan got up to leave. "Make sure you don't do anything or go anywhere without your folks knowing," she said. "Or someone going with you. There are plenty of people around at the college, but not in places like Janie Rose's apartment in Athens. That could be dangerous."

"Sounds like Mr Malachi covered that anyway."

"Promise me."

"Pinky swear."

Chapter Five

Branigan attended church at First Baptist Grambling with her parents on Sunday, then stopped by the grocery store on her way home. She was choosing red pears when she saw Sylvia Eckhart looking at lettuce at the next display stand.

"Dr Eckhart," she said.

"Well hello, Branigan," the professor said warmly. "And please, it's Sylvia."

"I guess you'll be called in on the Kappa Epsilon drinking party that ran in yesterday's paper."

"Already have," said the professor. "The dean called me at home Friday night."

"At least the girl survived."

"No thanks to them, by the sounds of it. The dean is personally bringing charges."

"Is that unusual?"

"Oh, yes. We have an emergency session tomorrow."

"Can we send a reporter?"

"No, I'm sorry, the proceedings are private. But if you submit a request, we will give you the action taken. That's how the college traditionally handles it."

Branigan thought for a moment. "I haven't talked to you since my interview with Mackenzie Broadus. I'm still puzzled over how the school didn't know such a thing."

"Believe me, we were too. Off the record, there were quite a few meetings after your stories were published over Christmas; how two young women left school without exit interviews."

"Two?"

"Mackenzie Broadus and Maylene Ayers."

"What about Janie Rose Carlton?"

"Oh, she had an interview with her adviser. Didn't say a whole lot, apparently, and certainly nothing about Mackenzie's accident. And of course, Ina Rose Carlton told us she had transferred to UGA. Her case wasn't unusual. But it was as if the other two girls had disappeared. Your interview with Mackenzie explained a lot."

Branigan squeezed a pear and put it in her cart. She looked around to make sure they weren't being overheard, and lowered her voice. "It's still hard to believe those girls were able to keep an accident like that quiet. And that Janie Rose and Maylene were upset enough to leave school."

"Well, your story implied they felt guilty because she was paralyzed. At least that's what I got from it."

"Yeah, that's what Mackenzie thought." Branigan stopped abruptly. "Oh, I almost forgot. Something else surfaced."

Dr Eckhart waited expectantly.

"The man accused of beating Maylene to death says he took videos of Rutherford Lee students and tried to extort money from them."

"*What?*" Dr Eckhart dropped a head of lettuce back on the pile and turned her full attention to Branigan. Now she too looked around to make sure no one was listening. "He was *blackmailing* them?"

"You remember I told you about the 'rehab' beating of Max Brody under the Garner Bridge last winter? Well, apparently this man caught it on his cell phone and was able to scare a student out of several hundred dollars not to release it. When that succeeded, he started doing it at other frat and sorority parties."

Dr Eckhart looked horrified. "Nothing like that has come before the Honor Council."

"So the blackmailer didn't follow through and tell the college about any of this?"

The professor shook her head.

"That's what isn't clear," Branigan said. "Why didn't he use what he filmed? Detective Scovoy is back talking to him."

"Well, I hate to say it, but it could be evidence for the council. Let us know if you find anything."

She and Branigan exchanged goodbyes and parted ways.

* * *

Reaching the last aisle of the grocery store, Branigan reached into the ice cream freezer for mint chocolate chip, then had a thought. She left the ice cream and pondered her carton of milk, finally deciding it could stay safely in her trunk for awhile.

After packing her groceries into the Civic, she drove to Rutherford Lee. She might try bluffing some of these sorority girls.

As she pulled through the brick arch of the school, she saw plenty of activity – students biking, jogging, walking in twos and threes, and gathered on a playing field off to her right for what looked like intramural soccer. On an impulse, she exited the traffic circle to the right and drove to the football stadium, which was on the opposite end of the campus from Greek Row. She parked, and entered an open gate below the stadium's press box. She passed across a concourse and under concrete stands, then emerged into the mid-afternoon sunshine.

On either end of the field, gleaming bright yellow against the manicured green grass, were the goalposts. Mackenzie Broadus hadn't mentioned which side she'd fallen from, so Branigan walked to the side with the scoreboard, pushing her way through waist-high shrubbery to get into the end zone. She stood beneath the crossbeam, which looked dizzyingly high from this angle. She imagined the beautiful college freshman, inebriated, attempting daring gymnastics in the dark, and felt a sudden chill.

How many lives had that senseless accident affected? Two of the girls here that night were dead. One was paralyzed. And not only paralyzed but scared. What could Mackenzie be scared of that was worse than life in a wheelchair?

Well, Branigan thought again, *two of the girls here that night were dead.*

She felt a chill as a shadow passed over the football field, and looked up to see a scuttling cloud block the sun. For the first time in a lifetime of visits to the campus, the place struck her as foreboding, a pretty façade that hid a deep fissure.

She headed back to her car.

* * *

Young men and women were out in the yards of almost all the Greek Row houses, many playing frisbee in the intermittent sunshine, music blaring from the porches. As she drove by the Kappa Epsilon Chi house, Branigan could see over the revelers onto the raised porch, and saw a familiar white head. She slowed. It was Sylvia Eckhart, and she had her arm around someone. Branigan slowed to a crawl, trying to see what was going on. The girl looked up, and Branigan recognized the *Swan Song* reporter, Anna Hester. Even from the car, she thought she could see the stubborn thrust of Anna's chin.

Dr Eckhart turned to see what Anna was looking at, then waved at Branigan. Branigan returned the wave and continued on to the Gamma Delta Phi house three doors down.

Dr Eckhart hadn't wasted any time in getting to the Kappa Ep house, Branigan mused. She wondered if she was asking the young women about Ralph's videos. Or maybe warning them? After all, she had been a Kappa Ep herself.

Unlike the other houses, the Gamma Delta Phi house stood closed and silent. No one was out enjoying the winter sun. *Heck*, thought Branigan, *it may be against their rules to wear shorts or jeans in the yard.*

She climbed the porch steps and rang the doorbell. Emma Ratcliffe opened the door dressed in a draped blouse, close-fitting pants and knee-high boots. *The dress code must relax on Sunday*, Branigan thought.

"Emma, can I talk to you and Marianne and Catherine again, please?" she said. "More questions have come up about the deaths of your sorority sisters."

Emma opened the door. "Sure. Let me get them, and we can sit in the library for privacy. Can I get you coffee or tea or water?"

"No, thanks. I don't want to trouble you."

"No trouble at all."

"Well then, sure, water would be great." Branigan knew that if she could frame her visit as a social call, she could win more time with them.

Six women were sitting in the parlor, and they looked at Branigan curiously. Emma didn't introduce her, but showed her into a rather formal library separated from the parlor by double French doors. Branigan placed her purse on a stiffly upholstered armchair. While Emma disappeared, she took in her surroundings. The walls were lined with framed group pictures of sorority members dating back to the 1980s. She walked around the room, glancing swiftly over the pictures, stifling laughter at the nearly identical dark hair and slender build of those in the more recent classes.

Back in the 1990s, there had been a little more diversity, she noted. A handful of blondes, some overweight girls, stylishly cropped hair, more interesting faces. To one side in all of the photos stood a slightly older woman whom Branigan assumed was a faculty adviser.

The same woman was in several of the pictures from the early 1990s, then in 1996 there was a different one. Branigan stopped, peered more closely. That year's adviser looked familiar. She moved on to 1997. There she was again. But not in 1998. Branigan moved back and looked again. The woman appeared to be in her early thirties with auburn hair, a warm smile, her arm linked with that of the co-ed on the end of the back row.

Branigan imagined her with white hair, and then had it. It was Sylvia Eckhart.

Emma Ratcliffe came into the library, followed by Marianne Thurman and Catherine Reisman, who carefully shut the door.

"Dr Eckhart was your adviser?" Branigan asked, pointing at the picture where she stood.

"Not that I know of," said Marianne, coming closer for a look. Her eyes took in the picture, then the years engraved on a brass plate. "Yeah, that does look like her, doesn't it? I guess it's possible. I think she's been at the school a long time."

"But she was a Kappa Epsilon Chi in college."

"That doesn't matter," Marianne said. "We have to have somebody from the college staff or faculty, and sometimes there's no one who's been a member. Like Dr Andrews, our adviser now. She wasn't a Gamma Delt, but she agreed to advise us."

She took a seat at the game table. The young women looked at Branigan expectantly.

Catherine was the first to speak. "I thought you finished this story before Christmas."

"We did," Branigan said. "But the police have never caught Janie Rose's killer."

"Okay," said Marianne. "How can we help?"

"I never got back to you ladies after the story came out about Mackenzie Broadus's accident. I'm still confused about how that stayed so quiet. How no one in your sorority knew about it, especially when Janie Rose and Maylene left school."

The young women exchanged glances, and there was an awkward silence. Marianne cleared her throat. "Miss Powers, if you're asking if we feel bad for not being more sympathetic or more alert to our pledges, the answer is yes. We feel awful."

"I'm not trying to make you feel bad. I'm just wondering how it happened. I can see how Mackenzie didn't talk, because apparently she left the night of the accident and never came back. But I can't imagine that Janie Rose and Maylene didn't tell *someone something*. Everybody talks to somebody."

Emma raised her eyebrows. "Maybe they talked to each other?"

"Yeah, maybe. But are you sure no one in this sorority knew anything about Mackenzie falling?"

All three women shook their heads, dark hair swinging. Emma and Catherine looked to Marianne. Finally she spoke. "It does sound strange, I know. But that was a year ago. If anyone knew anything, it would've come out by now. We never heard a whisper."

Branigan continued to press. "This campus is such a small community. It's hard to believe that three girls left school and there wasn't gossip. There wasn't speculation. Especially when all three were in one sorority."

Catherine spoke up. "Sure there was speculation," she said with a shrug. "Was Janie Rose pregnant? Did Maylene run off and join the Peace Corps? Was Mackenzie homesick? But no one knew the first thing."

"Why would you think Janie Rose was pregnant?"

Catherine threw up her hands. "We didn't really. People were just guessing. And when Dr Carlton said she had transferred to Georgia, we figured everything was all right."

Emma stepped in. "You have to realize that Rutherford Lee isn't for everybody. It's hard academically. Really hard. So freshmen leaving isn't all that uncommon."

"But freshmen leaving *without the administration knowing* is uncommon," Branigan said.

Emma shrugged. Marianne spoke again. "We really don't know what to tell you, Miss Powers. Were we properly looking out for our pledges? Clearly not. And we regret it and we're trying to do better with this year's class. But we honestly didn't know what was up with those three. There's no more to it than that."

Branigan looked thoughtfully at their poised faces. "Tell me about this year's pledges," she invited.

For the next ten minutes she listened as the three talked about the winter's rush season, about the "excellent" pledge class they had recruited, about last week's initiation ceremony. She asked a few innocuous questions, then inquired about the seniors' post-graduation plans. Emma had applied for several jobs in Atlanta, and Catherine was headed to graduate school in psychology. Marianne explained that she had been offered a job with the national Gamma Delta Phi organization. Branigan tried to keep a straight face. *Oh my, a lifetime of this*, she thought. She glanced at the other two. Emma stared vacantly ahead, but something passed over Catherine's face. What was that look? Did she find Marianne's career choice as stifling as Branigan did? Or did she wish for it herself?

Branigan made a show of gathering her purse, and stood. She took a shot in the dark.

"Catherine, after two years as pledge chair, I'm surprised you aren't looking for a national post too."

Catherine's face colored. She started to answer, but Marianne jumped in. "They'd seldom take two from one chapter. They generally start with the president, and when I took it, that was that."

She smiled at Catherine – condescendingly, Branigan thought. She looked at Catherine again, but the involuntary flush was receding, and Catherine had a polite smile on her face.

"Is there anything else you can think of that I neglected to ask?"

The women, all smiling now, more relaxed, shook their heads.

"Oh, I almost forgot," Branigan said. "The police found out that Ralph Batson, the man charged with killing Maylene, was taking videos of some fraternity and sorority parties in the hope of blackmailing students. He got money from the Robies, but the police aren't sure if he ever approached anyone else. Did he approach you?"

The women looked at each other, apparently puzzled. "No," said Marianne. "And I think we'd have seen him if he'd been at one of our parties."

Emma and Catherine nodded. "I mean, wasn't he kind of tattooed?" Emma asked. "And dirty?"

Branigan laughed. "Well, yeah, I guess he would stick out. But he claims to have video of Janie Rose and Maylene."

She watched the women's faces carefully. All were composed. Marianne swallowed. "He claims to have a Gamma Delt video? I don't see how that's possible. And he certainly never tried to contact us."

"He didn't specify it was a Gamma Delt party," Branigan corrected. "He just said a video with those 'dead girls'." She waited a few beats, but no one rushed into the silence. Emma and Catherine looked at Marianne, and Marianne held Branigan's gaze.

"Well, I've taken enough of your time, and you've been most gracious. I'll let myself out."

She walked out of the library, wishing she could have left a bug to capture the conversation after her departure.

She was trying to shake things loose.

CHAPTER SIX

Malachi Martin dragged a rusting lawn chair out of the dim chill of the bridge's shadow and plopped it in the February sunshine. He unzipped his insulated coveralls and pulled his arms out, letting the sleeves dangle at his waist. He hardly noticed that his view consisted of a knee-high mound of trash.

Malachi wasn't looking at his surroundings. He was looking at what wasn't where it should be. He was having a hard time figuring out why so many things were missing in this case. And yes, he admitted to himself, he thought of it as a "case". Miz Branigan seemed to be neck-deep in a murder case once again.

First, there had been no diary or journal or personal writing of any kind in Janie Rose Carlton's apartment. He knew the Grambling police would've gone through her luggage. And even though not terribly high tech, they would've been all over her Facebook page and laptop files. What kind of college girl didn't write down *something*?

Second, where were the family or friends who knew something? What kind of college girl didn't *tell* somebody something? If she was being threatened by somebody her father knew, wouldn't she tell him? Or her mom? Or a hall mate?

Third, Ralph's cell phone. Ralph said it showed the dead girls. And it showed them in such a way he thought it might make the po-lice think Ralph didn't kill Maylene. So, *what was on that video*? Detective Scovoy should know by now. And where was it? Did the murderer go after it? That would mean he'd come right into Tent City, under Malachi's nose. Or did a Tent City dude take it, not realizing what he had?

Malachi turned to look at the tent where Ralph and Maylene had stayed – the tent where Elise lived alone, now that Slick had disappeared. Wait a minute. Was Slick missing too? Nah, he was always taking off and coming back, taking off and coming back. And Malachi knew how that would go down: the two would have a spectacular fight that everyone in Tent City would hear, then Elise would take him back into her tent.

He returned to the bridge's shadow and shook Elise's tent flap. "Elise, it's me. Malachi."

Elise's head popped out, a yellow scarf sliding off her head, pupils huge, a sleepy smile on her face. Malachi knew she'd been smoking crack.

"It just me," he said. "No po-lice. You got Ralph's phone?"

"Nah, if I did I'da pawned it." She cackled. "Mal'chi, you know good and well who done took that phone."

He stood silently, waiting.

"Maylene done took it."

Malachi dropped to his haunches to bring his eyes down to Elise's level. Her body was starting to weave. "How you know?" he asked.

"Saw her do it."

"When?"

"Aw, I dunno know, Mal'chi." Elise smiled and stretched.

"Elise. Think. How Maylene dig it up 'thout Ralph knowin'?"

"Ralph warn't here. He was off buyin' beer or sum'pin. She dug it up, just like your po-liceman did, pretty as you peas." She giggled. "Please. Pretty as you *please*."

Malachi stood and walked back to his rickety chair in the sun.

Okay, so if the phone was on Maylene's body, the Grambling police had it, and for some reason hadn't looked at it. Or they'd sent it to her family in Gainesville. But no, Detective Scovoy was no slouch. He would've looked. So there was only one other solution.

Maylene's killer took the phone.

And Maylene's killer was supposedly Ralph.

That was one more thing missing from this case, Malachi thought. *Logic.*

CHAPTER SEVEN

B ranigan walked up the street to the Kappa Epsilon Chi house, curious to see what had transpired between Sylvia Eckhart and Anna Hester. But Anna was no longer on the front porch, and a conversation with some sisters in the yard revealed she'd gone to the *Swan Song* office.

Branigan stood on the sidewalk trying to decide what to do. Beside the Kappa Ep house was a spacious side yard, then the beginning of the fraternity houses. The first was Rho Beta Iota. Branigan decided it was time to meet Jones Rinehart.

A handful of frisbee throwers directed her to the front door. The young man who opened it – in a T-shirt, Bermuda shorts and barefoot – motioned her inside. A scarred pool table took up most of the living room, and neon beer signs with exposed cords dotted the walls. The room's sagging brown sofas appeared to be Salvation Army rejects, and the once-matching carpet was worn and stained. Branigan doubted there was much dating between the Robies and Gamma Delts.

"Could you find Jones Rinehart for me, please?" she asked the student who'd let her in.

"Prez?" he asked. "Sure, he's around here somewhere."

He bounded up the stairs hollering, "Rinehart! Some lady here to see you."

Branigan felt instantly older. *He'll ma'am me next*, she thought.

Sure enough, the young man called from the top of the stairs, "He'll be right down, ma'am." She shuddered.

Seconds later, a good-looking young man with dark hair and Paul Newman eyes walked down the stairs, a beer in his hand. He was followed by a young woman who looked vaguely familiar.

The woman spoke first. "You're Charlie's Aunt Branigan," she said, sticking out her hand. "I met you at a Grambling East soccer game. Maggie Fielding."

"Of course. Maggie," Branigan said, relieved at the introduction. "Liam told me you and Jones had visited Charlie."

"Can I get you a beer?" Jones asked.

"No, thanks," Branigan said. "Actually, I'm here about Charlie. Or rather, about Charlie's wreck, and the deaths of Janie Rose Carlton and Maylene Ayers."

"Have a seat," Jones said, slumping onto a couch. Maggie sat beside him, and Branigan sat carefully on the second couch, hoping the stains weren't fresh enough to transfer to her pants.

She wasn't sure how to proceed with Maggie in the room. Finally, she addressed the girl. "Maggie, I need to ask Jones about some things he may want to keep private. I'll need you two to decide if you should stay or not."

Maggie looked at Jones, who shrugged. "No problem," he said. "She can stay."

"All right then." Branigan pulled out a pen and notebook. "The man charged with killing Maylene Ayers told police that he blackmailed you over an incident that occurred last winter under the Garner Bridge."

Jones's face went still. He placed his beer can on a side table and twisted to face Maggie. "Maggie, maybe you'd better leave after all. I think Miss Powers may have some of her facts wrong."

Maggie stood, looking confused. She started to say something to Jones, then thought better of it. "Call me when you're done," she said. "Miss Powers, good to see you."

After Maggie had left, all trace of Jones Rinehart's politeness evaporated. He looked stonily at Branigan.

She returned the look. "I believe you paid Ralph Batson to prevent him from releasing videos of you 'rehabbing' Max Brody," she said.

Jones's face darkened. Branigan was suddenly glad there were other people nearby. He nodded almost imperceptibly. "Did he give it to the police anyway?"

"He's trying to. But his cell phone is not where he said it would be."

Jones looked hopeful for a moment. Branigan answered his unspoken question. "But he did tell the police all about it."

"Damn." He put his head in his hands. "Look, I know this is no excuse, but I was drunk, okay? We were all drunk. Including, I might add, the man in the tent."

Branigan stared at him. "But you beat up a homeless man as a fraternity pledge function."

Jones's shoulders sagged, and he leaned back into the couch. "Yeah. We did."

"And then you paid Ralph Batson $300 to keep it quiet?"

"Yeah. Are the police bringing charges?"

"No. Max Brody is dead."

"What? We didn't kill him." Jones's voice rose to a whine.

Branigan decided she didn't like Jones Rinehart; that he was both a bully and a coward. She let him suffer a moment longer.

"No, I didn't mean to imply that," she said finally. "He was one of the homeless people killed last summer. You may have heard about it."

Jones looked relieved. "Yeah, I did. But I didn't know the name of the guy we…" His voice trailed off. "So there won't be charges then?"

Branigan shook her head irritably. "I'm not here to get you into trouble, Mr Rinehart. I'm here to ask you some questions about Ralph Batson. He claims that after successfully extorting money from you, he thought he'd try it with other fraternities and sororities. Do you know anything about that?"

Jones picked up his beer, some of his swagger returning. "Yeah, he knew some of us Greeks had money."

"But did you hear anything from other students?"

"Yeah, maybe something at the Sigma Eta house. And you might ask Sophie over at the Kappa Eps. Maggie said a creep had taped their Halloween party where some underage girls got drunk and threw up. But they told him to take a hike."

"They didn't pay?"

"I can't swear to it. But from what Maggie said, I think Sophie told him to get lost. I wish I'd thought of that."

Branigan was quiet for a moment. "I'll talk to Sophie. But did anyone else have a run-in with Ralph? Maybe the Gamma Delta Phis?"

Jones snorted. "Like what? He videoed them in public without pearls?"

Branigan sighed. "Let's go back to your interactions with Ralph. Was there any violence?"

"The first night he followed us back to the house, he tried to show his little video to a couple of the brothers. He also threw a few punches. But there were lots more of us." He snickered. "I broke his nose."

Branigan could picture Jones Rinehart punching the much burlier Ralph – *if* his frat brothers were holding Ralph down. "And later with you? Did he threaten you?"

"Not physically. When he came back sober the next day, he threatened to take the video to the college president. That would've gotten me kicked out of school, maybe arrested. I didn't want to take the chance."

"Did you spend a lot of time with Ralph?"

"It felt like it. But no, not more than half an hour total."

"What did he talk about?"

"Mostly about how his recording would ruin my life. He had a whole scenario about how that would play out."

"Like what?"

"Like my parents refusing to pay for my senior year. Like being kicked out of school and prevented from going to law school. Like me living in Tent City, where everybody'd know I had attacked one of their own." Jones rolled his eyes. "He was pretty convincing, the douche bag."

"How many times did he come by?"

"Three. I didn't have cash the first time. I paid the next two."

"Did he ever say anything about Maylene Ayers?"

"The girl he killed? No, he didn't say anything." Jones stopped and thought for a moment. "But I have to admit, something changed during that spring semester. I honestly thought he was going to keep bleeding me – until I ran out of money or figured out how to make him back off. But then he just stopped coming around. I thought he'd found a richer vein of frat boys. But maybe Maylene settled him down."

"Did you know Maylene?"

"Saw her around, but didn't know her. She was pretty hot, but a do-gooder, you know? Always collecting coats and stuff for the homeless. Not exactly my thing, as you might imagine." He tipped back the last of his beer and crushed the can.

Branigan closed her notebook and stood. "Anything else you think I should know?"

"Can you let me know if that cell phone surfaces?"

Branigan didn't bother to answer.

Branigan stood for a moment outside the Rho Beta Iota house, wondering how a friend of Charlie had got mixed up with the self-involved Jones Rinehart. She wondered if she should tell Charlie to warn Maggie, then decided it was none of her business.

Heaven knows I'm in no position to offer dating advice, she thought.

She walked back to the Kappa Epsilon Chi house, climbed the porch steps and knocked. Something was nagging at her about Anna Hester. The wannabe reporter was one of the last people to talk to Maylene. Did she know something that she didn't use in her story? And did Sylvia Eckhart rush over to tell her about Ralph's little video hobby?

The girl who answered Branigan's knock invited her in, but reported back minutes later that Anna's roommate thought she was still at the *Swan Song* office.

"Is that in the student center?" asked Branigan.

"Yeah, third floor," said the young woman.

"I hate to keep bothering you, but is Sophie Long in?"

"She's in the kitchen." The girl trotted to the kitchen, shouting, "Sophie!"

Sophie Long appeared at the doorway, a sandwich in one hand.

"You're letting your hair grow out," Branigan said.

"Yep, interviews this semester," she said. "I needed a real world 'do."

"It looks good," Branigan told her honestly.

"Thank you. Can I help you? Would you like something to drink?"

"No, and I don't want to keep you from your supper either. I have just one question for you."

Sophie sat on one of the couches and motioned for Branigan to have a seat. "Fire away."

"It's about the man who's accused of killing Maylene Ayers. Apparently he took some videos of fraternity and sorority parties here at the college and was trying to extort money for them. Did he do that to you?"

Sophie laid her sandwich on a napkin. "Yeah, Ralph something, the jerk. He got some of our underage girls drinking and throwing up."

"But you didn't pay?"

"I was tempted," Sophie admitted. "But I finally decided, 'You know what? I don't have enough fingers to plug this dam.' I told him to do his worst. As it turns out, we blew it anyway with this year's pledging. Which, of course, was all over *The Rambler*." She shrugged. "This time next year all this sorority silliness isn't going to mean a thing. And it can't end soon enough for me."

"Why do you say that?"

She poked a finger through her sandwich, as if she'd lost her appetite. "Just that it all seemed kind of wild and fun my first three years. But being president, I started feeling some responsibility. And I found out I had no control over these girls."

"Over their drinking, you mean?"

"Over their drinking, their bad decision-making, you name it. If that girl had died at our pledge party, I could've been named in a lawsuit. And this whole thing with our hearse, people looking at us like we're involved. I'm ready to graduate and get out of here."

"Who's looking at you like you're involved?"

"Other students. Faculty members. Or who knows? Maybe I'm imagining it."

Branigan remained silent in case Sophie wanted to add something. When she didn't, Branigan spoke quietly to make sure they couldn't be overheard by the girls in the kitchen. "Sophie, do you think one of the Kappa Eps ran Janie Rose and Charlie off the road?"

Sophie's eyes remained downcast and she stabbed again at her sandwich. "No-o-o," she said slowly. "It's not that exactly. No, I wouldn't say that."

"But?"

"But... but... I don't know." Her eyes slid to Branigan's and away again. "I'm wondering if I should resign before anything else happens that I can be held responsible for."

"I can understand that," Branigan said. "Especially if you feel you have no control over what the other sisters do."

She waited, hoping Sophie would continue, but the girl wrapped her sandwich in her napkin in a gesture of finality.

"One more thing," Branigan said. "Did you hear about anyone who did pay Ralph?"

"Those idiot Robies," Sophie said, her voice gaining a hint of her former confidence. "But we heard he had something bigger on them than drinking. I was never clear what it was. We heard everything from making pledges steal from a downtown store to throwing water balloons off the Nicholas Inn onto homeless people." She stood.

"Okay," said Branigan. "I won't keep you any longer. Thanks for your help."

Sophie hesitated. "Were you looking for Anna too?"

"Yes. I understand she's at the newspaper office."

"Should be. She pretty much lives up there."

Branigan had the impression the young woman wanted to say something else, so she pretended to go through her purse in order to give her time. When Sophie didn't speak, Branigan tried once more. "You look like you want to say something."

When Sophie spoke, it was in a near whisper. "It really didn't occur to me until after you were here last time. But the hearse driver who killed Janie Rose Carlton had to be someone we know. Someone who's been in our house."

Branigan nodded. "Yes."

Sophie's eyes looked tortured. "I feel like everything I ever knew has been jerked out from under me." She shuddered, as if swept by a cold draft. "I can't wait to get away from this school."

CHAPTER EIGHT

Malachi sat on the bench in front of Bea's on Main Street. Weak afternoon sunlight filtered through the bare limbs of a silver maple. He liked the way the sun fractured all over him, dancing almost, when the wind blew. His coveralls were zipped to the neck to ward off the chill that was moving in with the late afternoon wind. He was reading Sunday's *Grambling Rambler*, which he'd taken from the newspaper's recycling bin.

Miz Branigan didn't have a story today, but that Miz Marjorie did. It was a story about a little boy whose soldier daddy surprised him in the middle of a school spelling bee. His winning word was *artillery*. His daddy, dressed in khaki camouflage, walked on stage to give him his trophy. The fourth-grader had burst into tears.

Malachi rubbed under his own eyes.

Reading about the soldier reminded Malachi of the cash rolled up in an inside pocket of his coveralls. He patted it. He didn't like to carry this much cash on him. Way too dangerous for the places he went, the people he saw. But he'd cashed his veteran's disability check on Friday and had kept $200 for a week in a motel. That'd give him a shower and a warm place to sleep when it turned colder tomorrow, as it was supposed to. He was looking forward to watching TV in his underwear, out of these heavy coveralls.

Cars drove lazily up and down Main, careful of the pedestrians who were jaywalking with their over-priced coffees. Malachi didn't see the point of buying a cup for two dollars when he got it free at Jericho Road. A black Mercedes pulled into a spot right in front of Bea's, and Malachi recognized the dead girl's father from the hospital back in December, the one Miz Branigan was talking to on the way through the emergency room. Malachi wondered where his wife was. The father wore a gray running suit. His jaw was clenched just as Malachi remembered. The man was aiming for a heart attack.

He passed Malachi without a glance, and headed into the bakery. Three minutes later, he came out, coffee in hand. If he could afford that Mercedes, Malachi figured, a two-dollar coffee wasn't going to bother him none. He passed Malachi again, unseeing. The man got into the black car, but he didn't pull out. He sat staring through his windshield. Then he got back out of the car and walked south.

Malachi placed his newspaper in a garbage can on the sidewalk, and slowly followed him.

Mr Carlton – Malachi finally remembered his name – walked quickly down Main Street and entered Farnsworth New and Used Book Emporium. The owner, old Mr Farnsworth, didn't mind you sitting and reading, as long as you weren't taking up space from his paying customers. Malachi was careful not to abuse his welcome.

Fifteen minutes later, Mr Carlton came back out, that jaw clamped as tight as ever.

He headed north, toward his car. At one point, Mr Carlton whirled around to stare behind him, eyes sweeping over the street and sidewalk. But his eyes didn't linger on the homeless man twenty feet behind, as Malachi knew they wouldn't. He stomped back to his car, got in and slammed the door.

Had Malachi not seen the familiar shape of Taxi Blue, the local cab company, he would have let it end right there. But with money in his pocket and his interest high, he tapped the window of the taxi. The black driver began to smile, then saw Malachi. He looked him over, braids under a do-rag, the insulated camouflage coveralls. "No, brother," he said in the lilting accent of an African immigrant, Kenyan maybe, or Nigerian. Or heck, maybe even Jamaican.

Malachi unzipped his coveralls and pulled out three twenty-dollar bills and showed the man. "I got money," he said calmly.

The driver flashed a huge smile. "Then get in, brother."

Malachi climbed into the back seat and pointed to the black Mercedes. "Follow that car," he said.

"Yes, brother."

The Taxi Blue driver followed Mr Carlton's Mercedes four miles from downtown. By the time they reached the brick archway of Rutherford Lee College, Malachi wondered if the man was going to see his wife. Miz Branigan had said she was a professor here. But would she be in her office on a Sunday?

Malachi watched as the Mercedes drove slowly to the north side of campus, to a row of houses with huge Greek letters above their porches. Mr Carlton stopped in front of one of the houses, but he didn't get out. He simply sat for a minute, his car idling.

Then he slowly returned to the middle of campus and parked next to a lakeside building. He got out and set off walking around the lake, fists in his pockets, head down.

"How much?" Malachi asked his driver.

"You don't want a ride back to town, brother?"

"No. How much?"

"Eleven dollah," the man said. Malachi thought he sounded disappointed.

He handed the man a twenty-dollar bill and waited for his change.

CHAPTER NINE

The February sun was setting by the time Branigan returned to her car after talking to Sophie Long. She was tired and hungry, and didn't want to talk to any more college students. She longed to unpack her groceries, heat up some chicken noodle soup and snuggle on her couch for the rest of the evening.

But since you're here... she told herself. Morosely, she drove to the student center, dusk falling fast. Students filled the brightly lit dining hall, which was noisy with their chatter and the clink of cutlery and dishes. She skirted the cafeteria and walked up a wide, winding staircase to the second floor, where student service administrators had their offices. A combined movie theater and lecture hall took up one end of the floor, but it was dark and empty. Carpet muffled the cacophony from below, and all the offices appeared to be closed for the weekend.

Branigan exited the second floor to access a stairwell, unheated and weakly lit. She climbed to the third floor, letting herself in through a door with a push bar.

The top floor appeared to be for the school's media outlets. Signs mounted at right angles to the wall marked offices for the literary magazine, the radio station, a TV studio and, oddly, the chaplain's office. At the far end of the hall was a sign for the student newspaper, *The Swan Song*. From the pencil-thin light under the doors, the only rooms that seemed to be occupied were the radio station and *The Swan Song*.

She strode quickly to the newspaper office, wondering again what Sylvia Eckhart and Anna Hester had been talking about that afternoon. Had Sylvia been warning her fellow Kappa Eps about Ralph's recordings of compromising sorority functions?

Two separate doors opened into the newspaper office suite, but light emanated from only one. The top half of the doors held glass panels, so Branigan stood at an angle to peer into the lighted room before knocking. In the murky hallway, she could see in without being seen herself. Anna Hester was working on a laptop at a desk against the left-hand wall. She paused, flipped open a notebook, then began typing furiously.

She paused and picked up a smart phone from her desk, apparently responding to a ring that Branigan couldn't hear. She spoke for only a moment before returning to her work. Branigan raised her hand to knock on the door, but before she could, Anna reached for her purse and withdrew a black flip phone. Branigan hesitated. Why would she have two phones? She continued watching as Anna stared intently at the flip phone and then turned back to the keyboard and began typing again. Could that be Ralph's phone?

Branigan knocked. Anna swirled in her chair, sliding the flip phone back into her purse in one fluid movement. As Branigan entered the office, the girl eased her laptop closed.

"Miss Powers. What are you doing here?"

"Call me Branigan. I've been talking to Sophie and some of the other Greek Row residents today and wanted to run one more thing by you."

"Okay."

"It turns out that the man in jail for killing Maylene Ayers recorded some fraternity and sorority functions with the idea of blackmailing students. Sophie confirmed that he did try that with the Kappa Eps." Branigan watched Anna closely, but the girl's face gave away nothing. "Did you meet Ralph when you interviewed Maylene?"

"No. She was by herself."

"So you don't know him?"

She shook her head.

Branigan realized she was going to have to be more confrontational. "Ralph claims he taped Maylene and Janie Rose

Carlton before their deaths. He says the video will help prove he didn't kill Maylene. But his phone has disappeared."

When Anna didn't speak, Branigan added, "Do you know anything about that?"

"Why would I?"

"You were one of the last people to talk to Maylene."

"So?"

"So she lived with Ralph and he buried the phone under their tent. It would make sense that she knew about any video he had."

"But as you pointed out the last time we talked, Maylene didn't confide in me."

"Didn't she?"

"Miss Powers, you gave me an ethics lesson because you thought I'd betrayed her. Now you're suggesting she trusted me so much she gave me some kind of video?"

Branigan was silent, wondering how much this girl knew, wondering if her knowledge placed her in danger. She changed tack. "Are you working on a story for next Saturday's *Swan Song*?"

"Yes."

"Will it be something the police are interested in?"

Anna couldn't help preening slightly. "Maybe."

Branigan nodded. "Anna, be careful. Two of your fellow students are dead. If you don't want to tell me, that's fine. But if you know something, you *do* want to tell Detective Scovoy." She grabbed a business card from her purse and scribbled Chester's cell phone number on the back. "My number's on the front and his is on the back," she said.

Branigan turned to leave. She heard a quiet click. It sounded as though it came from the adjoining room.

"Is someone else here?"

"No, just me."

"Do you mind if I look?"

"Not at all. You're making me nervous."

Branigan walked through the open doorway next to Anna's desk, blindly searching the wall with her palm until she found a light switch. The room leapt into brightness. It was empty. She tried the door to the hallway and found it unlocked. She poked her head out, but saw that the hallway was empty as well.

"Do you always come up here by yourself?" she asked Anna, returning to the first room.

"Well, yeah, but the radio guys are just down the hall."

"Do they know you're here?"

"I don't know."

"Do you want me to drive you back to the sorority house?"

Anna glanced out of the window at the inky blackness that had fallen. She grabbed her laptop and purse. "Yes, actually, I think I do."

Anna turned off the office lights, and they exited.

"You don't want to take the elevator?" Branigan asked as Anna walked past it.

"It takes forever. The stairs are faster."

As the women entered the stairwell, they heard a door close on the floor below. Branigan held a finger to her lips, then ran down the stairs. She pushed the door bar and looked onto the second floor hall. A dark figure had reached the end of the hall and was starting down the wide staircase to the dining room below. A figure somehow familiar.

Branigan sprinted down the hall, leaving Anna behind. She reached the staircase only to see the figure disappear out of a side door next to the bottom step. She hurried down, pushing through the door and into a shadowy alley between buildings. The lakeside patio fifty feet away was well lit, but back here, next to the building, the college wasn't trying to show off anything. Branigan darted from the alley to her right and saw no movement, so she turned back toward her left. Shrubbery taller than she was hugged the side of the building. She ran a few steps toward the patio, toward the welcoming light.

A padded arm reached out and grabbed her.

Branigan was in mid-scream when her brain registered the bulky coveralls, the nylon do-rag, the dreadlocks.

The scream died. "*Malachi?*" she hissed.

"Miz Branigan," he said in surprise. "Why you followin' me?" He extricated her from where she'd half fallen into the bushes.

"I'm not. I mean, not unless you were in the newspaper office on the third floor. Were you?"

"Nah, I ain't been up but to the second floor." He peered into the darkness. "I follow that Mr Carlton here. But I ain't seen him after I got inside."

"Harry Carlton came to the student center? Not his wife's building?"

Malachi nodded, looked around once more. "He come in whatever building this is."

"What was he doing here?"

Malachi shrugged. "Like I say, I lost 'im."

"Could he have gone to the third floor?"

"Dunno."

Anna came alongside Branigan and looked from her to Malachi. "Why would Janie Rose's dad be in the newspaper office?" she asked.

Branigan looked at the girl but couldn't make out her expression in the gloom. Obviously, she knew more than she was letting on. But would she have agreed to meet Mr Carlton? Or, more to the point, would Mr Carlton meet with her? Or had he been in the office to find out something? For that matter, had he been in the office at all?

"So you weren't supposed to meet Mr Carlton in your office?" Branigan asked her.

"No, why would I?"

Branigan stood on the sidewalk, brushing leaves from her coat sleeves. Malachi stepped out to join her. Anna looked from one to the other without speaking. Then the three headed toward Branigan's car, none of them entirely at ease in the presence of the others.

Branigan was beginning to understand Sophie Long's dread. She too wanted to get free of this campus.

CHAPTER TEN

*C*harlie Delaney exited her doctor's office and actually skipped across the parking lot. Her mother started to call her back, but her dad shook his head.

"Let her go," Liam said. "Lot of pent-up energy."

Both her arm and her leg cast had been sawn off. As Liam and Liz leaned against Liam's SUV, their daughter danced like a six-year-old across the asphalt. "At least I'm not twirling, Mom!" she cried.

"I can't watch," Liz laughed as she got into the car. "Come on, you goofball, it's cold."

Charlie fell into the back seat, breathing hard. "Boy, I'm out of shape. And my ribs hurt."

"That's not a bad thing if it'll keep you from overdoing it," said her mom.

Winter had returned to the South, and though the sun showed up occasionally between flying clouds, the wind was frigid. The three stopped for fast-food tacos, then Liam dropped Liz and Charlie at home.

"I've got to meet with a client," Liz said, gathering up giant binders of fabric swatches. "We'll be downstairs. What are you going to do with your first cast-free afternoon?"

"I've got homework," said Charlie. "But first I'm going to call Chan. This is too major for a text."

"I won't be tied up long. Tell your brother hi for me."

The next morning Charlie accompanied her dad to Jericho Road so she could take his car for the day. Breakfast was ending and many of the departing homeless people hugged the young woman with whom they'd shared Sunday worship and Friday night pizza. Charlie asked after their children, friends and even the pets some of them kept in the encampment under the Garner Bridge. Her dad had taught her the importance of remembering names in a population that felt unnoticed, unheeded, unseen. Tiffany Lynn hung back, waiting to see her.

"Tiffany," Charlie said, catching a glimpse of her. "I've been trying to find you ever since I saw the Good Samaritan painting. It's amazing."

"Thank you," the artist said. "Good to see you outta yo' wheelchair."

"That's been awhile. I'm even off crutches now."

"Yeah, that too. Miz Charlie, they ever catch the fellow what did this to you?"

"No, and I'd sure like to get hold of him. I'm not quite so forgiving as Saint Dad."

Tiffany laughed. "I ain't so sure Pastor would be forgivin' this time neither."

Charlie drew a cup of coffee from the nearly empty urn and filled it liberally with milk. She wandered back to her dad's office and wasn't surprised to find Malachi Martin mopping the hallway.

"Mr Malachi!" she cried. "Mom told me you came to the hospital, but I never saw you."

"Just checkin' to see you was all right, Miz Charlie."

"I am now. See? No casts."

"I see that. Congrat'lations."

"I have to admit, it gives a whole new meaning to feeling free."

"If you looking for your daddy, he in there." Malachi nodded to Liam's office, its door ajar. "He got somebody with him."

Charlie tiptoed over the damp floor, and listened at her father's door. Hearing soft voices inside, she stepped away. "I won't bother him now," she told Malachi. "Thanks for coming to the hospital."

She left a message with Dontegan at reception that she would check in with her father by noon. Then she hurried into the gray-white day, texting as she went.

Do u have 15 mins to meet this AM?

Maggie Fielding shot back immediately:

No time 2 come 2 your house.

Have car. Can meet at RL coffee shop.

OK. See u @ 9:30.

Charlie was winded by the time she reached her dad's SUV. Eight weeks off her feet had wreaked havoc with her muscle tone and stamina. She eased into the driver's seat and caught her breath. At least she had plenty of time to drive to Rutherford Lee. Like many residents of Grambling, she was familiar with the campus. Her family went to the occasional football and basketball home game, and she had attended soccer camp there for three summers during high school. She shook her head to think how much sprinting she'd been capable of this time last year. "Girl, you got some territory to make up," she said aloud.

Charlie drove through the college's brick arch, barren now of the climbing roses that would return in the spring. There had been a few days at UGA when she'd wondered if she'd made a mistake in not coming here instead. One day in the campus post office, used almost exclusively for care packages these days, she'd received a handwritten letter from her dad. Reading it, she had slid to the floor, her back against the wall of small, metal-doored openings, and cried. She'd wanted to leave home, she really had. She knew it was the best thing. But breaking up the foursome that had been her mom, dad, Chan and her hadn't been easy. She wondered now what it'd been like for her parents, sending her and Chan off at the same time. They'd put a brave face on it. But that letter, telling her how proud he and Mom were, how much they loved her and Chan, the hopes they had for them…. It wasn't what she needed to hear at that homesick moment.

She rounded the entrance fountain, meandered on the one-way road with its adjacent bike lane. She wanted to get some visuals on the events that had rocked her life this winter, so her first stop was the football stadium. She couldn't see anything from the parking lot, so she got out of the SUV. Pulling her coat tightly around her, she made her way through the empty concourse to the field where groundsmen in the college's navy and yellow windbreakers were consulting in one end zone.

She took a seat on an aluminum bench on the home side, near the yellow goalpost, and imagined the scene of a year ago. She'd read her Aunt Branigan's story a dozen times, and tried to think how a brief drunken accident could send things spiraling so darkly out of control. Mackenzie Broadus was paralyzed, possibly because of a mistake Janie Rose Carlton and Maylene Ayers had made in moving her. She didn't know Mackenzie or Maylene. But there was a solemnity to Janie Rose at Georgia that hadn't been there in middle and high school. They'd attended different high schools but kept enough mutual friends to see each other occasionally. So what caused the change? Was it guilt? And the way she'd acted in the Jeep that last morning. Was it fear? Of what? Had she recognized the Kappa Ep hearse and known something that Charlie didn't?

There was no obvious link between Janie Rose's death and Maylene's. But how odd that both girls were present at Mackenzie's accident.

Charlie had a sudden thought: *Could it be some unbalanced person from Mackenzie's family, seeking revenge? Her father or a brother or a friend?* She made a mental note to suggest it to Branigan.

Charlie paused to catch her breath after climbing the steps to exit the stadium. *I'm pitiful*, she thought, walking slowly back to the car. She drove past the chapel and then to Greek Row, curious to see where the hearse had come from. She'd like to see it again, but knew it was still in the police compound.

Students walking and biking to class on this Tuesday morning were concerned mostly with staying warm. No one glanced at

Charlie as she crept by the elegant Gamma Delta Phi house. So that was where Janie Rose had lived. Three structures over, Charlie saw the Kappa Epsilon Chi letters on the last house before a vacant lot. She crawled past, staring at the brick façade. She realized she didn't know if Maggie lived here or in a dorm or in an off-campus apartment. She looked around, thinking she might spot her friend. When she didn't, she drove on to the student center and walked across the frigid lakeside patio into the coffee shop.

Maggie was already seated, and waved to Charlie from a booth. "No crutches?" Maggie called excitedly. The two hugged, and she handed Charlie a laminated card. "Get something to drink with this."

Charlie waved her off. "I had coffee at Jericho Road," she said, sliding into the seat facing Maggie. "I don't need anything else."

"It's so good to see you up and walking," Maggie said. "How's it feel?"

"Good," said Charlie. "Though I kinda got caught off guard by how out of shape I am."

"You'll get that back in no time," her friend assured her. "What's brought you to Rutherford?"

"I want to meet Janie Rose Carlton's freshman roommate. Can you find out who she is and where I could find her?"

"Yep. Actually, I rushed her and she pledged Kappa Epsilon." Maggie's fingers flew over her phone's keypad. "Her name is Ashley Paul. I have no idea if she's in class right now, but we'll see." She looked up. "What else?"

"Janie Rose's mother told my Aunt Branigan that she was dating someone from Louisiana. Can you find out who that was?"

Maggie's face froze. After a moment she said, "You're kidding, right?"

"Why would I be kidding?"

Maggie continued to stare at Charlie. "Maggie, what?"

"Jones dated Janie Rose the semester before we started dating."

Charlie's heart began to pound as she remembered Jones leaning over her hospital bed, insisting upon straightening her pillow. She tried to speak, but a croak came out. She cleared her throat and tried again. "I thought he was from Virginia."

"Why'd you think that?"

"When you guys visited my room, he said he was going home to Alexandria."

"Oh. Well, it's Alexandria, Louisiana."

Now it was Charlie's turn to stare. "Why didn't you say anything before?"

"What was there to say? We didn't want to remind you of Janie Rose's death when you were recovering. And they'd stopped dating months before the accident. It was never serious."

"But…" Charlie stopped. It was serious enough for Jones Rinehart to visit Janie Rose at UGA as late as Thanksgiving. He must have been dating both women at the same time. But she didn't want to say that to Maggie, who was wearing Jones's engagement ring.

"I… I… guess I don't need to talk to him then," she stammered.

"Your Aunt Branigan already did," Maggie said. "Something about a homeless guy who was taping frat parties and trying to get money from students. Jones said it was the Robies and a lot of other Greeks. Including us."

Charlie couldn't get the vision of Jones and Janie Rose out of her head. Her mind was spinning wildly. Janie Rose had dated Jones. When they stopped, was she scared of him? Was Jones at the hospital to see if Charlie recognized him from the hearse? She was afraid her face would betray her confusion. "Do you know why they broke up?" she asked.

Maggie shrugged. "They'd only dated from the middle of the fall until Janie Rose left school last winter. I don't think he saw her but a time or two after that. It wasn't serious enough for them to continue long distance. Then we started dating. And that was that."

Charlie knew that wasn't true. Janie Rose had mentioned at least three visits from her Rutherford Lee boyfriend during the same semester he was supposedly seeing Maggie. Should she say something?

Before she had a chance, Maggie's phone beeped, alerting her to a text. "Ah, here you go. Ashley has an hour between classes. She's on her way over."

"That's fantastic. Thank you so much."

The awkwardness between them didn't dissipate, but Charlie's heart rate slowed and they managed to find neutral ground until Ashley arrived. Maggie gave Charlie a quick hug and hurried away.

Ashley Paul was a muscular, wide-shouldered girl with a flawless complexion and wiry brown curls that fell past her shoulders. Charlie struggled to wrest her attention from Janie Rose's former boyfriend and focus on her roommate.

"Thank you for meeting with me," she said. "I was the one driving the car when Janie Rose Carlton was killed."

"I'm so sorry," said the girl. "I read about your accident."

"The police haven't found out yet what happened. I'm trying to fill in some blanks in my mind."

"Okay."

"So you were roommates freshman year?"

"Yeah, I'm from Nebraska and didn't know a soul here. So the housing office paired me with a local girl. I think they do that so you'll have your roommate's family if you need support."

"But you didn't get along?"

Ashley looked surprised. "No, we got along fine."

Charlie paused for a moment.

Finally, Ashley spoke again. "Why would you think we didn't?"

"The Gamma Delta Phis told my aunt – she's a reporter for *The Grambling Rambler* – that was the reason Janie Rose moved into the sorority house. That she didn't get along with her roommate."

Ashley's face cleared. "Yeah, she probably did tell them that. But it wasn't true. It was just that Janie Rose was hell-bent on being a Gamma Delt. At every possible level."

"What do you mean?"

"Well, Janie Rose was super into rush and into being one of those Stepford girls."

Charlie laughed. "Yeah, my aunt did mention that your Gamma Delts have a type."

"To put it mildly. They still think it's the 1950s. They all want to be engaged by the time they graduate." Ashley shrugged. "Which is fine. Whatever. But Janie Rose really liked them and wanted to live in that sorority house the minute she could. She heard that one of the sisters was moving out and she made a beeline over there to get her room. I didn't know she pulled me into it, but I'm not really surprised."

"But you didn't want to be a Gamma Delt?"

Ashley pulled a face of mock horror. "No! I wasn't one hundred per cent sold on going Greek at all. But I play soccer, and half the team is Kappa Epsilon. So I joined. But it's pretty laid back."

"Except for the hearse."

"Yeah, there is that," Ashley conceded. "Our one big silliness. The police still have it. I'm not sure we'll ever get it back."

"Did you know Janie Rose's boyfriend, Jones Rinehart?"

"Sure. They started going out sometime in the middle of that first semester. It was a pretty big deal because he was this hot frat guy. An upperclassman."

"Was it serious?"

"I guess. I mean he sure was around a lot. I hate to say this because I love Maggie, but after awhile you can get kind of sick of Jones. He's not terribly bright and he's arrogant. Not a great combination."

"Do you know why he and Janie Rose broke up?"

"They didn't while I was living with her. After she left the dorm, I lost track of her. Then I heard she'd left school entirely."

"Did you know why?"

"Not at first. But one day I ran into Dr Carlton in the library and asked. She said Janie Rose was headed to UGA and everything was fine."

"When was that?"

"Around graduation. Late May."

Charlie paused for a minute. "And I guess you read about the reason she left? About Mackenzie Broadus falling off the goalpost and being paralyzed?"

"Yeah, we all read that. It was all anyone talked about when we got back from Christmas break. But I didn't know Mackenzie or Maylene Ayers other than to say hi."

"Were you good friends with Janie Rose? We hung out some in middle school and at Georgia, but I still wouldn't say I knew her well."

"I'm not sure I'd say that either. One thing I do know is that she was going to be a writer. She wrote in that blue journal every night."

Charlie perked up. "So she *did* keep a journal while you lived with her. She told me she journaled. What did it look like?"

"Very nice. Blue leather cover. Kind of an unusual size – maybe eight by six inches."

"What kind of stuff did she write in it?"

"Everything, I think. I never read it, of course, but she'd spend five to fifteen minutes a night on it, sometimes more."

"And obviously she took it with her when she moved out of your dorm room?"

"Oh, yeah."

"It wasn't found in her suitcase or in her apartment in Athens."

"Then somebody took it," said Ashley. "There is no way Janie Rose Carlton was living *anywhere* without that journal."

CHAPTER ELEVEN

B ranigan signaled for Jody to meet her in a conference room, but before she could step away from her desk, her phone rang. She held up a finger to ask Jody to wait, and answered it.

"Miss Powers? This is Tony Broadus, Mackenzie's brother. Do you remember me?"

Branigan sat down in surprise, and pulled a notebook and pen to the center of her desk.

"Of course I do, Mr Broadus. How may I help you?"

"I've called the Grambling police and they won't tell me anything, so I thought of you."

"Okay."

"Are they still working on the murders of those girls? Those friends of Mackenzie's?"

"Absolutely."

"Can you tell me if they're close to finding out who killed them?"

She still didn't know what Detective Scovoy had learned from interviewing Ralph, so was able to truthfully plead ignorance. She added: "Why are you asking now, Mr Broadus?"

"We – that is, my parents and I – are worried about Mackenzie. She seems really anxious. We're wondering if she will get better once all this is over. Settled."

"Do you mean she's worse now than when I was there?"

"Yes. No." He hesitated a moment. "I don't really know. It's hard to put my finger on it." She could hear the pain in his voice. "But we can't stand seeing her like this."

Branigan let the silence stretch out.

"I thought… I thought… I mean, I wasn't sorry when I heard

they were dead, those girls who moved her. I know that sounds awful. But I wasn't. Now, though, it's like it's even worse for Mackenzie. I thought it would be better, but it's worse."

Branigan was furiously taking notes. "Mr Broadus, do you know something about these murders?"

"No!" He sounded confused. "No! Why would I?"

She backed off. "Do you think Mackenzie knows more than she's telling us?"

"No! At least I don't think so. Why would you ask that?"

"It's just that I never got over the feeling that Janie Rose and Maylene's reaction to her accident was rather drastic."

"Are you kidding me? They were responsible for her being paralyzed. I hardly think there's any reaction that would've been too drastic."

"So you do think they were responsible? That's not what you said last month."

"I think I said I didn't blame them. That's a little different."

"Is it?"

"Miss Powers, I shouldn't have bothered you. I'm sorry."

"Wait a…" But he had already hung up. Branigan was left staring at her scribbled notes: "I thought it would be better, but it's worse."

She shut the conference room door behind Jody, and he looked at her expectantly.

"I need you to do something for me," she said.

"Let me guess. Call Scovoy."

She blushed. "How did you know?"

"I heard you call him twice this week and it sounded like you weren't getting what you wanted. So I'm guessing you're too embarrassed to keep calling."

"You're scary," she told him.

"And you're going to set Tan-4 off. You know how he feels about us dating sources."

"I know. And this guy was not my source until we downsized so much that we're all cop reporters."

"Details, details."

"So will you call him? I need to know what Ralph said was in his video that he thinks exonerates him."

Jody sighed. "And in return I get…"

"My undying gratitude."

"Big whoop."

Jody spun around in his chair and caught Branigan's eye. "He lawyered up."

"What do you mean?"

"When Scovoy went to interview Ralph Batson about the video, Ralph asked for a public defender."

"Why didn't Scovoy just tell me that?"

"I think he kept hoping Ralph would talk through his attorney and tell him what was on the video. But the attorney is advising him to keep quiet for now."

"That's maddening."

"I'm sure his attorney is hoping it's something he can use at trial or for a lesser plea. He doesn't want to squander it too early."

"Even if it can help catch a killer?"

"The attorney swears there's no direct link. And of course, without the video, the police would have only Ralph's word for it. Not the most reliable witness."

"Still, it could point us in the right direction," Branigan fumed.

"The right direction on a story we're not even working on?"

"Shhhhh," Branigan warned.

An hour later, Branigan finished a Valentine's Day story for Julie on a local bachelor auction to benefit the county's no-kill animal shelter. She was torn between the inanity of the fundraiser and her genuine respect for the shelter's work.

"Just hold your nose and knock it out of the park for us," the shelter director told her. He was acquainted with Cleo and the line of German shepherds raised by Branigan's grandparents.

"I'll do my best," she'd promised him. And she had.

She was giving the story a final read-through when the downstairs receptionist called. "A Charlie Delaney here to see you."

"Send her right up," Branigan said.

She met Charlie at the elevator. "Your casts are off!" she cried delightedly when the girl emerged.

Charlie grabbed her arm. "Aunt Brani, you are not going to believe what I learned today. Where can we talk?"

Branigan led her to the conference room she and Jody had used earlier, and closed the door.

"What's going on?"

"I hardly know what to tell you first," Charlie began, taking a moment to sit and catch her breath. "Jones Rinehart dated Janie Rose Carlton before he started dating Maggie Fielding."

Branigan's eyes widened.

"And I never told you this because I wasn't sure it wasn't all in my head. But on my last night in the hospital, the cop at the door was called away, and Maggie and Jones invited Chan to go downstairs with them for hot chocolate. I told him to go, and I fell asleep. When I woke up, Jones was standing over me. He said he'd left his phone in the room, and then he offered to straighten my pillow. I don't know if I'd been dreaming or what, but for some reason I was absolutely convinced he was going to hurt me. I hit the button to call the nurse, and he ducked out real quick."

"Charlie! You should've told us."

"Like I said, I'm not sure *what* he was doing. I may have imagined the whole thing."

Branigan hugged her. "I'm so sorry. I thought we were protecting you better than that."

She thought for a moment. "But he dated Janie Rose Carlton? How did you find that out?"

"I went to Rutherford Lee today and talked to Maggie and then to Janie Rose's freshman roommate. The other bombshell is that Janie Rose definitely kept a journal. Her roommate said there was no way she'd live in an apartment in Athens *or* go home for Christmas without her blue leather journal."

"So Malachi was on the right track," mused Branigan.

"And one more thing I thought of."

"There's more?"

"Well, just a wild idea really. Has anyone considered that someone close to Mackenzie Broadus killed Janie Rose and Maylene? Maybe they blamed them for her accident? Or at least for being paralyzed."

Branigan swiveled in her chair as she remembered the phone call from Tony Broadus. "Yes, I have considered it." She pictured the manicured subdivision in Columbia, the frightened young woman in the wheelchair, her handsome and protective brother. She remembered Tony Broadus's soft murmur, *What are you gonna do?*, and the quote in the notebook lying on her desk: *I thought it would be better, but it's worse.*

But would he know about the hearse? And who but Ralph could have killed Maylene with Ralph's crowbar? What was that saying you heard all over TV crime shows these days? *When you hear hoof beats, think horses, not zebras.*

Ralph was the one who blackened Maylene's eyes, who punched her in the face. Who else would beat the pretty co-ed to death?

"Aunt Branigan? What are you thinking?"

Branigan wrenched her attention back to Charlie. "I'm thinking you have done amazing work, young lady. But it doesn't sound like you kept to your pinky swear."

"Dad knew where I was. And I was in a public place the entire time."

Branigan eyed her skeptically. "While you're on a roll, I wonder if you'd have better luck with Anna Hester than I have."

"Who's that?"

"She's a sophomore Kappa Ep and a reporter for the Rutherford Lee newspaper. I think she knows something and she's writing it up for this Saturday's student newspaper. I even wonder if she has Ralph's cell phone."

"How would she?"

"Sunday night I went to see her. Before she knew I was there, I saw her answering one phone and then looking at another one as she was writing. And she knew Maylene Ayers, which is a strong connection to Ralph."

Charlie knew Branigan was assembling her thoughts as she talked, so she let her continue.

"I got the feeling she knows a whole lot more than she was saying. Like maybe she's trying to pull a rabbit out of the hat and beat the police and everybody on this thing. But being the only one to know something can be dangerous. I tried to get her to share what she knows with Detective Scovoy."

"You want to go right now?" Charlie asked. "I don't have to check in with Dad's car until noon."

"Sure. Let's take my car and talk strategy on the way over."

CHAPTER TWELVE

Malachi stayed in his motel room until noon on Tuesday, enjoying the rattling heat and television and stash of Vienna sausages, Slim Jims, Saltines and beer he'd brought with him. He'd had two hot showers in two days.

But now he was getting antsy. He pulled aside the curtain and looked out at a pure white sky. Weatherman wasn't calling for snow, but that's what it looked like.

He pulled on his coveralls and backpack, and headed to Jericho Road.

Once Dontegan let him into the basement, he groped behind the water heater until he found the plastic grocery bag containing the maintenance uniform with the name "John" stitched above the shirt pocket. He took a quick sniff. It'd do.

He changed in the half-light that came through a cobwebbed window. *Ol' Charlotte woulda been at home down here*, he thought. That got him thinking 'bout sitting with his granny by the fire on days like this, days too cold to farm, days made for readin'. Pop would be out tending the animals, but Granny knew the best use for a day in February. "That boy is goin' to college," she always told Pop, "the way he loves books." It hadn't worked out like that, though.

Malachi pulled a heavy jacket from behind the heater and switched his coveralls for it. If these coveralls got gone, he'd regret doing this, sure 'nough. But Pastor and Dontegan kept the basement locked unless someone wanted a bike. Malachi would chance it.

He yanked his backpack onto his shoulders, Slick's unreturned tools clanking inside. He grabbed his bike and wheeled it into the late morning cold. Most days, as a homeless man, invisibility came his way unwanted, unsought.

Today he was counting on it.

* * *

After stashing his bike and down-filled jacket behind the towering shrubbery alongside Rutherford Lee's student center, Malachi retraced his steps of Sunday night. Through the side alley door and up the stairs. On a weekday morning, the second floor offices were open, and staff and students walked the carpeted hallway. No one paid attention to the maintenance man carrying a wrench, hammer and who-knew-what.

Malachi pushed through the second floor door into the unheated stairwell where he'd peeked after losing Harry Carlton two nights before. This time, he went all the way to the third floor, quickly eyeing the signs above each office.

From what Miz Branigan had said, that girl she'd been with Sunday worked for the student newspaper. Yep, there it was: *The Swan Song*. Must have something to do with all those birds on the lake.

Malachi knocked, and when no one answered, he looked both ways down the hall, then slipped a long pick from the tools in his hand. Seconds later, he was in the office, door locked behind him.

The room had desks and filing cabinets on three walls, a worn leather couch on the fourth. He turned to his left and went to work.

CHAPTER THIRTEEN

On the drive to Rutherford Lee, Branigan suggested that Charlie call Detective Scovoy and fill him in about Jones Rinehart dating Janie Rose Carlton. "It may not mean anything," she said, "but he needs all the information available."

She listened as Charlie placed the call, heard Chester's questions through the phone. As their conversation wound down, Branigan whispered, "Tell him about Jones being in your room, too."

Charlie related that story, rather haltingly and full of caveats, to the detective. She listened a moment then handed the phone to Branigan. "He wants to speak to you."

"What do you make of Charlie's story?" he asked.

"She's not a nervous Nellie," Branigan said. "If she felt threatened, something was probably going on. But she's not sure."

"And very strange that no one mentioned Jones Rinehart's relationship to the dead girl," he said. "Makes me wonder if he was visiting Charlie to see if she could identify him. And he'd know about the hearse and could get the key easily enough." He paused. "This may sound kind of out there, but do you think Charlie would consider undergoing hypnosis? To see if she could reclaim a memory of seeing anyone in that hearse."

"Interesting thought," Branigan said with a sideways look at Charlie's profile, her red-gold hair gleaming even in the sunless day. "But not for me to say. You'd better ask Liam and Liz and Charlie."

The girl turned. "Ask us what?"

"If you'll be hypnotized."

Charlie looked puzzled.

"We're pulling in," Branigan said into the phone. "I'll tell the Delaneys to call you."

"Branigan, wait. Are you free to have dinner Friday night?"

Her stomach fluttered with unexpected pleasure. "Sure. Tell me where to meet you."

"No, a real date. I'll pick you up."

"Sounds good. See you then."

Branigan handed Charlie's phone back as they veered into the winding turn-off to Rutherford Lee. Branigan slowed before entering the roundabout, and was surprised to see two campus police cars enter the top of the roundabout then exit in quick succession.

"What do you think's wrong?" Charlie asked.

"Don't know. But we're going the way they're going, so we may find out."

Branigan followed more slowly, but was able to see the school's police cars up ahead. They pulled onto the lakeside patio at the student center, parking haphazardly before the doors burst open and uniformed officers spilled out. Branigan counted four.

"That's got to be every cop on duty," she said. "What *is* going on?"

She parked in an adjoining lot, and they ran across the patio and through the doors the officers had used. The dining hall was a third full with an early lunch crowd. Everyone was still serving themselves or eating, clearly not cognizant of whatever was going on. Branigan and Charlie heard the officers' radios squawking overhead and bounded up the stairs to the second floor. Branigan could hear Charlie gasping next to her, and put an arm around the girl.

"Take it easy," she cautioned. "We don't want that leg to snap."

Apparently the occupants of the second-floor offices hadn't been alerted yet. Branigan saw only one woman peering curiously from a doorway. But on the spacious landing that served as a theater lobby, a girl sat on the carpet outside the women's bathroom, head buried in her arms, weeping. A female officer knelt next to her, speaking quietly, as her colleagues fanned out into the darkened theater and the men's bathroom.

Branigan pulled out her *Rambler* ID, but the officers were making no attempt to keep anyone away.

She and Charlie watched as the male officers completed their search of the men's room, then the theater, and turned their attention to the administrative offices. Now people started coming out, glancing at the crying girl shielded by the female officer.

Branigan found a position where she could see the line of offices. A middle-aged woman hurried out of one marked *Vice President, Student Services*, and bent to speak to the crying girl. Together, she and the officer helped her to her feet. The girl turned unsteadily and Branigan was shocked to see blood streaming from her head and down a face that was already swelling. But she was more shocked to see that she recognized the girl.

It was Catherine Reisman. The pledge chair from Gamma Delta Phi.

Catherine's eyes registered shock when they met Branigan's. Then Branigan saw them slide to something behind her. She wheeled to find Anna Hester staring at Catherine.

Anna ignored Branigan and Charlie, and approached her fellow student.

"Catherine, what happened?" she asked. The woman from the vice president's office shooed Anna away. "Not now," she said. "You can get your story from Chief Ellsworth."

"Call me," Anna mouthed. Catherine nodded woodenly.

"We need to get her to the infirmary," the administrator told the officer. "If you haven't finished questioning her, you can do it there."

The officer spoke into the radio on her shoulder. Branigan strained to hear. "White male, five-eight to five-eleven, black ski mask, blue jacket. In other words, could be anybody on this whole campus."

By now the landing was beginning to fill with curious students from the dining hall below. A low buzz followed the administrator, the officer and the student to the elevator. Catherine Reisman gave Branigan an imploring look as the elevator doors closed on her battered face.

Branigan felt the hairs on her arms rise, and she looked around at the confused swirl of young bodies. She shivered. Something was perilously wrong here, hidden beneath the surface of this affluent campus and its bright, attractive students. But it was impossible to tell whether the threat was coming from within or from without.

Chapter Fourteen

Branigan motioned for Charlie to follow her into the women's bathroom. "This will be a crime scene soon," she whispered. "With criminal assault, the school will have to report it to the Grambling PD. I want to look around first. But don't touch anything." She wrapped a paper towel around one hand, then pushed open one door after another in the empty stalls.

"What are you looking for?" Charlie whispered.

"I don't know. I'm hoping something will jump out at me."

She peered all around the sinks and mirrors and paper towel dispensers. Using two paper towels to avoid leaving her own fingerprints, she carefully lifted the lid off the trash can and looked inside. On top lay a bunch of wet paper towels streaked reddish brown. She lowered the lid until it was the way she'd found it.

She pulled out her phone and punched in Chester Scovoy's number. "Have you gotten a call yet from Rutherford Lee?" she asked as soon as he picked up.

"Yeah, we're halfway there. Are you at the school?"

"Yes. Charlie and I stumbled right into the middle of it. The victim is one of the Gamma Delta Phis I've talked to a few times. Pledge chair."

"The same sorority those other two were from?" Chester's voice rose an octave. "What the hell is going on out there?"

"I don't know," said Branigan. "But I'm beginning to agree with you that hypnotizing Charlie might be a good move. Janie Rose and that wreck was where it all started." She put an arm around Charlie. "Meanwhile, I'll keep Charlie with me until I deliver her to Liam."

"Good idea. I'll see you in three minutes."

"Might be a little longer. We're headed upstairs to talk to someone."

Branigan and Charlie entered the frigid stairwell at the end of the hall and climbed to the third floor. They saw Anna Hester turning her key in the door to the *Swan Song* office. The door swung open and Anna screamed.

They ran to the doorway, and inside the room saw Malachi Martin, a wrench in one hand, the other held palm up. "The dean called for maint'nance," he was explaining calmly to Anna.

Charlie looked ready to speak, so Branigan laid a hand on her arm.

"I'm sorry," Anna said, exhaling and sitting heavily on a couch along one wall. "A girl was attacked on the second floor and I'm jumpy."

Branigan broke in. "Um… John…" she said, reading the name above Malachi's pocket. "The victim described her attacker as a white guy in a ski mask. And the Grambling police are on their way."

Without a word, Malachi gathered his tools and left, shutting the office door quietly.

"How did you get here so quickly?" Anna asked, her attention diverted from Malachi to Branigan.

"Complete coincidence. Charlie and I were coming to see you."

"Me? What about?"

Branigan pulled a rolling desk chair over to face Anna. Charlie took a seat at the far end of the couch and spoke up. "Anna, I'm Charlie Delaney. I was driving the day the hearse ran Janie Rose and me off the road. I still have a temporary bridge and got out of arm and leg casts two days ago."

Anna's eyes widened.

"Branigan told me about your stories in *The Swan Song*," Charlie continued, "and that you may have been the last person to see Maylene alive. I mean, other than her killer. I'm hoping you can tell us something that will catch this guy. Too many people are getting hurt."

"I don't know what I can tell you."

231

"Two big things are missing. Janie Rose kept a journal. A blue leather one she wrote in every night." Charlie waited a moment, but Anna didn't speak. "And a phone video that supposedly shows Janie Rose and Maylene."

Anna waited a beat too long, Branigan thought, before asking, "Janie Rose and Maylene doing what?"

"I have no idea. But that's what the homeless man who lived with Maylene said."

Anna remained silent.

"The thing is, Anna, you know these people. You know that Jones Rinehart dated Janie Rose, which we only found out this morning. You know who hung around your sorority house enough to know about the hearse and the key. You may even know things you don't know you know."

Branigan looked at Charlie with admiration. Well, Liam had been a reporter before he went into ministry. Maybe she'd inherited his instincts.

"I swear we are not trying to steal your story," Branigan broke in. "And we can credit you in *The Rambler* with anything you tell us."

"So you want to join forces?" Anna asked.

"You could put it like that," Branigan said with a flicker of hope.

"But what do you have to offer?"

Branigan and Charlie looked at each other. Precious little, both knew.

Charlie tried one more time. "That's not really the point. I'm not a reporter. I don't care about the story, though I'm sure Aunt Brani does. But I want whoever ran me and Janie Rose off the road caught, and I want to be able to go out alone again, and I want my nightmares to stop." Charlie halted, seemingly near tears. "That can't happen until all this is solved."

Anna looked lost in thought. Branigan and Charlie let the silence spin out, uninterrupted.

Then abruptly Anna stood. "An hour ago, I might've said okay. But it's possible I've been reading everything wrong. I've got to think it through."

Branigan sighed. "We have people watching Charlie," she told the young woman. "We're afraid the hearse driver thinks she saw something, even though she didn't. But no one's protecting you. The police are right downstairs. Tell them."

"Maybe," said Anna.

But Branigan heard the *no* in her voice.

Chapter Fifteen

As Branigan and Charlie walked down to the second floor, Branigan called her office to see if Bert wanted a story on Catherine Reisman's assault. Ordinarily, such an incident wouldn't make the newspaper, but the fact that it was the fourth involving a Rutherford Lee student pushed it to the forefront.

Bert wanted it. "Can you dictate a few paragraphs for online, or have you got your laptop handy?"

"I haven't talked to the police yet," said Branigan. "Let me do that, then I'll call it in."

Charlie sat on a bench to rest her aching leg while Branigan caught up with Detective Scovoy. Ordinarily, he wouldn't answer such a call either, but nothing was ordinary these days at the private college. The president and dean, along with the vice president who'd accompanied Catherine to the infirmary, were all on hand, talking to the detective. To their credit, as far as Branigan could tell, they weren't asking him to keep it quiet. They said they'd already sent out a text alert to students and parents with Catherine's description of her attacker.

A young man Branigan assumed was Anna's *Swan Song* editor stood at the president's elbow, taking notes. During her own college days, one student per year – usually the paper's editor-in-chief – took the role of interviewing the president. That kept the president from having to endlessly repeat himself, and ensured a bit of institutional knowledge on the part of the newspaper staff.

The young man now asked if Catherine had been raped. The vice president shook her head vigorously. Branigan pulled out her notebook, introduced herself to the administrators, and began taking notes on Detective Scovoy's briefing. After getting clarification on the time, place, Catherine's injuries, and other details, she asked

Scovoy if he considered this to be an isolated incident or somehow connected to December's murders of former students.

The administrators froze at the question. It occurred to Branigan that while assaults might be fairly common on a college campus, murders were not. And now she had dragged off-campus murders of former students into this on-campus assault. No wonder the administrators looked as though they'd eaten hot peppers. The dean began sputtering that perhaps they'd better wait for their internal media people to arrive.

"Not necessary," Branigan said. "I've got what I need."

Collecting Charlie, she walked out with Detective Scovoy. He'd interviewed Catherine at the infirmary before meeting with the administrators, and was headed to the campus police office for one more consultation.

"What do you think?" Branigan asked him when they were out of earshot of college personnel. "Serial killer on the loose at Rutherford Lee?"

"My, what an active imagination you have, Miss Powers."

"But is this connected? Or entirely random?"

"Good question. It certainly appears random. Girl alone in a restroom in the student center."

"But what about all those offices down the hall?" Branigan asked. "Weren't there a lot of people around?"

"There are smaller bathrooms along the hallway that they use. The bathroom she was in is a large one used by theater-goers."

"So what was she doing in there?"

"She acts occasionally in college productions. I verified that with the dean. She said she goes to the darkened theater sometimes to think. She used the bathroom while she was up there."

"Hmmm. Did she do that regularly enough for this guy to know her pattern?"

"That was my thought. But she said no one's been stalking her and there are no disgruntled ex-boyfriends. Unfortunately her description – black ski mask, blue jacket – are things easily discarded. That leaves us with 'white guy'."

"Yikes."

"Tell me about it."

Branigan and Charlie turned up the Civic's heater full blast before calling the story in to Bert. Charlie called her dad and promised to have his SUV back at Jericho Road within the hour.

"So what now?" she asked Branigan.

"I want to talk to Malachi and find out what he was up to in the newspaper office. And you and Liam can contact Detective Scovoy about hypnosis if you decide to do that. Are you considering it?"

"You know, I think so. I'd do just about anything to get my head cleared of this mess."

Branigan reached over and patted the girl's leg. "I know you would, Char. I hope it helps."

She started the car and headed back to the *Rambler* office. On the way, they saw a figure in a dark puffy coat cycling on the sidewalk toward town. Dreadlocks flew out behind his do-rag and baseball cap.

Charlie pointed. "There's Malachi now."

Branigan passed him, then pulled into an insurance office parking lot and waited for him to catch up. When he pulled alongside her window, she said, "We need to compare notes. Want to meet at Bea's? Or Marshall's? I'm buying."

"Then Marshall's, for some of they veg'table soup," he said.

"Deal."

Branigan returned Charlie to her SUV at the *Rambler* building. She offered to follow her the six blocks to Jericho Road, but Charlie was adamant in her refusal. Nonetheless, Branigan watched her lock her doors and pull out before driving up Main Street to Marshall's.

Malachi was standing outside the popular diner.

"Why are you out here in the cold?" she asked.

He looked impassively at her, and an instant too late she realized he wouldn't be welcome inside if she weren't accompanying him. Her face grew hot.

"I'm sorry, my friend. Let's get some soup."

Branigan felt a few stares as they settled into a booth, but no one said anything. Homeless people might feel invisible on the streets, but in here it was the opposite.

They ordered large bowls of vegetable soup, and Branigan added two sides of cornbread. She leaned across the table so the people behind her couldn't hear. "So what were you doing in the newspaper office?"

"Lookin' for that dead girl's diary or Ralph's phone," he said.

"Any luck?"

"Nah."

"Where were you looking?"

"Desk drawers mostly. Some filin' cabinets."

"Weren't they locked?"

Malachi gave her a rare smile. "You really wanna know that, Miz Branigan?"

She sat back. "Maybe not." She thought for a moment. "And if you got caught, your story was you were maintenance. Not too shabby, *John*. But it could've backfired with the cops sweeping through after the attack on the student."

"Sure coulda. Good thin' that such a whitey campus."

Branigan burst into laughter. "Don't let their diversity officer hear you say that."

He smiled slyly. "You gotta love people who spend a hundred years keepin' us out, then hundreds o' thousands of dollahs to get us in."

"You have a wicked sense of humor, Mr Malachi."

The waitress brought their soup, brimming with tomatoes, okra, onions, corn and green beans from the summer's bounty on the Marshall family farm. Branigan offered Malachi the basket of fragrant cornbread. He took the largest piece and slathered it with butter.

"But what made you think the diary and phone were in the office?"

Malachi took his time, chewing cornbread and taking a few spoonfuls of soup before answering.

"That girl," he said finally.

"Anna Hester?"

"Yeah, the way she act Sunday night."

"How did she act?"

"Like she the reporter and you some kind of groupie."

Branigan cocked her head.

"Miz Branigan, I read *The Rambler* enough to know you a damn good writer. I seen years you won all them Georgia Press awards and maybe even a national or two if I 'member rightly."

Branigan shrugged an assent.

"But that girl actin' like she's the Diane Sawyer of Georgia. So I have to wonder, 'What she got up her sleeve?' Tha's all." He returned his attention to his soup and cornbread.

"You got all that from walking her to my car Sunday night?"

"And ridin' to her sor'ity house."

"I know you're observant, but I can't imagine she was throwing off that many vibes."

He put down his spoon. "Miz Branigan, what you think is the No. 1 require-ment for a reporter?"

"Accuracy. Fairness."

"No, before that. What's the thin' makes you want to be a reporter in the firs' place?"

"Curiosity, I guess."

"Zactly! So you and this Anna hear somebody next door in her office on a Sunday night when ain't nobody supposed to be there. Then a homeless guy jumps out of the bushes and grabs you. Then you pretty much accuse her of meetin' with the daddy of one of them dead girls. And what does she say?"

"She didn't say much of anything."

"Zactly! She didn't say nothin'. She didn't ax no questions. Either she ain't got the curiosity God gave a cat, or she so focused on somethin' else she can't see what's in front of her."

Branigan sat back. "You amaze me. You don't look at what's there, but at what's not there."

He shrugged.

"I remember last summer, you kept harping on about the respect that *wasn't there* for Vesuvius Hightower's painting," she continued. "And you were right. That's what led you to the answer. And, incidentally, to pricing Vesuvius's work out of my range." She smiled. "But anyway, about Anna. You may be onto something. When I first met her, she *was* eager to watch me and Jody work. Later she became almost dismissive."

"Like the cat ate the canary, my granny used to say."

Branigan grinned. She found Malachi's mixture of sophistication and rural-speak hilarious. He was like no one she'd ever met – a homeless man with deep wells of knowledge and intuition.

"I've felt all along that she knows something about Maylene and Ralph that she's not saying," she mused. "Before I went into her office that night, I saw her messing with two phones. She slipped one inside her purse. I think it might have been Ralph's with the video."

"And since she knew Miz Maylene…" Malachi trailed off. He changed tack abruptly. "What kinda purse she carry, that Miz Anna?"

"Uh oh. What are you thinking?"

"You never mind. What kinda purse?"

"Black pebbled leather with a single shoulder strap. They're called hobo bags or slouch purses. They hold a lot of stuff."

"Hobo bags, huh? You think Jericho Road's coat room might have one?"

Branigan look puzzled. "No, but the Salvation Army thrift store might."

Malachi pulled a pencil and piece of paper from his coat pocket, and scribbled a note.

Branigan went back to her original concern. "I think she's trying to write a blockbuster story for this Saturday's *Swan Song*."

"Then one way or 'nother, we gonna know what she up to."

Branigan thought Malachi looked worried at the prospect.

CHAPTER SIXTEEN

Liz, Liam and Charlie sat down to a dinner of pork loin, mashed potatoes, French-style green beans with almonds, and sourdough rolls.

"Comfort food for the day you've had, my dear," said Liz, kissing the top of her daughter's head. "Or rather, the winter you've had."

"Thanks, Mom." Charlie spooned a huge helping of potatoes onto her plate. "This hits the spot."

Charlie and Liam had spent the afternoon on the phone with Detective Scovoy. He'd arranged for Charlie to visit a therapist the next morning – one who specialized in hypnosis. Nearing retirement, Dr Mellicent Hayes was easing out of her private practice and spending time at the counseling center at Rutherford Lee. She agreed to fit Charlie in between student clients mid-morning. Both the detective and Liz planned to be in the waiting room.

After dinner the Delaneys turned on the gas fire in their living room – Liz's one modern concession in renovating the early twentieth-century house – and settled in to watch *Forrest Gump* on HBO. They'd seen it before, lots of times in fact. But Liz and Charlie cried every time the young Jenny threw stones at the house where she grew up, and Forrest said, "Sometimes, I guess there just aren't enough rocks."

As the feather floated away at film's end, Charlie wiped her eyes. "Dad, do you think that's what happened to Tiffany Lynn?"

Liam had lost the thread of her thinking. "Do I think what happened?"

"Sexual abuse."

"Oh. Yes, it's possible. I think most of the homeless people we see – women *and* men – have sexual trauma in their backgrounds."

"And they never get over it?"

"I wouldn't put it like that exactly. But sure, sometimes it can victimize a person, sort of set them up for repeated incidents of abuse. Prevent the development of self-esteem. Make them define themselves by their relationships. That's where we run into trouble getting people away from their abusers."

"Like Maylene?"

"Like Maylene. We can see that a woman has so much potential, talent, intelligence, you name it. But if she can't see it, we'll talk ourselves blue in the face and make no headway."

"But the story in *The Rambler* about Maylene made it sound like she wasn't like that. She was smart, acted in theater, worked with the homeless. Her family sounded normal. What would make her stay with that loser Ralph?"

"That's the sixty-four-thousand-dollar question. I still have no idea what was going on there. We do occasionally see people from middle-class or even wealthy backgrounds who want nothing to do with their families. You never know what's really under the surface. But the fact that Maylene told her family she was in Atlanta rather than homeless in Grambling sounds like she deliberately misled them. Whether that was out of shame, or fear that they'd force her to come home, I have no idea."

"It's sad, isn't it, Dad? For people to live like that."

"Oh, yeah, Charlie. Very sad."

The hearse was inches from Charlie's driver's side door, flying down the road beside her Jeep. Next to her, Janie Rose was splayed against the seat, her face like white plaster.

Suddenly the hearse jerked toward the driver's side, and Charlie tried to scream as the Jeep sheered over the embankment, rolling over and over. She tried again to yell and couldn't. But someone was. Piercingly. And in the fogginess that surrounded her brain, she realized it was Janie Rose. Then the Jeep made one final roll and slammed into something, and all was silent. The silence was even worse than the screams.

Charlie was trapped. She felt herself trying to wake up, to open her eyes, to move an arm or a leg, but she seemed to be pinned under a great weight. Then she heard the far-off jangle of bells that came closer and closer until a sleigh passed the Jeep's cracked window. Outside, there was snow on the ground – and a white-haired Mrs Claus, wearing a red suit trimmed in white fur, drove a team of reindeer. Atop each reindeer was a giggling, tiny elf in a shiny green suit, turned-up slippers and a pointy green hat.

Charlie tried to scream again, and this time she must have managed some sound, for someone was touching her shoulder, shaking her, trying to break through the heaviness that was on her chest.

Charlie woke with an ear-splitting shriek, flailing against Liz's grasp.

"Charlie, Charlie, it's all right," her mother said. "You're having a bad dream."

She looked around wildly, heart pounding, not entirely sure Mrs Claus and those elves weren't there in her dresser mirror, behind her mother in the darkened room. Gradually, her heart slowed. But she had no desire to return to sleep, to risk the possibility of sliding back into the dream. She sat up.

"What was it?" asked Liz.

"I was back in the Jeep," Charlie said slowly. "But I actually *had* the wreck this time. The Jeep flipped and we hit the tree. And then there was snow on the ground and Mrs Claus and the sleigh and the reindeer and the elves were right outside my window." She glanced at her bedroom window as if a sleigh might appear there. She shuddered. "Mom, I know it sounds crazy. But it seemed so real."

"That's how dreams are."

"Do you think this therapist can get rid of them?"

"I sure hope so." She smiled and hugged her daughter. "Otherwise nobody's going to get much sleep around here."

Liz finished a rather fitful night in Charlie's double bed. They slept past 8 o'clock and had a leisurely breakfast of oatmeal and toast, dawdling over coffee and passing *The Rambler* back and forth.

Together they did the paper's word puzzles, trying to beat each other to the answers.

They left in time to be at Rutherford Lee's counseling center well before Charlie's 10:30 appointment. The center had its own private, pillared entrance on one end of an academic building that housed the history, psychology, English and foreign language departments. Inside its comfortable waiting room, Charlie and Liz joined Detective Scovoy.

Charlie was too nervous to read the *Time* magazine she picked up; she discarded it in favor of the week's *Swan Song*. She scanned an editorial page rant about the administration's refusal to allow guns on campus. *Hang tough*, she silently encouraged administrators. Her eye skittered to a column at the bottom of the same page on recent actions taken by the Honor Council. A thumbnail photograph of the author, Dr Sylvia Eckhart, showed an attractive woman with a sleek white bob framing her face.

Suddenly, Charlie's breathing quickened, and with a shaking hand she tugged on Detective Scovoy's sleeve.

He leaned toward her. "Charlie, what is it?"

Charlie pointed to the picture. "I don't have to be hypnotized," she said, pointing. "There's Mrs Claus. I remember now."

CHAPTER SEVENTEEN

B ranigan and Jody got soft drinks from the vending machine at the Law Enforcement Center as they awaited a statement on officers' interrogation of Sylvia Eckhart. Jody had already learned that Dr Eckhart was not being immediately charged but was being interviewed as a "person of interest". He wouldn't have gotten that much had he and Branigan not arrived at the LEC on the heels of Scovoy and the professor. They had Charlie to thank for that.

The police had sequestered Dr Eckhart for two hours, during which time a gray-suited woman entered the room. The reporters exchanged glances, knowing that the presence of an attorney raised the possibility of charges. The two were discussing which one should remain and which should return to the newsroom when the door flew open and a grim-faced Detective Scovoy emerged. "The PIO will have a statement at 2 o'clock," he said, referring to the department's public information officer. He strode off down the hallway.

By unspoken agreement, Jody followed the detective, and Branigan hurried to the parking lot to take up a position near Dr Eckhart's Prius. She remained out of sight until she saw Dr Eckhart shake hands with her attorney. The lawyer hoisted her briefcase into a black BMW and left. Branigan stepped forward to intercept Dr Eckhart before she reached her car.

"Branigan!" she said, visibly shaken to see her. "So you know?"

Branigan didn't know nearly as much as she'd like to, but hoped to learn more by pretending she did. So she nodded. "Charlie identified you as being at the wreck site. She said you came down the embankment and looked inside her car. Why didn't you help her?"

"I did! Who do you think called 911?"

Branigan was startled. "You forced the girls off the road and then called for help?"

"No! No! I wasn't in the hearse. I came along minutes later and saw the wreck and called it in. The police checked my phone and verified it."

"But why didn't you stay? And why didn't you tell anyone?"

"Because I was afraid that exactly what has happened would happen. I'm being charged with accessory after the fact and obstruction of justice. My lawyer talked them into letting me turn myself in tomorrow morning." She strangled back a sob. "I swear I didn't hurt those girls. I was not in that hearse."

Branigan looked at her skeptically. "But you know who was."

Dr Eckhart shook her head. "No. I didn't know it would come to this. How could I?"

Crying in earnest now, Dr Eckhart got into her Prius and wheeled out of the parking lot. Branigan saw an unmarked Crown Victoria pull out of a spot on the far end and turn in the same direction.

Branigan was waiting in the newsroom when Jody returned from the Law Enforcement Center. It turned out the police were being more cagey with information than Sylvia Eckhart had been. Jody suspected that the cops had gone along with her attorney's request for a day to get her affairs in order in the hope that Dr Eckhart would lead them to the hearse driver.

The reporters huddled with Bert Feldspar at the city editor's desk. "I don't have much on the record," Jody admitted. "The police haven't released the charges, since they don't have Dr Eckhart in custody."

"We have to have their confirmation," said Bert. "They might have been trying to scare the professor and won't actually charge her. We'd end up running a retraction." He turned to his computer. "Tell me the minute you get something solid, and we'll run with it."

Branigan and Jody retreated to the conference room and shut the door. "Let's not worry about what we can run for a minute," she said, "and think about what might have happened. Do you know what Dr Eckhart told the police?"

"I got this off the record from a uni, not from Scovoy. She denied everything except stumbling upon the accident. They verified that she did call 911, but she was gone by the time the Georgia patrol got there. That's why they know she's hiding something. It doesn't make sense that she'd leave the scene, especially since she's a colleague of Ina Rose Carlton. I mean, what kind of monster leaves a friend's daughter like that?"

"Why does she say she did?"

"Something about fear of being blamed."

"But why would she be blamed, if she's sitting there in a friggin' red Prius?"

Jody shrugged. "If she thought both girls were dead, there'd be no one to say it was a hearse and not a Prius that ran them off the road. Maybe the person in the hearse threatened *her* with that scenario."

"That's an interesting idea." Branigan paused. "But say it's not fear of being blamed. Is there anything else that could explain why Dr Eckhart would follow the hearse and then protect the driver?"

When Jody was silent, she answered her own question. "Maybe she's more afraid of the driver than she is of the police."

"Or if not fear, then what?" Jody followed her line of thinking. "Loyalty? Didn't you say she was a Kappa Ep? Could she be protecting them? The hearse *is* theirs. They're the most obvious candidates. Greeks gone wild."

Branigan ignored the quip. "But Jones Rinehart dates Maggie Fielding, who's also a Kappa Ep. So he would have easy access to the hearse key too. And he used to date Janie Rose Carlton."

"Have you given up any idea of Harry Carlton's enemies or creditors having a hand in it?" Jody asked. "I can't imagine what connection they'd have with Dr Eckhart. Unless maybe she knew the Carltons before they ever came to Georgia? Where is she from originally?"

"I don't think I know. She said she went to the University of Michigan. Maybe that's a place to start."

"And let's not forget Ralph. He's still a prime suspect for Maylene's murder. So if the two deaths are connected..."

"You're giving me a headache," Branigan said.

* * *

Back at her desk Branigan placed calls to her grandparents, the University of Michigan and the national Kappa Epsilon Chi sorority as she began to gather information on Sylvia Eckhart. Maybe something in her background would trigger an explanation for her bizarre behavior.

Mid-afternoon the receptionist rang her. "Catherine Reisman and Emma Ratcliffe to see you."

"Really? Send them up." Branigan walked to the elevator to meet the girls. Catherine wore a camel-colored fedora pulled low over her auburn bangs that didn't hide the angry contusions on her face as much as she probably hoped. Emma had an arm around her, as if to steady her friend.

Both girls wore knee-length overcoats over tapered slacks and boots. Emma was the first to speak. "Miss Powers, the police have questioned Catherine, but they won't tell us anything. We read your story about her attack this morning. We were hoping you could tell us if they're close to finding who did this."

Branigan ushered the girls through the newsroom and watched her colleagues' eyes follow them, openly inquisitive. Malachi had a point. Reporters *were* a curious bunch, and didn't bother hiding it. She started to invite Jody to join them, then thought the girls might be more forthcoming without him. She wanted to use this time to do more than share what she knew.

"Can I get you anything?" she asked. "Water? Coffee? Coke?"

The girls declined, shucking their overcoats to reveal cashmere underneath. "Okay then," Branigan said as they settled themselves at one end of the conference table. "How can I help you?"

Emma leaned forward, her blue eyes laser focused on Branigan. "Are the police near an arrest on the man who attacked Catherine? All our sisters are absolutely panicked that he's still on the loose."

Branigan hadn't expected that. "Your sisters?" she repeated. "Your sorority sisters are panicked?" She let the question dangle.

"Isn't it obvious? Two former Gamma Delts have been killed and now Catherine is attacked."

Branigan opened her mouth, but nothing came out. She turned to Catherine. "Catherine, you don't think it was a matter of being in the wrong place at the wrong time?"

Catherine shrugged, her eyes filling with tears.

"It hurts her to talk," Emma jumped in. Catherine nodded – gratefully, it seemed to Branigan.

"To answer your question, no, I don't think the police are terribly close on this," Branigan said. "The problem is Catherine's description. Once you remove the black ski mask and blue jacket, which the guy probably *did* remove very quickly, you've got a white male. That's half the students, professors and staff at Rutherford Lee. Plus any manner of vendor, cafeteria worker or campus visitor." She leaned toward Catherine. "Is there nothing else you remember? Age? Voice? Tattoos? Body hair?"

Tears began to spill down Catherine's cheeks. Branigan excused herself and walked through the newsroom, where she located a box of tissues on Lou Ann's desk. "Okay if I steal a couple of these?"

"Sure," said Lou Ann. "What's going on in there?"

"Something I hadn't considered before. I'm going to have to think about it."

She returned to the conference room and handed Catherine the tissues. "Came... fro... 'hind," the girl said, moving her face muscles as little as possible. "Coulden ... see."

"How did you know he was white?"

Catherine held out her left hand and pointed to it with her right.

"She saw his hands," Emma said unnecessarily.

"Were they smooth? Hairy? Did you scratch him?"

"Older," Catherine said. "Rougher... Diden scratch."

Emma jerked her head around to look at her friend, whose tears had resumed.

"Okay," Branigan said.

She turned to Emma. "Tell me about the sisters: what they're thinking, what they're saying."

"Well, when Janie Rose and Maylene died, they had been gone for a year. Nobody really thought anything of it." She corrected herself. "I mean, we were sad. Of course. But nobody thought it had anything to do with the school or the Gamma Delts." She took a deep breath, opened her blue eyes wide. "But when Catherine was attacked… I don't know, it was like it hit close to home, you know? It was like, 'Geez, does somebody have it in for us?'"

"I could see how you'd think that if it had happened in the house," Branigan said. "But over in the student center, in a relatively isolated bathroom, it seems more random."

Emma nodded vigorously. "It could be. And I sure hope you're right. Maybe we're being paranoid."

"What does Marianne think?"

"She's worried too, but trying not to show it. Trying to be strong for the younger girls. Lots of their parents called after the school sent out that text alert."

"Are any of the parents pulling them out of school?"

"Not yet. The college is spinning it as the kind of thing that can happen anywhere. They're saying to make sure we go everywhere in twos or threes."

"That's smart."

Emma reached for her coat. "Maybe we are overreacting, Miss Powers. But I hope they catch this guy soon."

Catherine reached for her coat, moving gingerly.

Branigan looked at her with sympathy. "I'm really sorry this happened to you, Catherine."

The girl tried to smile, but it came across as a grimace. She nodded and pulled her fedora lower for the walk through the newsroom. As she escorted them out, Branigan considered telling them about Sylvia Eckhart's impending arrest. The girls entered the elevator and the doors began to close. Branigan reached out an arm, and the doors glided back open. They looked at her expectantly, and she changed her mind.

"One more thing," she said. "I don't think I've ever seen you guys in your Gamma Delt shirts. What are your colors?"

"Green and white," said Emma. "Why?"

"Just curious."

Chapter Eighteen

Malachi dumped the clothes from his backpack into a laundry basket at Jericho Road. The navy uniform went right in with the white underwear and socks (well, at one time they'd been white). Also, a gray hoodie, jeans, camo pants and two Army green T-shirts faded nearly to the sand color of his old Desert Storm uniform. Dontegan wasn't big on separating colors. Darks, whites and in between went into the one load a week you got.

"They be ready in 'bout an hour," Dontegan said, shoving his clipboard at Malachi to sign. No one else was doing laundry on this Wednesday afternoon, but that Dontegan, he was a stickler for rules. Malachi signed and checked the box for *Chore*.

"What kinda chore you need doin'?" he asked.

Dontegan pointed to the kitchen. "Kitchen need moppin'. That Church o' God spilled pancake syrup on the flo' this mornin' and I ain't been able to get up th' stick-y."

Malachi headed for the mop closet. "Yo' got it."

An hour later, he was finished mopping and redressed in his maintenance uniform, toasty from the dryer. He got Dontegan to open the basement so he could fetch his bike, then rode it to the nearby Salvation Army thrift store. Chaining the bike to a rack out front, he made his way to the women's section, to the shelves that held pocketbooks and shoes. He pulled out the note he'd made when Miz Branigan was explaining a "hobo bag" or "slouch purse". But "black pebbled"? What the heck was that? He fingered the purses, getting more confused by the minute.

Finally, he looked around for the tell-tale red apron of an employee. He saw a heavyset black woman hanging up pants, and recognized her from meals at Jericho Road. Kalina. Kamina.

Katrina. Something like that. She'd moved from crack house to friend's house to abandoned house, he knew, but she must be staying in the Salvation Army now. If you moved into the shelter, you best get a job right quick or they'd get one for you.

"Ma'am," he said, approaching her.

"Mr Malachi," she said. "How you?"

"You in the Sallie?"

"Yeah, it got too cold where I been stayin'. Horace, he in jail since October. So I got in. Ain't too bad."

"I need some he'p. Can you show me —" he looked at his paper — "a 'black pebbled hobo purse or slouch bag'?"

She looked at him in a way that said Miz Branigan's description might not be everyone's, then led the way to the rack where dozens of purses dangled.

She picked up a red leather bag with a single strap. "I think this here a 'hobo purse'," she said. "And that one." She pointed to a similar black one. "But I don't know nothin' 'bout no *pebbles*. Wha's tha' mean anyway?"

"I dunno. I guess I'll take tha' black hobo."

She nodded and pulled it free of its hook. "It's three dollah."

Malachi followed her to a cash register.

His next stop was the outside barrel under the store's drive-through awning. Folks drove up and unloaded their stuffed trunks into grocery carts. But some things were so worn or tattered or busted that employees tossed them in the discard barrel on the spot. Malachi had heard workers talk about the drivers after they left. *Why rich people think anybody want they nasty ol' crap?*

The two men working with donations weren't near the barrel. Malachi rummaged through broken toys and stained clothes until he found a few things that would work: a cracked candy dispenser, a filthy baseball with the stitching coming unraveled, two bent forks, and best of all, a floral case with a busted latch that once held glasses. He didn't care a whole lot what went in the purse. He needed things of a certain size and weight.

With the discards inside, he hefted the purse onto one shoulder.

He'd never carried a woman's pocketbook, but this must be about right. He stuffed it inside his backpack, settled the pack between his shoulder blades, and jumped on the bike.

The February day was dreary and freezing. He hadn't seen the sun in two days, come to think of it. Malachi rode through the cold, eyes watering. He arrived at the college, face near to frozen but his body sweating inside the uniform and coat. He rode under the brick arch, around the fountain, and followed the campus road to the student center. He shoved the bike and coat behind those helpful shrubs, then slipped up the inside stairs.

The *Swan Song* office was lit up. He looked through the glass in the door, but could see only two young men. He walked back down the stairs, got his bike and rode to those big houses where all the fraternity and sorority kids stayed. He straddled the bike in front of the house where Miz Branigan had dropped Anna Hester. Should he go inside? He could say somebody had called maintenance. But he'd need to get into her room, and that wasn't likely to happen. He hadn't thought this through entirely, he admitted to himself.

Malachi wheeled around and rode back to the student center. Might as well look through the dining hall. It was half filled with students eating a late lunch. He pulled a baseball cap from his hip pocket and tucked his cornrows under it. That should be enough to keep Anna Hester from recognizing him. It'd been dark on the sidewalk and in Miz Branigan's car, and she'd never looked directly at him anyway.

He entered the dining hall hearing his granny shrill in his ear about wearing a hat to the table. He was glad to see a group of maintenance workers seated across the room. Their uniforms were steel gray, but he doubted anyone would notice his was different.

Walking into the serving area, he picked up a tray and filled a glass with ice and water, giving him time to scout the room. Finally, he spotted her. She was sitting with a girl and three boys at the far end of the table closest to some kind of conveyor belt that carried dirty dishes. He couldn't see her purse from this angle, but it had to be under the table.

Anna and the other girl stood and walked toward Malachi. He dropped behind the salad bar as if he'd lost his napkin, and watched as they stood in line at the self-serve ice-cream station. This was his chance. Staying blocked by the salad bar until the last moment, he stood and passed behind the girls, and walked rapidly to their table. The three boys were deep in conversation. Malachi placed his tray on an adjacent table, and dropped a spoon. He crouched as if to get it, sliding the Salvation Army purse from his backpack and across the floor in a single motion, and pulling Anna's black one from beneath the chair legs. The boys didn't look down. Malachi slipped Anna's purse into his backpack, sat down and drank his water.

His shirt was soaked with nervous sweat, but no one paid any attention to the maintenance man who got up, hoisted a backpack, and put his tray and plastic water glass on the conveyor belt.

Outside, he pulled on his coat and hopped on his bike, pedaling fast until he was past the college gate. He rode hard, his heart banging against his ribs and his breath coming in gasps, until he reached the insurance office parking lot where Miz Branigan and Miz Charlie had found him yesterday. He stopped with a screech of tires and yanked Anna's purse from his backpack, feeling its bumpy surface. So that was what "pebbled" meant. He reached a hand inside and found a smart phone, then plunged in again and came out with a cracked and battered flip phone.

His face split into a grin. He'd seen this phone before. Had seen it right outside his own tent when Ralph was yakking away.

CHAPTER NINETEEN

B ranigan, Jody and Bert were seated in Tan-4's plush office overlooking Main Street. It was late afternoon and they were trying to determine the extent of the story they had on Sylvia Eckhart. Without official charges by the police, they had to be careful not to overstate the case and face a retraction.

But they did have her interrogation as a "person of interest", and they did have her own admission to Branigan about being at the scene of the wreck, calling 911 and leaving. Branigan had quotes from the college administration (surprise and horror), from a colleague (disbelief), and from Kappa Epsilon president Sophie Long (puzzlement). After a very uncomfortable silence on the phone, Ina Rose Carlton had declined to comment.

Tan-4 leaned back in his leather chair, lacing his fingers behind his head. "Powers, the strongest thing we have is your interview. We can go with that. And you think the police are following her now?"

"That's what it looked like with that Crown Vic pulling out after her," Branigan said.

"Then I'm thinking we go online now with what we've got. 'College professor, Honor Council head, no less, happens upon deadly wreck in which a colleague's daughter is killed, and flees before the cops arrive.' That's weird as hell.

"Jody, you keep calling Scovoy and that bunch every hour. I want this the minute they move on charging her.

"Bert, hold room on the front for tomorrow. We've got about six hours for something else to break."

The reporters headed out the door, but Tan called Branigan back. Closing the door, he said, "I hear you're dating the lead detective on this story."

"Who told you that?"

"That's not important. What's important is putting a wall between you and him as a source."

Branigan hesitated. "Look, I can see why you'd think that. But it really hasn't risen to the level of 'dating' yet. We've literally been out for drinks once and dinner twice. I didn't think it'd reached the level that I needed to tell you *or* pull back from the story."

"That's not your call to make."

Branigan held his gaze for a moment. His face was impassive. "Fine," she said. "What do you want me to do?"

"I want Jody – and only Jody – dealing with this Scovoy. And after we wrap up this story, I don't want you handling any stories involving the Grambling PD."

"That's a little drastic, don't you think?"

"No, I don't. Look, Powers, it's not that I think you're going to be swayed by him or take it easy on him. But we've got to be above reproach when it comes to appearances. You can't be covering your boyfriend."

"I can't tell you how far off base that is."

"Maybe so. But that's the way it's got to be. So no more Grambling PD if you're going to keep seeing him."

Branigan walked out of Tan's office, making a herculean effort not to slam his door. She felt deflated and embarrassed. Not being allowed on police stories would put a serious crimp in her career. She'd have to think this through when she had more time.

Her ringing phone ended her reverie. It was the assistant to the national director of Kappa Epsilon Chi.

"Miss Powers, we've searched our records and they show that no Sylvia Eckhart has ever been a Kappa Epsilon Chi member – at the University of Michigan or anywhere else."

"That can't be right. What decades did you look at?"

"All the way back to the founding in 1952. We've got a national database. Are you sure you have her maiden name?"

"Oh, that must be it. Probably not. Let me get back to you."

She hung up and dialed her grandparents' number. When her

grandfather answered, she said, "Still on this Sylvia Eckhart angle, Granddad. Do you know what her maiden name was?"

"It's Eckhart," he replied. "She never married."

Branigan slowly rolled her chair in a full circle, head back, staring at the ceiling and noticing the loose tiles and water stains from some mysterious leak on the third floor. So Sylvia Eckhart had never been a Kappa Ep. Why in the world would she say she was? And why had she been on the front porch of the Kappa Ep house, talking to Anna Hester?

Branigan lurched up straight, so quickly the boomeranging chair back almost sent her flying to the floor. Was Dr Eckhart warning Anna Hester about Ralph's videos? Or was she confronting her?

She walked over to Jody's desk. "Sylvia Eckhart lied about being a Kappa Ep," she said quietly. "Why would she do that?"

Jody twirled his chair around. "That's interesting. You think maybe she got blackballed in her undergrad days and has it in for them?"

"That seems a little extreme."

"This whole thing seems a little extreme. Not to mention bizarre."

The reporters were silent for a minute. "Okay, how about this?" Branigan said. "Sylvia Eckhart is protecting someone or afraid of someone. Maybe it has nothing to do with the Kappa Eps and that stupid hearse. But the very fact that she lied must mean something." She threw up her hands in frustration.

Jody turned his back to her. "Time for my check-in with the Grambling PD. I'll get back to you in a minute."

As he dialed the number, the police scanner beside his desk squawked to life. Scovoy picked up his phone, but Branigan, three feet away, could hear bedlam in the background.

"What's going on?" Jody asked, brow furrowed as he tried to make sense of the noise hitting him from both the phone and the scanner. Branigan untangled the cacophony before he did.

"Rutherford Lee," the scanner crackled. "All available units."

"My car's on the street," Jody yelled. "I'll drive. Bert, we're headed to Rutherford Lee."

Branigan grabbed her coat and they rocketed down the stairs and out the glass door, startling the circulation employees as they hurtled past. They hopped into the mottled blue Buick Jody had driven as long as she'd known him. He yanked it out of its space, not bothering to look behind him.

They reached the brick arch of the college and raced onto the roundabout. Branigan rolled down her window to listen for sirens. "The student center," she said, pointing. The Buick rattled ominously as Jody took the speed bumps too fast.

The screaming sirens made it easy to locate the police. Four marked cars, blue lights spinning, were parked helter-skelter around the lakeside terrace of the student center, where a small crowd of students had gathered. Two paramedics were on the ground, obscuring the object of their interest.

Detective Scovoy knelt beside them, his head bent low.

Jody got as close as he could to the detective, while Branigan circled around the students and came up beside a young Hispanic man. He stepped aside and she had a straight view of a young girl's twisted body, an arm and one jeans-clad leg lying at impossible angles.

"She fell," said the helpful young man, pointing to the third floor window open above them. "Or jumped."

"What is that?" Branigan asked as she peered up at the open window.

"The student newspaper office."

Branigan had a sinking feeling she knew whose body lay on the patio.

With the police focused on the terrace, Branigan slipped into the dining hall, deserted at this time of day except for a few cafeteria workers using their down time to eat. She bolted for the stairway, passing several administrators hurrying outside.

No one paid her any attention as she entered the stairwell and raced to the third floor. She heard sobbing as soon as she pushed the door bar.

Sylvia Eckhart sat huddled on the hallway floor across from the open *Swan Song* door.

Branigan ducked into the newspaper office, searching for the police officer she expected to be tailing Dr Eckhart. Both rooms of the office were empty, but her gaze snagged on a woman's purse spilled open beneath the window, where a freezing wind whipped in. Branigan took a pen from her own purse and used it to gently lift one flap. Inside was a dirty baseball, a glasses case made of floral fabric, what looked like a child's plastic toy and, oddest of all, two forks. No phones. Mystified, she left the pocketbook where it lay. She figured she had only moments before Chester's officers stormed in.

She returned to the hallway and knelt next to the crying professor. "Dr Eckhart? What happened?"

Sylvia Eckhart looked at her with a tear-streaked face, mascara running.

"It's all my fault," she hiccupped. "I thought I was helping, but…" She trailed off.

Branigan pressed. "What happened to Anna?"

Dr Eckhart broke into fresh sobs. "Anna knew everything. Everything. I warned her…" Again she broke into violent, shuddering tears.

"Did you push her?"

That broke through. Dr Eckhart looked at Branigan with horror. "No! No! No! I was trying to prevent this!"

Branigan heard footsteps pounding on the stairwell. She knew her time was almost up. "Then tell me what happened."

"I came up to…" The stairwell door banged open and two policewomen burst through, guns drawn.

"Are you Branigan Powers?" asked one. When Branigan nodded, the officer kept her gun on Sylvia Eckhart, but spoke to the reporter. "Detective Scovoy is looking for you."

"Are you arresting Dr Eckhart?"

"Absolutely. Sylvia Eckhart, you have the right to remain silent…"

Chapter Twenty

B ranigan entered the second-floor conference room that college administrators had handed over to the Grambling police. Already, she saw, they'd brought in pens, pads and bottled water. When Detective Scovoy saw her, he motioned for the president.

"We also need an office," he said.

"No problem." The president turned to a younger colleague standing uncertainly at one end of the conference table. "Ed's is the closest. Ed, let's give them your office for the time being. Please clear enough space for them to use your desk."

"That's not necessary," Scovoy said. "I just need a quiet space for debriefings. Miss Powers, you're first."

He escorted her into Ed's office, which had separate doors opening onto the conference room and the main hallway. Closing both, he took one of two upholstered chairs and motioned for Branigan to sit on the other.

"Is she dead?" Branigan asked softly.

"No. I'm not sure if she'll make it, but the paramedics took her to St Joe's."

Branigan closed her eyes.

The detective didn't waste time. "As I'm sure you know, the girl is Anna Hester. She's a reporter for the student newspaper. She fell or jumped or was pushed out of the office's third-floor window. She was trying to talk when we arrived, but I could make out only two words. I need you to tell me what they mean."

Branigan leaned in. "What were they?"

"'Find Mackenzie.'"

Branigan sat back. She wasn't expecting that. "So she didn't tell you if she'd been pushed?"

"Well, that's just it. I'm not sure what she was trying to say. I know you wrote about a Mackenzie from Columbia. But she's in a wheelchair, right?"

"Wait a minute. You think Anna was trying to say that Mackenzie *pushed* her?"

Chester ran one hand through his hair. "That's what I'm asking you. Is it possible Anna was giving us the name of her attacker?"

"I sure wouldn't think so." Branigan stared at the ceiling, trying to collect her thoughts, remembering Mackenzie Broadus's unnamed fear, remembering her brother Tony's soft words, *What are you gonna do?*

"Run through that story again for me," Scovoy said. "I want to make sure I've got the details right."

"Mackenzie Broadus was a freshman classmate of Janie Rose Carlton and Maylene Ayers," Branigan said. "One night after coming back from Christmas break, they got drunk and went for a walk around campus. Mackenzie climbed up on the football goalpost and was doing gymnastics. She fell and broke her back. Janie Rose and Maylene took her to the hospital, and she was helicoptered to another hospital in Columbia. As far as I know, she lives there with her parents. And she's definitely in a wheelchair. That's no act." Branigan's eyes pulled away from the detective's face.

"But?" he pressed.

"Well, Charlie and I wondered if maybe someone who loved her, a brother or boyfriend or somebody, could be behind all this."

"Like they blamed Janie Rose and Maylene for her being paralyzed?"

Branigan nodded. "I met her older brother."

"And?"

"I just don't know. Was he upset about what happened? Sure. He *said* he didn't blame a couple of eighteen-year-olds for making a bad decision. But then he called me when you guys wouldn't give him information. And he said the girls *were* responsible."

Scovoy looked pensive. "That would explain what Anna said. She was definitely trying to tell me something." He stood abruptly and opened the door to the conference room. "Get Detective Rogerson on the phone," he called to a uniformed officer. "Let me know as soon as you've got him."

He closed the door again. "We'll send Jim to South Carolina to check alibis and see if Mackenzie will come to Grambling. If not, I'll need to go down there. But I hate to spend the time on the road. Give me the brother's name."

"Tony Broadus."

"He lives in Columbia?"

"I assume so."

He looked lost in thought for a moment. Branigan hated to interrupt, but her curiosity got the better of her.

"You arrested Dr Eckhart," she said. "I thought you had an officer following her."

"We did," he said. "She must have spotted him. She went into the dining hall and he took a seat to keep an eye on her. She went to the serving stations, but then disappeared. Must've ducked through the kitchen. By the time he figured it out and called in, all hell was breaking loose on the patio."

"Wow. So I guess she sneaked upstairs. Chester, she saw what happened."

"I agree. But she can't stop crying. I'm afraid if we keep pushing, she may have a complete breakdown."

"She must've gone to the *Swan Song* office to confront Anna."

"About what?"

"I think maybe Anna had gotten hold of Ralph's phone and was planning to write a story for the college newspaper. It comes out on Saturdays."

He stared at her. "So Anna was playing a dangerous game."

"That's what I tried to tell her. I begged her to tell you whatever she knew."

"And do you know what she was going to write?"

"No. I swear. I've been trying to find out."

Scovoy opened the conference room door again, and yelled,

"Get me that kid who edits the student newspaper. Send him in as soon as you have him."

Branigan thought for a moment about her next comment, then decided there was no reason to hold back. "There's something else. It may mean nothing. But we've found out that Dr Eckhart lied about her sorority affiliation. She said she was a Kappa Epsilon Chi, but the national office says she wasn't."

Scovoy stayed on his feet, pacing the office. "Strange thing to lie about."

"But if we can find out why, it may explain all the other strange things she's done. Like leaving Charlie and Janie Rose at the crash site. Like lying to protect the hearse driver. And like maybe – maybe – pushing Anna out of a window. Is that possible?"

Scovoy looked grim. "Anything is possible at this point."

A knock on the office door made Branigan jump.

A uniformed officer stuck his head in. "Detective, we got Rogerson on the line and your student editor is here."

"Good." Scovoy waved the editor into the chair he'd vacated. "I'll be just a minute," he said to the young man. He grabbed the cell phone from the officer and exited through the hallway door for more privacy.

With the detective out of the room and presumably putting Detective Rogerson on the road to Columbia, Branigan was left facing the student editor. *Was it only yesterday I saw him after Catherine Reisman's attack?* she thought blearily. She introduced herself.

"I'm Steven Hodges," he replied. "Do you know what this is about?"

Branigan figured news of Anna's fall must be all over campus by now. "It's about your reporter," she said. "Anna Hester." She thought about waiting for Scovoy to return, then decided there was no harm in finding out what Steven knew. "We understand Anna was working on a story for Saturday's paper, possibly about the deaths of Janie Rose Carlton and Maylene Ayers?"

The young man looked at her steadily. "Yes, and that's exactly the extent of what I know."

Branigan's shoulders sagged. "You don't know what your reporters are working on?"

"You'd think so, right?" he said wryly. "But Anna was a lone wolf. I would've seen it before we published, obviously. But she refused to tell me any more than that she had a big story with more information about those girls. She promised to turn it in a couple of hours before deadline. Which is today." He shrugged. "I warned her that might not give me time to vet it for Saturday's paper, but she said she'd take that chance."

"Where would her notes be?"

"On her laptop."

"Which is where?"

"She would've had it with her in the office."

Branigan was sure there hadn't been a laptop in the *Swan Song* office when she'd looked around. Only the purse on the floor.

She stood, certain now that Anna hadn't gone out of the window of her own accord. Another rap came on the office door, and Branigan jumped again. *Sheesh.* She needed to get her nerves under control.

An officer stuck his head in, obviously looking for Detective Scovoy.

"I'm here," Chester said, coming in from the hallway.

"Detective, some guy is insisting he has information you'll want to hear."

"Some guy?"

"Well, yeah." The officer looked uncomfortable. "Some maintenance guy, but not one of the college's."

Branigan jumped up to swing the conference room door wider. Suddenly the odd contents of the purse in the *Swan Song* office made sense.

"I bet Malachi's found what we've been looking for."

Detective Scovoy, Branigan and Malachi huddled around the office desk where Malachi had laid Ralph's phone. Jody slipped in, and Branigan moved over to make room for him. This story was so complicated, it would need both of them to keep the details straight.

"This that phone Ralph wuz telling Pastor Liam and me 'bout," Malachi said. "The one Ralph done buried under his tent."

Scovoy slipped his hands into latex gloves before handling it, though Branigan was pretty sure the phone had been through multiple hands by now.

"Do I wanna know where you found it?" he asked Malachi.

"I think Miz Maylene musta took it and give it to Miz Anna. Or Miz Anna stole it from Miz Maylene. But I'm not positive."

The detective scrolled to the first video, which rolled drunkenly for several seconds. Branigan had to look away before becoming nauseated. Finally, the scene lurched into focus. Numerous voices called out amid laughter. Then came the chant: "Ro-bies. Ro-bies. Ro-bies." Someone was on the ground, holding his arms over his head as laughing young men kicked him. Branigan's stomach clenched. She couldn't see his face but knew it was Max Brody.

The camera zoomed in on a black-haired young man, good-looking even in the dizzying beams of multiple flashlights, standing on top of a picnic table and swigging from a liquor bottle. "Make him an honorary Ro-bie, gentlemen!"

Branigan and Malachi exchanged glances. "Exactly as you described," she said quietly. Then to Scovoy: "That's Jones Rinehart, president of Rho Beta Iota."

The next few videos showed young men *and* women, dancing and kissing, yelling and vomiting, as Ralph had promised. Branigan recognized some of the Kappa Epsilon Chi girls. Anna Hester and a tall blond boy held cups aloft, as if toasting the videographer. Branigan wondered if that were Anna's Mike, and if anyone had informed him of her fall. She'd gladly leave that to Anna's sorority sisters.

Malachi's voice interrupted her thoughts. "This here the last one," he said. "It got Miz Maylene in it."

Detective Scovoy read off the date stamp. "February 9 of last year."

Again, the jerky video was dizzying at first. Ralph hadn't learned much about videography during his blackmailing stint. Like the scene under the bridge, it was night, but this time a group of girls held candles and chanted. It took Branigan a moment to make out what they were saying, then she realized it was simply "Go, pledge. Go, pledge. Go, pledge." She saw a painted white stripe on the ground, and a yellow bar rising vertically from the crowd.

Suddenly, the picture left the cheering girls and zeroed in on a young woman balancing on top of what Branigan recognized as a goalpost. The young woman had long brown hair and wore a sweatshirt and sweatpants, but she was barefoot. Branigan identified Mackenzie Broadus, weaving drunkenly, threatening to topple into the crowd. Branigan froze as she realized what she was watching. *Had Mackenzie performed her balance beam routine prior to the night of her crippling accident?*

The crowd urged her on. "Go, pledge! Go, pledge! Go, pledge!"

A voice from off-screen, amplified and rising above the crowd noise, commanded, "Give us one of those Olympic moves!"

Mackenzie turned toward the voice, her stricken face looking to the right of the camera. "I can't!"

The disembodied voice came again. "Of course you can, pledge!"

The shouts became louder. "Go, pledge! Go, pledge! Go, pledge!" Branigan could see large plastic cups lifted along with the candles.

Mackenzie shook her head. "I can't," she pleaded. "I've had too much to dr…" The rest of her sentence was lost. She wobbled precariously, arms pinwheeling, but regained her balance.

Again, the voice. "I'm warning you, pledge…"

Mackenzie appeared to gather herself, standing perfectly still for a moment. Suddenly, she leapt into a scissors kick, one leg going forward, one backward, then somehow coming together so that her feet caught the beam. Some in the crowd below gasped, but most cheered, lifting their cups.

"Drink! Drink! Drink! Drink!" they roared.

Branigan looked up from the video and caught Jody's eye in mute horror. No wonder Mackenzie's story hadn't made sense. This was no accident. It was a hazing.

Back on the video, the girl turned again toward the voice, and the camera caught tears rolling down her face. "I'm going to throw up," she warned, but the amplified voice was relentless. "No, you're not, pledge. Just one more Olympic move and you can come down."

Mackenzie looked around, panicked, teary. "I'll do it tomorrow," she sobbed. "I promise, I can do it tomorrow."

"Not tomorrow, pledge. Now!"

The girl rocked back and forth. She was crying hard now, her face contorted. She drew a deep breath, tucked her head and planted her hands for what promised to be a cartwheel. The crowd began to cheer, but it quickly became apparent that her legs were not following her arms in a straight line. First her right foot, then her left, missed the beam and she came tumbling off the goalpost with a whoomph, girls scattering, laughing and spilling drinks.

Then the laughter of those closest to the goalpost stopped, and was replaced with murmurs. And then a scream. Branigan recognized Maylene Ayers and Janie Rose Carlton running to Mackenzie. Suddenly, there was bedlam: shrieks and cries and feet running. The camera swung wildly over the crowd, then stopped on a girl with a megaphone.

"Pledges, freeze!" screamed Catherine Reisman. In the silence that followed, her icy voice commanded obedience. "Ladies, go back to the house immediately to meet with President Thurman. This is a mandatory meeting. Go now!"

Pulling the megaphone from her mouth, Catherine Reisman grabbed another woman. "Emma, stay with me," came her voice, thready without the amplification, but still discernible. "Pledges Carlton and Ayers, you stay too. Everybody else, back to the house." The camera was swinging crazily but Branigan was pretty sure she saw Emma Ratcliffe, Janie Rose Carlton and Maylene Ayers crouched on the ground. She could no longer see Mackenzie. There were another twenty seconds of swirling bodies and quiet crying.

Then the camera made one last swing, past Catherine's shoulder, at the departing girls. A flash of white blurred at the back of the crowd, then disappeared.

"Go back!" Branigan commanded. Detective Scovoy rewound the video. The flash of white appeared again. "Now stop."

The figure with arms out urging girls off the football field was blurry, but the white hair was unmistakable.

Sylvia Eckhart.

Detective Scovoy was the first to spring into action. "Branigan! Jody! Give me those girls' names. And their sorority."

Branigan hastily scribbled *Gamma Delta Phi* and the names *Marianne Thurman, Catherine Reisman* and *Emma Ratcliffe* on a notepad. Scovoy tore the page off and threw open the door to the conference room.

"Phillips! Myron! Mayfield! Head over to the Gamma Delta Phi house and pick up these three. If they don't come voluntarily, stay in that house until I return with a warrant. Do not let them out of your sight. Do not let them near their cell phones or computers. Everybody move!"

Branigan, Jody and Malachi stood by silently, not wanting to make Scovoy sorry he'd given them a front-row seat to the unfolding drama. As the detective headed out of the door, Jody spoke up.

"Are you bringing them back here?"

"No. LEC. We'll put them face to face with Sylvia Eckhart and let them know Mackenzie Broadus is on her way. We'll see who cracks first." He left the room.

Branigan, Jody and Malachi sank into office chairs, silently reeling at what they'd seen. Branigan shook her head in disbelief.

Finally she spoke. "How did they keep *that many girls* quiet about that pledge stunt? Is the stupid sorority that important to them?"

"Same way the Robies stayed quiet about beating up that homeless guy," Jody offered.

"Ralph diden know what he was dealin' with," added Malachi. "He's lucky he in jail, or those girls woulda got him too."

"I think you're right," said Branigan. "Just like they got Janie Rose and Maylene."

Malachi's response was so low the reporters had to lean in to hear. "They musta been 'fraid those two weren't gon' stay quiet no more. So they kilt 'em."

Chapter Twenty-one

In the end, it was Catherine Reisman, the one least able to speak clearly, who cracked first. She agreed to testify against her sisters.

Marianne Thurman held out until Mackenzie Broadus arrived from Columbia, accompanied by her parents and brother Tony. Detective Jim Rogerson wheeled Mackenzie into the interview room where Marianne sat, a can of Diet Coke clasped in two hands. *She might as well drink the real thing*, Branigan thought. *Her figure isn't going to matter where she's going.*

Branigan hung back from the two-way window in an adjoining room, afraid of catching an officer's eye and being asked to leave. But the Grambling police were too transfixed by the trio of creamy-complexioned and murderous college girls to pay attention to the familiar reporter.

Through the window, Branigan could see Mackenzie's hands trembling in her lap, but her chin was steady. Her father kept a firm hand on one shoulder, and her mother and brother pulled chairs close to her side.

Inside the crowded interview room, Detective Scovoy opened a notebook.

"Miss Thurman, Mackenzie Broadus has identified Catherine Reisman as the pledge chairman who forced her to perform gymnastics during a Gamma Delta Phi hazing incident on February 9 of last year. She has also identified Emma Ratcliffe as the rush chairman, and you as sorority president. Since we also have video evidence of the hazing, that much is not in question. What Miss Broadus is here to help us with is what happened subsequently."

Marianne's eyes came up to meet Mackenzie's. They flicked to Mackenzie's family and then to Detective Rogerson. Branigan saw her hands tighten until the top of the half-empty soda can crumpled.

Without waiting for a prompt, Mackenzie spoke up. "After I fell, Catherine and Emma told Maylene and Janie Rose they couldn't call 911. They made them take me to the old Grambling General." Branigan knew that was the dingy public hospital that provided most of the area's indigent care. "The doctors at Grambling General seemed glad to helicopter me to Columbia." Mackenzie's voice quavered, but she spoke clearly.

"Marianne was the one who threatened me," she continued. "While I was in the hospital in Columbia, she and Emma and Catherine came to my room. Marianne said that Janie Rose and Maylene were not talking and that I wasn't either. If I did, my mom might have a traffic accident that would put us in matching wheelchairs."

Branigan heard a stirring from the officers on her side of the glass. Marianne looked stunned.

"Miss Thurman, is that true?" Detective Scovoy asked.

She swallowed, then nodded, almost imperceptibly.

Mackenzie continued. "So I didn't say anything. I didn't say anything for months and months. I thought it was over. Then that reporter from *The Grambling Rambler* came to Columbia and told me that Janie Rose and Maylene were dead. I was sure Marianne, Catherine and Emma had done it, even though there'd been a man arrested for beating Maylene. I didn't know whether Janie Rose and Maylene had actually talked, or if those three simply decided they didn't want any loose ends. I was desperate for them to know I was sticking to the story we'd concocted for my family. So I told it to the reporter."

"Then what happened?" Scovoy asked.

"I thought everything had settled down again. But then three days ago, Anna Hester called me."

Branigan's head jerked up.

"She said she had discovered a video of my accident and knew it was a hazing. She wanted to know why I'd lied to *The Rambler*.

She said the real story gave a strong motive to the Gamma Delts to kill Janie Rose and Maylene, and she was writing that story for *The Swan Song.*

"I was scared to death and refused to comment. I couldn't sleep the last few nights. Then Detective Rogerson showed up. He said all three of them had been arrested and charged with murder."

She looked up at Detective Rogerson and her father, and drew in a tremulous breath. "I think I'll be able to sleep again now."

Detective Scovoy shoved a notepad and pen in Marianne's direction. "I don't think we'll need it, but here's your chance to make your confession. Might help you at your trial."

Emma Ratcliffe was silent until Catherine produced Janie Rose Carlton's journal, which the trio had taken from Janie Rose's suitcase on the side of US 441. The journal detailed how Jones Rinehart had made a casual remark to Janie Rose about Ralph's videotapes of the Robies and others. She asked if he had ever taped a Gamma Delta Phi function. When Jones innocently relayed the question to Marianne, the trio visited Janie Rose in Athens. Janie Rose chronicled their death threat – a threat, Branigan realized, that had triggered the anxiety Charlie had witnessed before the wreck.

Branigan and Jody pieced together an abbreviated online story late Thursday evening, and a full-blown story for Friday's print edition of *The Rambler.* That afternoon, Branigan picked up Malachi at the county library and drove to the Delaney house, where Liam, Liz and Charlie waited. Liz put out cheese and crackers and soft drinks, and ordered Branigan: "Spill. We read the story, but we still can't connect the dots of how you guys got there."

Branigan took a deep breath. "It didn't click for me until Charlie told us about that dream of seeing Mrs Claus and the elves in green hats. I began to think her subconscious was trying to tell her what she'd seen, either through the hearse window or after the wreck. Clearly she'd seen Sylvia Eckhart. When I found out the Gamma Delta Phi colors were green and white, I figured those would have been the colors of their stocking hats in the Christmas concert.

So I wondered if Charlie saw one of those hats through the hearse window."

"And it came out in my dream as elves in green hats," said Charlie. "Weird. But go back to the beginning. It started with that pledge hazing, right?"

"Right. It turns out that Sylvia Eckhart was a Gamma Delta Phi at the University of Michigan. But that's not the kind of thing she'd have bothered to tell the faculty or administration. She'd actually even been a chapter adviser to the sorority at Rutherford Lee when she first got here. So when she became Honor Chair, she tried to look out for them. I think it was mostly minor stuff until Marianne and Catherine and Emma took over.

"That hazing last February was chilling. According to Ralph Batson's video, Catherine pretty much drove Mackenzie to that accident, but no one else stepped forward to stop her. Marianne Thurman took all the girls back to the house and managed to shut the conversation down. That's the most amazing part of this whole thing to me – that so many people knew something and kept it quiet. It's mind-boggling."

Liam and Malachi looked at each other. "That couldn't happen on the street, could it?" Liam asked.

Malachi shook his head. "Don' nothin' stay quiet out there."

"Did the sorority have that strong a hold on its members?" asked Liz.

"Possibly. But Marianne told them they'd be implicated too," Branigan said. "I don't know if that's true or not, but they were scared enough to bury the story. Then Marianne, Catherine and Emma kept their same leadership positions a second year to ensure that everything stayed quiet.

"The problem came," she continued, "with Janie Rose and Maylene. They'd been friends of Mackenzie and they couldn't live with the guilt of her being paralyzed. Janie Rose had an emotional breakdown, then left school. Apparently, Maylene started asking questions. Marianne, Catherine and Emma shut her down by threatening her family. She was afraid to lead them to Gainesville, so she moved in with some of the homeless people she'd met during her mission projects.

"I think she intended to stay only a couple of days, but then she fell in with Ralph and discovered his video of the hazing. She couldn't decide what to do about it, and I imagine her crack smoking didn't help. Ralph fell for her – as much as Ralph could fall for anyone – and he stopped his blackmailing schemes. But then he reverted to type and began hitting her."

"So what changed?" Charlie asked. "It sounds like the Gamma Delts were home free."

"They were. Until Jones Rinehart mentioned to Janie Rose about Ralph's video of the Robie attack on a homeless man, which triggered the Gamma Delt panic attack and road trip to Athens. That's why Janie Rose was already anxious when she and Charlie headed home for Christmas."

Liz interrupted. "I thought I remembered you talking about Janie Rose being threatened by a man when she lived in the Gamma Delt house the year before."

"An associate of Janie Rose's father did stop by. But apparently he was looking for his niece and Janie Rose pointed him to her dorm. Emma Ratcliffe made it into something else to throw me off."

Charlie pulled a blanket off the back of the couch and put it over her shoulders. "They were so afraid Janie Rose was going to talk they were willing to kill both of us?" Liam put his arm around her.

"Yes. They took the hearse key from the Kappa Epsilon house. They told Sylvia Eckhart they were going to Athens to find Janie Rose's diary, but she was nervous enough to follow them. They left before dawn and laid low in Athens until they saw Janie Rose leave her apartment. They went in looking for her diary and didn't find it, so figured she'd taken it home with her.

"They waited until Charlie and Janie Rose left the UGA campus after their exams. They ran them off the road, then took Janie Rose's diary from her suitcase. I'm pretty sure that Dr Eckhart was horrified, but she had covered up the hazing incident and was in too deep to back out. She's been living in fear of those three for a year."

Liam turned to Malachi. "So Ralph didn't kill Maylene after all?"

"No," he said. "Them girls did it with the crowbar she wuz carryin'."

"That's the scary part," Branigan said. "Maylene recognized the hearse that was abandoned in the woods. When I told her about Charlie and Janie Rose's wreck, she went to the hospital to find out from Charlie if the Gamma Delts were behind it.

"But remember the nurse said she came back later that night? Or at least a slim girl with long brown hair was back? It wasn't Maylene. It was Catherine. I'm afraid to think what might have happened if Liz hadn't been in Charlie's room."

Charlie shivered involuntarily, and her dad hugged her closer. "So then Jones Rinehart wasn't trying to hurt me in the hospital?"

"I don't think so. He was just being his obnoxious self."

"I feel kind of silly."

"Don't," Branigan said. "Your mind was telling you that you were in danger. You couldn't have known where it was coming from."

"And he been known to hurt people," Malachi added.

Liz broke in. "We are so grateful to you two for warning us that Charlie was in danger," she said. "But go back to Maylene for a minute. What was she doing way out at the bus station?"

"Anna Hester had been digging around," Branigan explained. "The story outing Maylene as being homeless in Grambling was going to be in *The Swan Song* the next morning. Maylene knew the Gamma Delts would know where to find her. Plus, it'd be only a matter of time before the story got back to the Ayers family in Gainesville. So she was going home. But Anna mentioned the story to Emma Ratcliffe, not realizing the implications at that point."

"Thas the worst part of all this," Malachi said. "Miz Branigan and Pastor Liam done fin'ly talked Miz Maylene into leavin' th' street, and she tho't she had 'til that Saturday back in December. But them girls found out and tho't she ready to talk about that girl falling off the goalpost. I don't think she woulda. She just wanted to go home."

Liam gave Branigan a sad smile. "And the fact that Ralph was a known abuser made him an easy target to take the fall," he said.

Branigan pointed to Malachi. "It was Malachi – and Ralph – who led us to the video that broke the story. And then Malachi managed to get it. Even the police don't want to know how."

Malachi ducked his head to hide a grin. "Had to do with 'pebbles'."

"So how did you figure that out, Mr Malachi?" Charlie asked.

"Elise in Tent City tol' me Miz Maylene dug up tha' phone. When it diden turn up on her body, I figgered the killer had it. But then Miz Branigan started talkin' 'bout mebbe Miz Maylene gave it to that college reporter."

"Wait a minute," said Liam. "Maylene died in December. If Anna Hester had the video at that point, why did she hang on to it for so long?"

Branigan took up the story. "According to the little bit the police have been able to get from Anna, she didn't realize at first what she had. Maylene hadn't confided anything, just shoved the phone at her. She thought Maylene was directing her to Ralph's voicemails and text messages.

"It was only on Sunday that Sylvia Eckhart told Anna – and the Gamma Delts – about Ralph videoing sororities, having no idea Anna had his phone. Dr Eckhart was trying to find out what was on those tapes. That's when Anna put it all together and looked at the video function on his phone.

"After Anna saw the hazing video – and recognized Dr Eckhart on it – she returned to get a comment from her. But Anna didn't know that Dr Eckhart had helped cover up the murders. Dr Eckhart was trying to run interference and protect Anna from Marianne, Catherine and Emma. But it was too late."

Malachi added: "Those girls tried to get to Miz Anna on Sunday night, but Miz Branigan showed up in her office. We thought Miz Janie Rose's daddy might be up there, but he warn't. He just walkin' all round the school, half crazy with grief."

"That was the night I saw Anna with two phones," Branigan said, "and figured she might have Ralph's video. I actually heard someone in the room next to hers. Turns out it was Catherine and Emma. We took Anna with us then. Too bad we couldn't help her later."

"It wasn't your fault," Liam said. "What I don't understand is why she wasn't more scared of those girls, especially after she saw the video?"

"Good question," Branigan answered. "I don't know if she was so blinded by the thought of an exclusive that would beat *The Rambler*, or if she thought she was invincible or what. But apparently they never threatened her. They went straight for the kill."

"What, exactly, happened yesterday?" Liam asked.

"All we know is that Anna was in the newspaper office finishing her story before handing it in to her editor. Sylvia Eckhart got there in time to see Marianne and Emma leaving with Anna's laptop. They'd grabbed her purse too, but saw it was full of Malachi's crazy substitutions and left it." Branigan shook her head. "Dr Eckhart looked out of the open window and realized what they'd done. She was too broken up to even try to run. That's when I found her in the hallway."

"But Anna's going to be okay?" asked Charlie.

"We still don't know. Her family's with her. She'll be in the hospital for a while."

"Okay, one last thing," said Liz. "Was the assault on Catherine Reisman a coincidence?"

"Oh, no," Branigan answered. "Marianne, Catherine and Emma orchestrated that to lay the groundwork for the attack on Anna in the newspaper office. They wanted to create the idea there was a *male* attacker on the loose.

"Detective Scovoy was suspicious of Catherine's injuries from the start. He found a bloody paper towel in the bathroom trash that led him to a bathroom wall that'd been wiped clean. But there were still traces of blood smeared on it."

"What's that mean?" asked Liam.

"That Catherine allowed Marianne and Emma to bang her face on the wall."

Liz and Charlie instinctively brought their hands over their noses.

"Marianne convinced her she was going to have to get plastic surgery for the bump in her nose anyway. Now she could get it sooner."

"You are kidding!" Liz exclaimed in horror.

Branigan rolled her eyes in agreement, and continued. "The point was to direct everyone's attention to the idea of a violent *man* roaming the student center. Catherine and Emma came to see me the next day, maybe trying to get information and maybe planting the idea of Gamma Delts being targets. I'm not really sure. When they told me their sorority colors, I got an inkling that it might be them. But I had completely bought into their goody-two-shoes reputation. I couldn't make sense of it until I saw the hazing video."

The five sat back in silence for a minute.

"Who was driving?" Charlie asked. "The hearse?"

"Catherine. But Detective Scovoy says that as passengers Marianne and Emma will be charged exactly the same. And Marianne was the one who hit Maylene with the crowbar. Plenty of blame to go around."

Liam clamped a hand on Malachi's leg. "We thought the streets were rough, didn't we, my friend?"

Malachi stood to leave. "Streets can't hold a candle to mean girls."

CHAPTER TWENTY-TWO

B ranigan drove from the Delaneys' house directly to her farm, where she found not only Cleo but Chester Scovoy waiting for her.

"You didn't forget our date, did you?" he asked, as Cleo bounded happily between them.

"I most certainly did not," she said. "Just couldn't get away any earlier."

"Where would you like to go?"

"How would you feel about staying in?"

"Surely you don't want to cook after the week you've had."

"Not cook, maybe, but 'fix'. I can cut up some veggies and put out dips and wine and cheese."

"Sounds like dinner to me."

They walked through the dusk into the house. Branigan flipped the thermostat up and turned on the gas in the fireplace. "These two rooms will warm up real quick," she said, placing a bottle of pinot noir and two wine glasses on the kitchen island.

Chester filled the glasses. Holding them aloft, they clinked.

"To Greeks," he said sarcastically.

"Not going to drink to that," she said.

"Okay, then, to two murders and one attempted murder solved. And three murderers arrested."

Branigan took a sip. "I still cannot believe they went so far to cover up a hazing."

Chester ran his hand through his hair in a gesture Branigan had come to hold dear. "I'm no psychiatrist, but I think it had a lot to do with that damned legacy of theirs. They were so perfect with their hair and their pearls and their housekeepers and their engagements;

so almost … *typecast*. That pledge hazing would have brought all that crashing down."

"Not nearly as low as it's crashed now."

"You got that right. We had officers out there all day gathering evidence. They said the Gamma Delta Phi house was shut down, and the campus was full of parents packing up their kids. The whole school is taking a hit."

"I feel sorry for the administrators. There's no way they could've known."

"Apparently, those girls fooled everyone. As did Dr Eckhart."

"She fooled my grandparents," Branigan conceded. "They had a lot of respect for her."

"That's what is so weird to me – that a grown woman decades away from that sorority silliness could be drawn in."

"Maybe she was drawn in at first," Branigan said slowly. "But later, I think she was simply scared of them. Scared for herself, but also scared for Mackenzie and Charlie and Anna and anybody else who got in their way. She knew I was going to see Mackenzie early on, and she didn't tell them."

"That reminds me. I talked to Mackenzie and her family before they headed back to Columbia. Nice people. Her brother asked me to thank the good-looking reporter for her help."

Branigan grinned. "He did not."

"No, really. He couldn't leave for Columbia fast enough to suit me." Scovoy smiled. "And Mackenzie asked me to convey her apology for misleading you back in December."

"I understand why she did it. She was sending a message to the Gamma Delts that she was taking the blame for the accident, that she wouldn't tell the truth. That was a lot for her to carry by herself."

"Right up until Jim Rogerson got there and told her Marianne, Catherine and Emma were in jail. I'm telling you, those girls had everyone scared to death."

"I guess they looked pretty invincible for a while there." She moved to the refrigerator and pulled out baby carrots and broccoli and celery.

Scovoy popped a baby carrot into his mouth. "Oh, one more thing," he said. "We also made a copy of Ralph's video and gave it to the college president in case he wants to take action against Jones Rinehart and the Robies. Without a victim, there's nothing we can do. But he can make things hot for them."

Branigan nodded. "I don't know about you but I'm ready to talk about something else. Namely, that this was my last story involving the Grambling PD."

He eyed her warily over his glass. "It was?" He waited a beat, and when she didn't answer, he asked, "Did Tan take you off, or did you remove yourself?"

"A little of both," she said. "He's right. I can't see you socially *and* have you as a source. It got uncomfortable even this time. I found myself holding back on calling you when I would've pushed with anybody else. Luckily Jody was there to cover, but still, it was not a good situation." She blushed.

The detective smiled. "I think I'm flattered."

Branigan grew a little flustered. "I don't want you to think I'm expecting anything," she started. "I can still deal with Cannon County law enforcement. I'll just need to keep my distance from Grambling PD. No biggie."

She frowned as she attacked the celery, then glanced sideways to find Scovoy grinning.

"I have to tell you, it'll make my life easier," he said. He raised his glass again. "To the Cannon County sheriff and deputies. They don't know what's about to hit 'em."

ALSO FROM LION FICTION...

THE KILL FEE

POPPY DENBY
INVESTIGATES

"What a delight to escape into
the world of the irrepressible
Poppy Denby."

– Ruth Downie, author of the
Medicus series

"Do you know who that is, Poppy?" asked Delilah.
"I do indeed."
"So what does it feel like to dance in the arms of an
assassin?".

Poppy Denby's star is on the rise. Now the Arts and
Entertainment Editor at *The Daily Globe*, she covers an
exhibition of Russian Art at the Crystal Palace. A shot rings
out, leaving a guard injured and an empty pedestal in the place
of the largest Fabergé Egg in the collection. The egg itself is
valuable, but more so are the secrets it contains within – secrets
that could threaten major political powers.

Suspects are aplenty and Poppy is delighted to be once
again in the middle of a sensational story. But, soon the
investigation takes a dark turn when someone connected with
the exhibition is murdered and an employee of the newspaper
becomes a suspect. The race is on to find the egg before the
killer strikes again...

ISBN: 978-1-78264-218-3 | e-ISBN: 978-1-78264-219-0

THE RELUCTANT DETECTIVE

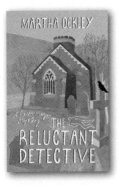

A FAITH MORGAN MYSTERY

"Couldn't resist touching the body, eh?" observed Ben.

Faith was defiant. "I had to check for a pulse."

Faith Morgan may have quit the world of crime, but crime won't let her go. The ex-policewoman has retrained as a priest, disillusioned with a tough police culture and convinced that she can do more good this way.

But now her worlds collide. Searching for the first posting of her new career, she witnesses a sudden and shocking death in a quiet Hampshire village. And of all people, Detective Inspector Ben Shorter, her former colleague and boyfriend, shows up to investigate the crime.

Persuaded to stay on in Little Worthy, she learns surprising details about the victim and starts to piece together a motive for his death. But is she now in danger herself? And what should she do about Ben?

Then a further horrifying event deepens the mystery...

ISBN: 978 1 78264 068 4 | e-ISBN: 978 1 78264 126 1